The Exar

So Little Done

Theodore Dalrymple

Monday Books

The Examined Life
© Theodore Dalrymple, 2010

So Little Done
© Theodore Dalrymple, 1995
(First published by Andre Deutsch Ltd in 1995)

A CIP catalogue record for this title is available from the British
Library

ISBN: 978-1-906308-16-2

Typeset by Andrew Searle
Printed and bound by CPI Cox and Wyman

www.mondaybooks.com
http://mondaybooks.blogspot.com/
info@mondaybooks.com

The Examined Life

All references to commercial products and entities and to people in this work are entirely fictional and bear no relationship to any existing products, entities or people.

The unexamined life is not worth living.

Socrates

Being party to the most intimate thoughts and feelings of patients is one of the privileges of medical practice. Recently a patient informed me that, though not an author by inclination, he had tried to write an account of his philosophy of life, which he hoped might be instructive to others. He brought this account with him to hospital and gave it to me, asking me to do my best to have it published. I agreed, and herewith fulfil my promise, appending extracts from his medical notes. I believe that the public interest justifies their publication, and in this case overrides the duty of confidentiality.

1

I'M DYING, AND I can prove it.

Not to my doctor, though. He insists that there's nothing at all the matter with me.

'If I'm not dying,' I said to him, 'how come I'll survive one day less for each day that I live?'

'We're all dying in that sense,' he said.

'That may be so,' I said, 'but it's no consolation to me. You've admitted that I'm right.'

'Anything else?' he asked, looking away from his computer screen for the first time. Doctors these days think they can learn more about their patients from looking at their computers than by looking at their patients themselves – let alone by examining them. 'A sprained ankle, perhaps?' he added.

He's admitted that I'm dying, and he asks me about my ankles! Talk about fiddling while Rome burns! I got up to go.

'I can see that you're not interested,' I said. 'My death will mean nothing to you.'

I reached the doctor's door without a reply. No doubt he thought of one after I had gone.

On the way home, I bought a newspaper. I do so on alternate days. In that way I combine the advantages of maintaining an interest in the world, which research has shown to reduce, or slow the rate of development of, Alzheimer's disease, with those of ignoring the news, which has been demonstrated to reduce the incidence of depression, that is to say research has shown that people who pay attention to the news are more depressed than those who don't.

But which newspaper to buy? The ink of some of them rubs off on to the skin more than others, and might be, indeed probably is, carcinogenic. Can you really afford to wait until the studies have been completed? It is very unlikely, after all, that newspaper ink could do your skin any good; man evolved long before there was any ink in the world, and has not had time to adapt genetically to its presence. Therefore, it is better to play safe and buy a newspaper whose ink doesn't rub off, or at least rubs off less than that of others: most carcinogenesis is dose-dependent.

Unfortunately, the headline that caught my eye – 'Fish Oil Cancer Scare' – was in one of the inkier papers. But the story was a very important one, of course, because up until then fish oil had been good for you. If fish oil causes cancer, I would henceforth have to avoid fish, or at least oily fish.

Of course, I could probably, though not certainly, find the story on-line. But looking at computer screens is not without its risks. There is the bad posture that leads to backache, only partially counterbalanced by ergonomic furniture. No one wants to spend what might prove to be his last day with a backache. Many people get headaches when they look at a screen, and, though so far I have not, there must surely be a first time. And goodness knows what invisible rays, yet to be discovered, emanate from the screen and scramble your neurones like an egg.

Here was the problem, then: on the one hand there was a medical story that might or might not have been of vital importance, depending upon its truth; on the other, was the dilemma of whether it was riskier to read the printed or the electronic version, if there was one. What was I to do?

I bent down to look a little more closely at the newspaper – there was a pile on the floor, where all the newspapers were arrayed. (Of course, I bent at the knee, not the back: I am always appalled when I see people bending at the back, careless of their own health and well-being. It seems to me grossly irresponsible of them, and I hope I shall not be thought uncharitable when I say that they almost deserve their backaches. The least the shopkeeper could do, if he had absolutely to place his wares on the floor, was to provide a large notice telling people to use their knees, not their backs, to pick them up.)

I was trying to establish whether the story was of such significance that I needed to read more than the first few lines.

The owner of the shop, a weedy Indian who was probably fed up with shoplifters but wouldn't have said anything had I been black, piped up that he was running a shop, not a library, and that if I wanted to read the newspaper, I should buy it. In a way, he was right, but as I handed over my money, I said, 'How do you know whether you want something until you know what's in it?'

The point was not to be right, but not to let other people trample on you. That kind of helplessness leads to disease: your aggression is turned inward by it. Not, of course, that I'm particularly aggressive, because aggression can lead to heart attacks and other serious conditions. You need a healthy medium.

The story about fish oil came from Russia. Forty thousand people who ate fish regularly were compared with the same number who didn't, and the fish-eaters had twice the risk of stomach cancer of the non-eaters, even when you controlled for alcohol intake. (I admit to being sceptical: how can you control for alcohol intake in Russia?)

Still, I was in the habit of eating herring or mackerel at least once a week, and now I would have to reconsider and modify my diet. One has not been given the powers of reason for nothing.

After buying the newspaper, I reached home. I live in a small block of flats, and I'm worried about the radon that the walls and fittings give off: that is, if they give off any. Nobody knows – or cares. Once I telephoned the Environmental Health Department of the local council, from whom I rent the flat, to find out, and after a prolonged message telling me that the department was there to make life safe for everyone, regardless of race, religion, gender or disability, and that my call might be monitored for training purposes, I spoke to someone with a disability, namely an inability to follow a logical argument.

'I'm worried about the radon from my walls,' I said, when this human voice eventually appeared at the other end of the telephone.

'I have to ask you a few security questions first,' she replied.

'Security questions?' I said.

'Yes,' she replied.

'What for?' I asked.

'It's our procedure.'

She seemed to think that she had given a completely satisfactory answer.

'But what if your procedure isn't right, or isn't necessary? What if it wastes a lot of time?'

'It's you who's wasting time,' she said. 'Are you going to answer my questions or not? If you don't, I'll have to hang up. What is your mother's maiden name?'

Of course I gave in. The danger from radon was more important to me than winning an argument. But I don't think she had heard of radon or its dangers.

'What makes you think you've got radon?' she asked.

'Everyone's got radon,' I said. 'It's everywhere. The question is, How much?'

'Let me rephrase the question, then,' she said, as if talking to a mental defective. 'What makes you think you have too much radon in your flat?'

'I don't know that I have too much radon in my flat,' I said. 'That's the whole point. But I do have a granite fireplace, put in by the last tenant, and granite is known for radon. I want you to measure it. I don't want the first evidence of it to be cancer of the lung.'

'Do you smoke?' asked the woman at the other end of the telephone.

'No, of course not,' I said. What did she take me for? 'I'm not suicidal. But radon gives you cancer even if you don't smoke.'

'I've never heard of that,' she said, as if that were evidence of the untruth of what I said, rather than of her ignorance.

'In Cornwall and Northumberland,' I said, 'they found that people who live in granite houses and didn't smoke had a higher incidence of lung cancer than people who lived in brick houses, and that was because of the radon.'

'That's news to me,' she said.

'What are you going to do about it?'

'There's nothing I can do about it. I mean, I can't come round and remove your fireplace, can I? For all I know, it's a listed building.'

A listed building? I was talking about life and death, and she was concerned about our architectural heritage! Anyway, my flat is not exactly a national treasure or an heirloom, more like a millstone round my neck. I'd like to live somewhere else, somewhere healthier, but I can't afford to move. My life is one long irony: I can't work to accumulate money to live somewhere healthy, or at least less unhealthy, until I've secured my health, and I can't secure my health until I live somewhere less unhealthy. The problem is that life is a precondition of everything else, and health is a precondition of life. That is why my health must always come first.

I brought my conversation with the woman at the Environmental Health Department to an end.

'Can you do anything about my radon or not?' I asked.

'We don't deal with radon,' she replied. 'We're more rats and cockroaches.'

'Thank you very much for all your help,' I said, putting as much sarcasm into my voice as possible.

'You're welcome,' she said. 'We're here to help. We're part of the council's Serving You Better campaign.'

I suppose I shouldn't have been surprised at her utter indifference to my health. After all, if even my doctor's not interested in it, why should she be? You're on your own in life, that's what life has taught me, and you have to look after your own health. No one else will do it for you.

Anyway, I returned home after my pointless visit to the doctor. Mrs Green, my next door neighbour, was returning with her shopping at the same time.

Mrs Green is a widow, and I'm not surprised, the things she eats and presumably gave to her late husband to eat. She is practically a murderer, as well as a suicide. She's seventy-five, overweight and crippled with arthritis. What's more, she smokes, though I've succeeded in giving her a bad conscience about it.

'What's the point in going to the doctor,' I said to her (she is always going), 'if you go on abusing yourself like that?'

'I know, dear,' she replied. 'But a little bit of what you fancy does you good.'

'Not if what you fancy is smoking, it doesn't,' I said.

'But I enjoy it.'

'Think of your lungs, your heart, your whole body. They're not enjoying it. Black tar is clogging up your lungs even as we speak. No wonder you're out of breath all the time.'

'I know you're right,' she said. 'But at my time in life...'

'You could live another fifteen years if you looked after yourself properly,' I said.

'It's lonely without Bert,' she said.

'Bert might still be here if...'

I know I shouldn't have said it, perhaps it was cruel, but it just slipped out, I couldn't help it. The fact is that I'm addicted to the truth, and fatalism about health makes me angry. The truth will not only set you free but help you to live longer. Ignorance is death.

Mrs Green had her shopping bags with her. I could see a lot of plastic packaging peeping out, of the type that had a lot of oestrogenic chemicals in it. I tried some time ago to interest her in the dangers of these, but she said that she was a woman anyway, so feminising hormones were good for her and anyway she was too old to worry about them.

'The older you are, the more you should worry about them,' I said. 'A rational man worries about things in proportion to the danger. The older you are, the greater the risk of developing cancer.'

'When you've lived as long as me, love,' said Mrs Green, 'you don't care no more.'

How irresponsible, immoral even! Who says it is only youth that is careless? The problem with old people is that they think that they have paid their dues, and that they can therefore do anything they like, with the right to be looked after, irrespective of whether they've brought their illnesses on themselves by their disregard of the most elementary precautions.

I looked a little more carefully into Mrs Green's shopping bags. What was the first thing I saw? A packet of pork pies! Salt and fat incarnate!

'Look at all that salt and fat!' I said to her, hardly able to control myself.

'Where?' she said, looking down. Was she just feigning ignorance and stupidity, or were they real?

'Those pork pies!' I said. 'They're deadly. They fill but they do not nourish.'

'Pork pies? I've been eating them for years. love.'

'Precisely,' I said, dryly. Is it not strange how people, when accused, often admit to aggravating circumstances as if they were mitigating?

'Those pork pies will kill you in the end.' (Sometimes it is necessary to use dramatic language to make one's point, without, of course, straying from the truth.)

She opened her eyes wide.

'What's wrong with them?' she asked.

'What's *wrong* with them? What's *right* with them, you mean? They go straight to your arteries and clog them up – among other things.'

'They're not poisoned, are they?' She was beginning to look suitably alarmed now.

'Only by the food industry,' I said. 'Actually, though they're not poisoned, they *are* poison.'

'Because them terrorists wouldn't stop at nothing, would they? Glass in your pork pies – I wouldn't put it past them.'

'Terrorism!' I said. 'I'm sick of hearing about it. I'm not in favour of terrorism, of course: even if you survive an attack you can suffer from severe problems, both physical and psychological, afterwards. But the psittacosis that you can catch from parrots probably kills more people in a year than terrorism. And who's afraid of parrots? Why can't people get their priorities right?'

I think this was a little too difficult for Mrs Green to follow, so I put the matter in concrete terms.

'Don't you realise,' I said, 'that you're twenty thousand times more likely to die of heart disease than of terrorist attack? You've been poisoned by the food industry all your life.'

'Poisoned? Why?'

'For profit, for money,' I said.

'Well,' she said, ever dim, 'I can't see why. I mean, I haven't got nothing worth taking.'

Literal-mindedness and concrete thought: these are the great enemies of the ideal, namely health.

'They don't want to poison you personally, in your capacity as Mrs

Green,' I said. 'They want to poison *everyone*. They're not interested in *you*, they're interested in *us*.'

She looked relieved at this: some people are concerned only with themselves, and the rest of humanity might as well not exist for them.

'I keep myself to myself,' she said. 'I don't bother no one, so I don't see why anybody should want to poison me.'

I changed tack.

'I see you haven't brought any fresh fruit or vegetables again,' I said.

'They're difficult to peel and eat,' she said defensively. 'And digest. They repeat on me.' Guilt was written all over her face; she knew she was rationalising. 'You see, my hands... artheritis,' she added, her voice trailing away, as very well it might, considering that she didn't even pronounce the name of her condition correctly.

'It's a vicious circle, Mrs Green, a vicious circle. First you get arthritis because you don't eat properly, then you don't eat properly because of your arthritis.'

'Some of them prepared meals are very tasty,' she said, any port being good in a storm.

'I'm not talking about taste, Mrs Green, I'm taking about health. *Your* health,' I said, raising my voice for emphasis.

'Yes, well...'

'Yes, well what?' I could see I had her at an advantage now. 'There's no real reason why you couldn't buy ready-chopped vegetables, is there?'

'No, I suppose not, but they're expensive.'

'Or fruit?'

'No.'

I pitied her poor bowels. They had so little to work on other than semi-cooked, pre-digested, soft junk: a real rope of sand. I shuddered to think about the state of her colon.

'Anyway, love,' said Mrs Green, obviously embarrassed by the exposure of her own irresponsibility, 'it's been lovely talking to you, and I wish I could go on, only I've got these varical veins and they begin to play up if I stand too long.'

'Did you know,' I said, 'that diets low in vegetable fibre cause varicose veins?'

'And I've got to feed the cat,' she added.

'Haven't you heard of toxoplasma,' I said, in a way halfway between a question and an exclamation. 'You get it from cats.'

But she had opened the front door and slipped inside – on reflection, she'd been searching for her key for a little while.

2

IF MRS GREEN hadn't scurried away in that guilty way, like a thief in the night, I would of course have informed her of the evidence of the connection between low-fibre diets and varicose veins. In Africa, for example, where people eat a lot of roughage (admittedly because there is not much else for them to eat), even old people don't get varicose veins, however much of their lives they've had to spend standing up in the bush and so forth. The reason for this – I don't see any reason to be squeamish about it, because we're talking about a perfectly natural process here – is that they do not have to push down so hard to expel their waste matter, which is soft, bulky and malleable like an elephant's (varicose veins, incidentally, are known only to humans, so that one might almost call them the defining feature of humanity), and so the pressure in the veins in their legs – I'm talking now of Africans, not elephants, although of course the same argument applies – is not raised so high that it blows the valves, as it were, although actually I am speaking literally now, and varicose veins develop, together with varicose eczema and then ulcers.

In a very important sense, then, Mrs Green's condition was self-inflicted, though she didn't fully realise it. Ignorance is no excuse for an unhealthy lifestyle, however, and I still feel it is my duty to lay the truth before her and all those like her. What they do with the truth, of course, is up to them, and I have to admit that my success rate is not very high, such is the frivolity of most of the population. But at least I do not have to reproach myself when they develop precisely the conditions that could have been predicted from their lifestyle, such as heart attacks and bowel cancer. At least I have done my best for public health.

Of course, my conscience wouldn't have allowed me to simplify matters too much, or at least not unduly. I would have had to tell her that not all vegetables and fruit were equal, and that she would have to pick them with care, and that most of those she would buy in the supermarket were contaminated with all kinds of artificial fertilisers, fungicides and insecticides, to say nothing of hormones. Many of these things could be presumed to be carcinogenic.

This is not to say, however, that fruit and vegetables grown without all these chemicals are safe in any absolute sense; far from it, risk cannot be avoided as easily as that. Naturally-occurring fungi, for example, contain or secrete some of the most powerful carcinogens known. It is all a question, at least in the present state of knowledge, and until entirely risk-free food can be produced, of balancing risks, and of estimating and acting upon whichever poses the least such risk, though this does not mean we should cease to strive to eliminate risk altogether. In the meantime, all vegetables should be washed – and I don't mean just rinsed – several times in strongly-running water before they are even cooked, let alone eaten.

Unfortunately, as I know from the experience of talking to her every time I see her, Mrs Green doesn't have any concept at all of relative risk. For example, she'll lock her front door with three mortise locks in an almost religious fashion, but she'll consume saturated fatty acids until they come out of her ears, even though she's much more of a candidate for a heart attack than for a break-in and assault. Don't get me wrong: I'm not against three mortise locks, in fact I think five would be better, because break-ins do occur and old ladies are attacked in their homes, but I just wish she would apply precautions in proportion to the risk. It is all very discouraging really; but still I do my best.

I opened the door to my own flat and closed the door quickly behind me, checking that none of my fingers was in the way and putting on the chain. I noticed at once that there was a letter on the floor just inside the door. It was a brown manila envelope: something official, then.

I did not pick it up straight away, impulsively, but went to fetch my letter-opening gloves, that is the transparent disposable gloves that I use to handle anything of whose provenance I cannot be certain. It always amazes me that people who would not open an e-mail on their computer from a stranger because it might contain a virus take absolutely no precautions when they receive a letter. Are their computers more precious to them, then, than their lives?

For the last few years I have also used a mask, ever since the anthrax scare in America made me realise what I should have known before, that germs don't just stick to objects but can be transmitted from them in the air. For example, when you lift a letter – bending your knees, of course, not your back – you cannot help but create a current of air, and because bacteria are so small, any current of air, no matter how slowly and smoothly you try to move, must be able to carry them into the general atmosphere: and not just by ones or twos, but by the hundreds of millions. A mask, therefore, is essential equipment when lifting or in any way handling unwashed objects.

Of course, when I first put on my surgical mask in shops and supermarkets both staff and customers were wary of me. They looked as though they thought that I had come to rob the shop, and actually expected me to draw a gun. All I had in my pocket, it goes without saying, was an anti-bacterial spray, which I confess might have looked a little like a gun when in my pocket, but which I used very sparingly and only when absolutely essential, for fear of damaging the ozone layer, which might – no, let us not equivocate, which *would* – increase one's chances of developing a skin cancer. I have quite pale and delicate skin, and it is one of the things that I have against my mother that she let me play outside in the sun when I was a child and knew no better, without anything to protect me from the ultra-violet. I didn't know there was anything wrong with this at the time, I had not yet reached the age of responsibility for one's health, and so I think she was culpably careless of my health. What is a parent for, if not to protect a child from danger? And early sun means early cancer.

I remember very clearly the first time I donned a surgical mask at a supermarket. The girl at the checkout counter pressed her bell to call the manager. You could see on her face that she was a girl of limited intelligence and information, with a slightly pendulous lower lip and the eyes of a sheep. Almost certainly she read those magazines that contain snippets about the lives of so-called celebrities, as if they were more real or important to her than her own, and whose only items about health were ridiculous testimonies to the healing power of onions and such like (not, of course, that I deny the healthiness of onions of the right sort). I wouldn't mind betting that she was a devotee of horoscopes as well.

Some people think that horoscopes are innocent superstition, but not I. The fault, dear Brutus, lies in ourselves, not in our stars, that we are susceptible to illness. Instead of actively taking sensible precautions to preserve oneself, horoscopes encourage fatalism of the most unscientific kind. How many people have uttered the most terrible sentence in our language (most terrible because it has been responsible for more unnecessary deaths than any other), namely 'When your number's up, your number's up?' Death is not a lottery, chosen at random; it is the result of frivolity and negligence. (I am speaking of most cases, perhaps not all.)

The manager of the supermarket came running, and alongside him two security guards dressed, I could not help noticing, in artificial fibre that does not allow sweat to evaporate. You would have thought it was an emergency. By the time they reached me, the manager, no taller than five feet three and weighing at least eighteen stone, was completely out of breath.

'Your body mass index is far too high,' I said to him as he panted to recover his breath. 'That's why the slightest exertion tires you out. You need to do something about your index.'

'What do you mean?' he managed to gasp between two laboured inspirations.

'Your body mass index,' I said slowly and patiently. 'Your weight in kilograms divided by your height in metres squared, that is to say multiplied by itself.' (He didn't look to me like a man familiar with mathematical concepts.) 'If it's over thirty, you're obese. I hope you don't mind me saying, as it's only for your own good, but I think your body mass index is well over thirty, in fact it may be over forty.'

The manager, who had by now recovered a little, looked at me and said: 'What are you, some kind of doctor or something?'

'No,' I replied. 'Doctors are only interested in illness. I'm interested in health. You ought to look after yourself a bit better, in fact a lot better.'

The two security guards were leaning forward, trying to catch what I was saying. I admit that my voice might have been a little muffled because of the mask.

'Why are you wearing that mask?' one of them asked.

'Germs, of course,' I said. 'They're ubiquitous.'

'You what?' he said.

'Ubiquitous – they're everywhere.'

'They are for us, too,' he said, 'and we're not wearing masks.'

Exactly the same argument as the doctor uses when I raise the subject with him.

'It was of no consolation to the victims of pneumonic plague during the Black Death that there were millions of other victims, was it?' I said.

'The Black Death?' said one of the security guards to the other. 'What's he going on about?'

I could see from their faces – brutal, devoid of ideas – that they would never be able to understand, so I turned to the manager, who had rivulets of sweat pouring down his face.

'What did you have for breakfast, for example?'

'Coffee, toast, a boiled egg... Look, we're not here to talk about me.'

'Was the coffee boiled?' I asked.

'Was the coffee boiled? What's that got to do with anything?'

'You sell coffee to the public and you don't know? You don't issue a warning? Boiled coffee raises your cholesterol whereas when it's not boiled it doesn't.'

'That's the first I've heard of it. Anyway, it's got nothing to do with me. You're frightening my staff with your mask.'

'Don't be ridiculous,' I said. 'They're surrounded here by every unhealthy food known to man and I wager you allow them to buy it at reduced prices as compensation for their miserable wages. It's their diet they ought to be frightened of, not a mask that would protect them from harm if I were suffering from a contagious pulmonary, that is to say lung, disease.'

I put in the word 'lung' because I thought the girl at the till would understand it.

The manager, forced to see sense, turned polite.

'I think, sir,' he said, 'you should just pay for your things and go.'

I handed my credit card to the girl with sheep's eyes and entered my number in the machine, having first put on a disposable glove. I wiped the card on one side with a propyl alcohol-impregnated tissue when she handed it back to me. Of course, I couldn't wipe it on the side with my signature because it would come off and probably damage the strip (an enquiry to the credit company on this very point went unanswered). But it is better for a card to be half-clean than wholly dirty, since most infectious diseases are transmitted in proportion to the number of bacteria consumed or breathed in or entering via blemishes in the skin, such as we all have.

When I took off my glove, I asked whether they had a special container for biological waste.

'You should get one,' I said to the manager when he told me that they had not.

My mask occasioned no further alarm on subsequent excursions to the supermarket. Familiarity breeds respect; it is not true that a prophet is without honour in his own shopping centre.

3

I RETURN TO THE brown manila envelope. It had to be opened with a letter opener, for it is surprising how often, if you open a letter with your fingers, you cut yourself on the edge of the paper, even through a glove, thus creating a portal for germs. No doubt many times this happens without serious ill-effects: but it is the once that is dangerous, not the ninety-nine times it is not, that counts.

I keep the letter-opener in the bathroom; it has a slightly more clinical aspect than the rest of my flat, the tiles being white and easy to clean (I won't say disinfect, that would be presumptuous and to tempt fate).

However, I do claim to disinfect the letter-opener. Not only do I have a small autoclave but also a stainless steel dish full of chlorhexidine, so that I don't have to sterilise immediately before use.

I was ready now to open the letter. I sat down in preparation for doing so, for, though not an emotional person, indeed a rational one, one never knows when shock will strike, and it is best to be prepared for all eventualities. Falling from standing can result in worse head injuries than falling from a seated position, and indeed most people who suffer from serious head injuries had been standing shortly before receiving them.

Gingerly, I opened the letter, unfolding the single sheet of paper and shaking it lightly to ensure that there was nothing else in it that might be harmful.

It was from the Department of Work and Pensions. Of course, it had been written, printed and folded by a computer, which was reassuring from the point of view of contamination, but one cannot but help feel that the impersonality of the modern world must have adverse health consequences, even severe ones. We are, after all, social animals.

The letter used no form of address such as 'Dear Sir'. Instead, it went straight to what, no doubt, it considered the heart of the matter, but which in my view it dealt with in very superficial fashion:

> It has been determined that your unavailability for work may not be justified by your current state of health, and you are therefore required to attend a medical examination at the time and location stated below.

I was angry but not surprised. Officialdom has no heart and very little more, perhaps even less, head. It thinks that people have nothing better to do than attend to its demands. Then I noticed that the so-called medical examination, of the kind that I had undergone only six months previously, was to take place on the very day after the letter arrived. If it hadn't been for fear of stirring up a cloud of dust, some of which might have entered my lungs, I should have crumpled the letter up and thrown it at the wall, or perhaps the ground (less wrenching for the shoulder).

How could they expect me to work? My last work, as a general administrative assistant in an office producing nothing but further administration, had been disastrous for my health. Even the thought of it was enough to put my blood pressure up. I knew that this was so because I tested it with my home blood pressure machine. (I find it almost inconceivable that in these days of strokes and heart attacks, there are still households without this essential piece of equipment, but I suppose human history is nothing but a record of people's irresponsibility and indifference to their health.)

My procedure for establishing the connection between emotion and blood pressure was the following: I would sit in a chair with the machine attached to my arm and think of something pleasant and relaxing, such as a cup of ginseng tea. (I do not, of course, claim for ginseng all the virtues that have been claimed for it, since they have not been tested scientifically, even taking into account that all scientific knowledge is provisional, but it seems to me unlikely that a root or herb that has been in use for more than two millennia by the most intelligent people in the world could be completely without beneficial effects, even if we do not quite know what they are.) Relaxation, in other words, is brought about by the thought of relaxation, and when thoroughly relaxed I would take my blood pressure.

It would be normal – perfectly normal, though I am the first to admit that even this level is not entirely without its risks.

Then I would think of something stressful. (I know the word 'stress' is inexact and perhaps even overused, but we all know what it means.) I would think of my last attempt to work, or of receipt of a letter from the Department of Work and Pensions.

The exact nature of the work I performed is not important. It is in the nature of the kind of work I do – office work – that it should be completely – or at least ninety-five per cent – unnecessary, redundant, supererogatory. There is nothing more stressful than being busy while bored, unless being busy, bored and useless is worse.

On receipt of the letter, I could not help but remember my superior (that is to say, superior in the hierarchy, not in any other sense) in my last job. He was called Jones.

Jones was stupid, he limped and had yellowing teeth that were more like fangs than a regular set. It was clear, as I told him repeatedly, that his teeth were like that because he sucked peppermints all day, but he would never explain how he came by his limp. Nevertheless, I was able to surmise. His limp, too, was connected to his habit of sucking peppermints.

Most people who suck peppermints all day have something to hide, namely their breath. Some suffer from halitosis – or rather, other people suffer from their halitosis. But most peppermint-suckers drink too much and seek to disguise the smell of stale alcohol by that of peppermint. It doesn't work, of course: the combination is far worse than either alone, but man was a self-deceiver ever.

But what, you ask, is the connection between sucking peppermints and a limp? Surely the answer is obvious. A man who drinks so much that he feels the need to hide it from others is much more likely to have an accident and thereby come by a limp than a person who is always sober. I suspected that Jones had staggered in front of a car and sustained a serious injury, perhaps a compound fracture that had never fully healed. Here was living proof that, the improvements in orthopaedic surgery notwithstanding, prevention is better that cure. Of course, he could also have had gout (more common in drinkers) that, neglected for long enough, would have produced deformities in his toes, particularly his big toes, and resulted in a limp.

Jones's limp was thus his own fault. I am not a puritan, far from it, but the facts of physiology make drinking to excess a danger to health. It is up to man to find pleasures that pose no risk to his health, though I concede that Nature has rather carelessly endowed him, if not with bad habits themselves, then at least with a propensity to form them.

Indeed, you might even say that the search for harmless pleasure is man's highest moral duty, since pleasure he must have, and all other moral duties depend upon his being alive or bodily able to perform them (for who demands morality of the dead?). Thus, the man who looks after himself, from the point of view of his own health, is the most fundamentally decent kind of man there is.

Incidentally, I am not boasting: it took me a long time to recognise this truth. Like many another foolish young man, I indulged in sport, completely disregarding the broken legs, sprained shoulders and so forth to which it might so easily lead, to say nothing of the long-term arthritic complications of having overstrained the joints. Really,

I think it is quite wrong – cynical or evil, even – for the government to encourage young people, who don't know any better, to indulge in sport when it (the government) knows perfectly well that sport is the commonest cause of injury, as is obvious from the emergency department of any hospital on a Saturday afternoon.

I am not against exercise, don't misunderstand me, but it should be taken with caution. Walking, for example, is very good for you, provided it is vigorous enough but not too vigorous, especially on hard surfaces such as pavements, that can cause erosion by the repeated small impacts on the surfaces of your hip joints.

And of course it is very important that you should choose where you walk with care. Everything in life is a question of the balance of the risks of harm against potential benefits, and there is no point of walking for the sake of your health in an area where you are likely to be attacked. Such activities as mountaineering I deplore, for the most obvious reasons.

In order to demonstrate that I am not a killjoy, let me add that I am not against sex, in fact I am in favour of it – provided, of course, it is solitary. Masturbation gives you all the pleasure and health benefits, but none of the risks, of sex with another person (of course I am assuming that you do not suffer from angina, which is a contraindication to sex and which, let me not mince my words, is probably the consequence of your bad habits anyway).

Masturbation sets the heart racing, and cardiologists tell us that we should raise our heart rates to the maximum for at least five minutes per day. There is, in fact, no reason why we should not do this several times a day; and the great advantage of masturbation is that it avoids the risk of infection by the other party to the activity. I am not talking here only of venereal disease, though I do not wish to minimise the risk of that. The fact is that close proximity to another person, however you feel about her (or him, nature in this respect draws no distinctions), risks the transfer of alien noxious organisms, not only bacteria but fungi, rickettsia, protozoa, worms, insects, arachnids, viruses and even perhaps prions yet to be discovered. We all have our own flora and fauna, with which by long familiarity we are in balance; and it is wrong, both practically and morally, to upset that balance for a few moments of sensuous pleasure that might lead to severe illness. It is wrong morally because health is the precondition of right action. Health is therefore the categorical imperative.

So sex, yes, as much of it as you like, provided it involves or implicates no one else.

I did not mean to imply, however, that all forms of raised heart rate are good for you: for example, those induced by letters such as the one I received from the Department of Work and Pensions. They lead to a release of glucocorticoids from the adrenal glands (if I have understood correctly), and this in turn leads to a rise in your blood pressure and your blood sugar level. If this happens often or regularly enough, the changes become chronic, physiologically institutionalised as it were, and then, before you can say non-steroidal anti-inflammatory, you have had a heart attack or a stroke.

It is not just a question of the receipt of such letters. Because man is a conscious being endowed with imagination and memory, he cannot avoid thinking about such letters once he has received them – mind over matter is one thing, but mind over mind another – and so the effect is long-lasting.

I went once to a lawyer to see whether there was any redress. I had, unfortunately, to select him from among those in the *Yellow Pages* who promised free initial consultation (only those who have secured their health can afford the best legal advice). I was unimpressed by the look of his premises: an old shop-front with a window rendered opaque with whitewash, on which were painted in faded gold lettering, 'Criminal, Divorce, Commercial'. No accident or negligence, I noted; but then his office had not been redecorated for years. The words in largest lettering were 'Legal Aid'. Those who need good lawyers most can afford them least, an example of how everything in the world is distributed in inverse proportion to the requirements of natural justice.

You couldn't just open the front door of the lawyer's shop (it hardly deserved the name of office, let alone chambers) and walk in. You had first to use some kind of security intercom system, which gave you the impression that you were regarded, virtually by definition, as a potentially violent criminal, or else why would you need legal advice in the first place?

Pulling on my glove, I pressed the button that said 'Press to enter.' Had it sounded inside? There was no way of knowing. I waited; there was no reply. It would hardly be surprising if, in a shabby place like this, the apparatus did not work. I pressed again; no reply. I rang – or did not ring – a third time.

'I'm not deaf,' crackled an angry female voice over the loudspeaker. 'Wait your turn.'

My turn? As far as I could see, I was the only person trying to get in; not surprisingly, perhaps, if this is the way clients were treated.

I waited a little longer – what else could I do? – and then the voice said, 'Yes?'

I said that I had an appointment with Mr A...

'What was your name?'

I tried to ignore the impertinence: to dwell on it would only have raised my blood pressure, perhaps to dangerous levels (there is, of course, no entirely safe level). I gave my name, speaking at a distance from the mouthpiece for fear of its embedded filth. A buzzer sounded, but by the time I realised that it was a signal for me to open the door, it had stopped. I pressed again on the intercom button but, as I did so, the buzzer caught me unawares again and I missed the opportunity once more.

It was like one of those situations in which a socially inept person tenders his hand to an interlocutor to shake, withdraws it just as he reaches out for it, and then puts it out again once the interlocutor has withdrawn his own. (The whole business of shaking hands is, of course, dangerous and irresponsible, and is something I never do. The Moslem men who will not shake hands with a woman are in my opinion only half right: they should not shake hands with anyone. If I were in charge, there would be a law prohibiting it.)

Eventually, the receptionist and I managed to co-ordinate my entry into the office. As I entered, I heard her say, 'See you on Saturday at three o'clock, then,' and put the phone down. She hadn't been attending to my situation at all.

'You're early,' she said.

'I wanted to make sure I was on time,' I replied, 'because it's important.'

'Mr A... is very busy and his time is fully occupied,' she said.

What was that supposed to mean? That my affairs were not important, that I was only one among many? Not for me, I wasn't. That is what people, even intelligent people, have always failed to understand.

'Take a seat. He's running late.'

She made it sound as if it were my fault. In the meantime, of course, I had been observing my surroundings.

The receptionist sat at a grey-painted steel desk, second-hand or army surplus, I should imagine. Beside her computer – far from the latest model – was a can of Coca-Cola. I would be being less than honest if I did not admit that there was a flash-flood of anger through my mind.

Who knows what is in that sickly-sweet brown concoction? The formula has never been revealed. We know, of course, that it has caffeine in it, and that caffeine is addictive. If you take it for long enough, and often enough, and in sufficient quantity, you get a headache if you stop which can then be relieved only by – caffeine! The commercial equivalent of the perfect murder, if you ask me.

And please don't tell me that the caffeine in Coca-Cola comes from the kola nut, and that people in West Africa have been chewing kola nuts for centuries. Since when has the condition of West Africa been something to imitate rather than avoid?

But caffeine is the least of it (perhaps). What about the other ingredients that we know nothing about, not even what they are: carcinogens, teratogens, allergens? How on earth are you supposed to know that a product is safe, especially if made in a factory, unless you know what is in it?

Needless to say, none of these vital questions (and I use the word 'vital' advisedly) passed through the mind of the receptionist, not even fleetingly I suspect. Her eyes were those, if I may be allowed a short flight of fancy, of a carnivorous heifer, in other words malicious and predatory without alertness. I know that Coca-Cola probably does not have meat extract in it, though we can't positively know this in the absence of knowledge of what it does actually contain; but even carnivores sometimes resort to grass and other vegetable matter.

Of course, it was not entirely a coincidence that I found her with this can of Coca-Cola. It would have been more of a coincidence, statistically speaking, if I had not done so, for she was, in a manner of speaking, Coca-Cola made flesh. I doubt that she was ever without her can to comfort her. Her fat flesh was the consistency and colour of putty (before putty has dried, of course), and indicated millions of empty calories consumed without thought or even pleasure.

Moreover, I could almost visualise the atoms of aluminium that leached out of the can into the liquid, and from there entered the neuro-fibrillary tangles in her brain that would lead her eventually to suffer from Alzheimer's disease. I am fully aware that it has been disputed that aluminium causes Alzheimer's, but where health is concerned there is no hypothesis without fire, if I may so put it. Besides, it has been demonstrated that those who do not use their intellectual faculties are in danger of losing them, such as they are, and of developing the disease later in life, and the receptionist was decidedly not one for thought. Caution was all the more advisable in her case, therefore, but it was clear that she had thrown all caution to the calories.

The reception area and waiting room was very small, and would have been very dark had it not been for the subliminally flickering fluorescent tubular lighting. Abandon hope – that is to say, convulsion-free periods – all epileptics who enter here! Since epileptics must require lawyers at least as frequently as others, if not more frequently, insofar as they have more accidents than average, the use of a fluorescent light tube in such an office was little short of criminally negligent. Didn't the lawyer care about anyone but himself?

On the other hand, I thought I might at least be able to interest her in her own health, that is to say her survival. I suppose that, at heart, I am still an optimist, believing that people can save themselves if they are given the opportunity, which is to say the knowledge of how to do so.

'There's no natural light in here,' I said. 'Only artificial.'

'What do you mean?' asked the receptionist.

'It's not good for your bones,' I said. 'They need sunlight, or they start to lose strength. There's no sunlight in here.'

'What do you expect?' she said. 'It's an office, not a holiday resort. And it's winter.'

Obviously a hopeless case, probably a victim of seasonal affective disorder (ironically a problem of lack of sunlight, too). I decided to sit down. There were four chairs, all of them different.

The first was a low, utility armchair with dark upholstery of artificial leather in which there were some clearly-demarcated cigarette burns. They allowed people to smoke in here (or at least did not stop them from doing so)! On reflection, I realised that I had detected immediately the poor quality of the air, but, distracted by more serious and immediate dangers, I had put it to the back of my mind. Of course, in the long-term, the poor quality of the air would be a very serious problem, none more serious in fact. I had to decide very quickly whether, in view of the polluted atmosphere, I should continue with my appointment. I decided to take the risk, because there was no guarantee that anywhere else would be any better.

I rejected the second chair on ergonomic grounds: it was as if it had been designed with the purpose of giving people backache.

The third chair was better from the design point of view, having a straight wooden back, but unfortunately it had a cloth upholstered seat that, it would be fair to assume, had not been cleaned in its entire career. Anyone who seen pictures of the microscopic fauna that inhabit even clean upholstery will not lightly take the decision to sit down on an upholstered seat, especially if he has been preceded there by numerous other people of whose level of hygiene he cannot be at all sure.

Fortunately, the final chair was of plastic, and not that plastic with an uneven, pitted surface, such as you often find in temporary usage at public events, though it is perfectly obvious that such a surface must result in the accumulation of germs and other pathogens, but smooth plastic of the type that is easily cleaned.

So I took out the isopropyl alcohol wipes that I have always with me and wiped the surface thoroughly. I am not sure whether the receptionist was watching me, but when she saw me standing, waiting for the isopropyl alcohol to dry (for it is only when it has dried that it has exerted its bactericidal effect, and unfortunately many people, including, I am horrified to say, doctors, do not realise this and think that the act of wiping alone is what counts), she asked me why I did not sit down.

'I am waiting,' I said, 'until the seat is sterile.'

'Suit yourself,' she said, and then, to my disgust, took out a sandwich.

The Earl of Sandwich – he who invented the simulacrum of a meal that has borne his shameful name ever since – was one of the greatest malefactors in human history. Was not the sandwich the beginning of the slippery slope towards the fast food that is now clogging up millions, perhaps billions, of people's arteries and irritating their bowels into cancer? The Earl was the first to give mankind the impression that it did not matter much what it ate, so long as it filled the stomach and gratified the mouth *en route*. His culpability was all the greater since as an earl, presumably, he had a household full of servants upon whom he could call to prepare the healthiest and most nutritious of meals. He had no need of the quick fix, so his crime against humanity was completely without extenuating circumstances.

The sandwich represents an attitude to health and nutrition that is nothing short of irresponsible. And they are particularly noxious nowadays because of what people put in them.

Nevertheless, I said nothing. The receptionist wouldn't have listened to me anyway; and, besides, am I my sister's keeper?

I sat down. In front of the chairs was a coffee table of the cheapest type, piled with magazines also of the cheapest type, that is to say those concerned with the lives of celebrities. It has been proved, of course, that people who are the most interested in the lives of celebrities are the least happy and the most likely to need, or perhaps I should say to take, antidepressants; though whether an interest in celebrities causes unhappiness or unhappiness causes an interest in celebrities has not yet been fully established.

I had not brought anything with me to read – books are like magnets to iron filings when it comes to contamination by the outside world, which is why I absolutely refuse to join any public library and buy all my books via the internet, on the strict condition that they have been machine-wrapped in cellophane immediately after printing, the oestrogenic effects of cellophane notwithstanding (everything in life is a matter of relative danger, the least danger possible being the nearest we can come to safety). I repeat, because the previous sentence might have been rather long to take in at a single reading (but it is important to miss out nothing that is vital, which is to say that could affect one's own health or that of the public), I had not brought a book with me; and since an unoccupied mind is prey to anxieties that are themselves detrimental to the health, whether they are justified or unjustified, I decided to read one of these magazines.

They were well-thumbed and out of date, of course. Their out-of-dateness did not worry me, for what can happen to a celebrity except illicit affairs, children born out of wedlock and court cases for possession of cocaine? Scandal springs eternal. But the well-thumbedness was another matter altogether. I hardly need point out that it was a serious problem. And I discovered that, while I had brought my disposable gloves with me, I had inadvertently omitted to bring my face masks. How could I have made such an elementary error? Was I beginning to dement? I would have to perform the mini-mental state examination on myself when I returned home (the examination is the one that doctors use to detect dementia in their patients). Of course, it could just have been the high state of emotion associated with this case: I am, after all, only human.

'Excuse me,' I said to the receptionist, in a reconciliatory tone whose falseness I did not think she would be able to detect. 'Where do you keep your face masks?'

'What?' she said, looking up from the computer screen on which she had not really been concentrating. She probably thought I was talking about her make-up.

'Face masks, to cover your mouth to prevent germs from getting in – or out, for that matter.'

'We're lawyers, not doctors,' she said.

I didn't correct her grandiose 'we', and point out that she was not a lawyer but a secretary – if that. In any case, the absence of face masks was absolutely typical and only to be expected. We might as well be living in the age before the germ theory of disease and aseptic surgery.

This left me with a dilemma: should I go to the nearest pharmacy, or not, to obtain some? The dilemma had two legs, the first practical as to whether the pharmacy was near enough, the second the more difficult theoretical question of whether the risk of infection by going into public space, frequented by many carriers of dangerous germs, especially a pharmacy which one would expect to be frequented by a more than average proportion of contagious people, was greater than that of staying put in the lawyer's office and handling magazines that, by their appearance, must have been pawed by scores, if not hundreds, of people, many of them bacteriological undesirables of the highest class.

As it happened, the receptionist was able to tell me that there was a pharmacist just round the corner, by the church. The proximity of the pharmacy decided the question: sometimes, one just has to be guided by chance.

The church, I noticed, was still in use though semi-derelict. Church attendance is, of course, an equivocal thing from the point of view of health. It has been shown that it improves people's mood and even survival, though it has risks from the point of view of infectious diseases, unsafe roofs and so forth. It is not necessary for me to attend, however, nor would I derive any health benefits from doing so, because I look after my health in other ways. And church attendance has never been shown to be good for people who are careful of their health in other ways. I would put it like this: health is a destination that can be reached by more than one route – perhaps.

The pharmacy was a small one, run by an elderly Indian. The only customer, apart from me, was a lady in a woollen hat, full no doubt of allergenic fomites. She was asking advice from the pharmacist about what cough medicine to take.

'None,' I said firmly.

She turned to me and smiled the fatuous smile of the indiscriminately well-disposed. Of course, I myself was genuinely well-disposed, but she had no reason yet to think so.

'Don't take any,' I said. 'None of them is any good and most of them are harmful.'

'Excuse me, sir…' said the pharmacist.

Ignoring him – he had a vested interest in a sale, after all – I picked up the first bottle that came to hand. (There were several different types arrayed near the counter, and if any of them was any good it would have had the monopoly. The main difference between them was in their colour, that is to say in their colorant, each of which might have had different harmful effects on different people according to their differing predispositions, or what the common man is apt to call his 'system'.)

'Look what it contains,' I said. 'Look!'

'I haven't got my glasses,' said the woman.

'Excuse me, sir,' said the pharmacist again.

'Look!' I said. By now I was getting angry: not for myself, of course, but on her behalf. She was about to be sold poison, perfectly legally and in broad daylight. 'Look! Chlorpheniramine. Do you know what that means?'

'No,' she said.

'Sir…' said the pharmacist.

'It's an antihistamine.' I turned to the pharmacist. 'Isn't that right?' He was about to answer, evidently thinking that my question was a request for information rather than rhetorical. Of course I knew perfectly well what chlorpheniramine was. 'By itself, it would make you sleepy, but look at this.' I stabbed my finger at the label with the list of ingredients. (The product, incidentally, was called Chestoclear, a name so dishonest that a politician might have devised it.)

'I haven't got my glasses,' said the woman, as if that absolved her of the responsibility of knowing what she was about to take.

'I know that,' I said. 'It doesn't matter, I'll tell you instead. Codeine, that's what it says, codeine. I suppose you know what that means?'

'No,' she confessed.

'No, I thought not.' People will swallow anything, but they don't know any pharmacology. 'Codeine,' I continued, 'is an opiate, just like morphine or heroin. And I suppose you know what that means?'

'Sir,' said the pharmacist, 'really, I…'

Really, he what? I didn't wait to find out. I listed the side effects for the old lady, ending with constipation (because all old people are worried about the state of their bowels, which is not wrong in itself, but only when it is to the exclusion of all other aspects of their health).

'And,' I said, 'the somnolence caused by the codeine is additive to that caused by the chlorpheniramine. So if you took this poison, it's quite likely that you would fall asleep for hours on end. And for someone of your age, that would be very dangerous.'

'I wouldn't mind a good sleep,' she said. 'I haven't had a good sleep for months. I can't get off, and when I do I wake up soon afterwards.'

'Aha!' I pounced. 'You're precisely the kind of person who'd get used to taking this stuff, and take more and more of it to try to reproduce its initial effect. Before you knew where you were, you'd be hooked. The manufacturers love people like you.'

'Can't you mind your own business?' said the pharmacist.

'Yes, that's what you'd like, isn't it?' I said, turning to him. 'Everyone to mind his own business, while you poison the population in peace. But what's going to happen to this poor lady here, of whose ignorance you want to take advantage, once she's addicted? That is, if she survives to get addicted.'

'What exactly do you mean by that?' said the pharmacist.

'Well,' I said, 'isn't it obvious? She goes deeply to sleep, slips down the bed and gets bronchopneumonia. Then it's curtains for her, and all because she had a little cough, a tickle at the back of her throat that would have gone away by itself if left untreated.' I turned to her again. 'I presume you've checked it with your doctor?'

I did not, of course, mention my own reservations about doctors. Our situations, after all, were very different. Doctors have their uses when you are completely ignorant of health matters, as she obviously was.

'No,' she said. 'I didn't like to bother him when he's so busy.'

'Typical!' I exclaimed. 'It could be anything, your cough: the beginning of heart failure, cancer, anything. Especially at your age. Of course you should go to your doctor, it would be stupid not to.'

To do her justice, she looked alarmed. The fecklessness of youth has often been remarked upon; that of age, never.

'Perhaps I will,' she said.

'Get out of my shop!' shrieked the pharmacist. 'Get out!'

These Indians are meek and mild, obsequious even, until things don't go their own way, and then they show their true colours.

'With pleasure,' I replied in a dignified way. 'At least I'm not prostituting myself.' I went towards the door. 'I wouldn't buy anything from you if it killed me.' And I left.

4

ON THE WAY BACK to the lawyer's office, I worried that I should have said 'If it killed me not to,' but I am sure the pharmacist would have known what I meant. Of course, not buying the face masks I had gone there to purchase might in fact kill me, but there are some principles so important that they are worth dying for.

When I arrived back at the office, the receptionist said, with the nearest to sarcasm that someone at her intellectual level could reach, 'Got them?'

'No,' I said. I didn't want to go into details, so I added, 'They didn't have any.'

'Shame,' said the receptionist.

By now I was so agitated that I forgot to put on my gloves and picked up one of the magazines with my bare fingers. Also, I did not re-wipe the seat: as Hume says, reason is the slave of the passions. A little bit of emotion, and one omits the most elementary precautions. Our life hangs by a thread.

Of course the magazine was complete rubbish, not worth taking the slightest risk for. It assumed that you knew who all these celebrities were, calling them by their first names (or even diminutives of their first names) as if they were personal friends of yours or members of your family. Mind you, I wouldn't have known who they were even if they were called by their surnames, for most of them were either pop singers, something to do with television, or footballers. I never listen to pop music because it destroys high-pitch hearing; television emits dangerous rays and its flickers can cause epilepsy; and it goes without saying that football crowds spread diseases, either actually or potentially.

'Are Dean and Caz an item?' was the title of the lead story. (I think the answer must be No, because the magazine was three years old

41

and any liaison between them must have ended by now. Don't these celebrities realise that constantly changing partners – horrible word – spreads venereal disease and increases the risk of Aids, from which so many of them die?)

The very next stories proved my point. 'Is Wayne cheating on Sharleen?' and 'Gemma has Lee's love child.'

Nevertheless, there was one interesting and important article in the magazine, though of course it was not written from the correct, medical point of view. Its title was 'A peanut nearly killed me!' and it told how a woman called Peggy Smith had eaten a peanut and had swelled to several times her normal size within seconds and nearly choked to death. Luckily her son, a soldier in the Special Air Service, was there and applied mouth-to-mouth resuscitation. At least they teach something useful in some parts of the army!

As usual, it was partly her own fault: her face may have swelled up to four times it original size, but its original size was far too big to begin with, and fat people are much more likely to choke to death than thin ones.

This is not to say that peanut allergy – indeed, allergies to many other things – is not an extremely important problem. No serious, intelligent or responsible person can avoid thinking about it. It can strike at any time, and you have to be prepared because there is always a first and unexpected time, a first and unexpected time that can be and often is catastrophic. (I don't mean, of course, that everyone becomes allergic in the end – I am not a hypochondriac or a neurotic – but only that every person who becomes allergic is allergic for the first time.)

Whenever I go past a restaurant and see people eating in it, oblivious of the dangers, I admit that I think 'The poor fools! I bet not one of them has a syringe of adrenaline with him. Probably they don't even have one at home.' The astonishing thing is that not one in a thousand people, no, not one in ten thousand, carries such a syringe, though disaster can strike at any time, and when it does, it is already too late.

Have all these people in the restaurant not heard, I wonder, of the case of the man who collapsed and died as a plate of hot sizzling prawns was carried by the waiter past his table? He breathed in the fumes, and within seconds he was dead. It goes without saying that if he had had a syringe of adrenaline with him, or if, better still, the people dining with him had had one, and had appreciated what was happening to him and known what to do about it, he might – no, he *would* – still be alive.

That there are many other reasons not to eat in a restaurant I need hardly add: among them, cockroaches and people who handle food who haven't disinfected their hands before doing so (washing is not enough). But I suppose we have to make concessions to human nature as it is, and it seems as though some people are not happy unless they are taking risks, for example by mountaineering or eating in restaurants. This is not say, however, that the risks from the public health point of view should not be reduced as much as possible. I suggest, therefore, that as an absolute minimum all people who insist upon eating in restaurants should undergo training in cardiopulmonary resuscitation and recognition of anaphylactic shock, and that they should be obliged to show the certificate that they have done so before being allowed to enter. These certificates should be valid for a year and renewable only after a refresher course.

Furthermore, every potential anaphylactic – and that is all of us – should have to show his adrenaline syringe and artificial airway before he enters, and should have a metal bracelet round his wrist to indicate where on his person these things are to be found. Failing any of which, he should be denied entry.

As for me, I always carry these things with me, and I do not even go to restaurants. I wouldn't been seen dead in one. But restaurants are not the only place where anaphylaxis strikes: just think of wasps. As far as I know, no government in the world has undertaken a wasp elimination programme, and if any were to try to do so I dare say the ecologists would protest, though as far as I am aware no one has ever demonstrated what good wasps do, though the harm that they do is so obvious that I need not point it out.

Moreover, we live in a peanut-saturated environment: you have only to think about the number of products that carry a warning that they might (not even that they do) contain peanuts to appreciate this. How would peanuts get into tinned soup, for example, unless they were ubiquitous? So even if you are extremely conscientious about avoiding peanuts, as I am (though I am not allergic to them, or at least not yet allergic to them, 'yet' being the most important word in the English language in this connection), you can never be sure that you will not encounter them somewhere or other.

Because we live in a peanut-saturated (I nearly said peanut-dominated) environment, allergy can strike at any moment, capriciously. One moment you can encounter peanuts with impunity – bury yourself up to the neck in them, if you wish – and the next, a single molecule of peanut is enough to kill you. There must be an explanation, because there is an explanation for everything, at least everything worth explaining, but we cannot yet say for certain what it is. All that one can say for certain is that there has been a devastating increase in the number of people who are allergic to peanuts and that we cannot predict who will be next to fall victim to this modern plague. In the absence of a complete prohibition of the cultivation and sale of peanuts, which in any case would probably result in a illegal trafficking of them and an epidemic of allergy to something else, onions for example, because the immune system is like Nature as a whole and does not like a vacuum, the precautionary principle, which, when stripped of its sophisticated intellectual and statistical justifications can be boiled down to the folk wisdom that it is better to be safe than sorry, requires that we carry an adrenaline syringe with us at all times. Not that I expect anyone to take me seriously; there are too many vested interests involved, though I think it only fair to point out that my suggestion would stimulate the syringe and needle supply industries, as well as the pharmaceutical manufacturers of adrenaline, not to mention the cool-box manufacturing industry, because – obviously – if one is going to be from home for longer than a few hours, and given the rate at which adrenaline degrades at room temperature and loses its efficacy, one will need a means of keeping the adrenaline at a cooler temperature.

Needless to say, Mrs Smith, no doubt ghosted by the real author of the article, did not draw any serious conclusions at all from her brush with the near-fatal peanut. This is what she wrote:

> I nearly died. These terrifying moments brought me nearer to God. It was His will that I should be saved and it was thanks to him that my son was near me when I swallowed the peanut. Every day I give thanks to Him that I am still alive.

Heavens above! Can't she, or her ghost-writer, think? If God wanted so much for us to live, would he have invented peanuts? – which, incidentally, kill in more ways than one, being among the principal causes of choking in childhood. Surely it would have been much easier and more economical not to allow the development of peanuts in the first place; there would then have been no such thing as peanut allergy and Mrs Smith wouldn't have needed her son to save her.

What offends me about her attitude is its passivity, its implied fatalism, its *che sera, sera*. We don't have to die like lambs to the slaughter if we take a few simple precautions. If the peanut incident had happened to me, I would have been out demonstrating against peanuts, or rather against a government so culpably indifferent to the health and welfare of the population under its jurisdiction that it allows a peanut anywhere near a food factory. I wouldn't do this for my own sake, of course, because demonstrating in public obviously carries health risks of its own, but for the allergy-sufferers of posterity – who, if current trends continue, will soon be a hundred per cent of humanity.

On that sad note, I happened to lower my eyes, and I immediately caught sight of something suspicious under the chair in front of me. I thought I recognised what it was, but I wanted to make sure before I accused anybody. I got down on my hands and knees – recklessly, you might say, but clearly my public duty outweighed my duty to my personal safety – and picked it up. It was just as I thought.

'Look at this!' I cried. I didn't have to exaggerate my indignation.

'What is it now?' asked receptionist, as if I were likely to be making a fuss over nothing.

I stood up and held the offending object out to her on the palm of my hand. She looked at it; I could see from the expression on her face, or rather the lack of it, that she had not the faintest idea of its significance.

'Can't you see what it is?' I asked.

'Yes,' she said. 'It's just a child's marble. So what?'

'Just a child's marble!' I said. 'Just a child's marble! Is that all you can say?'

'Yes,' she said.

'Think what a marble can do, think of the public danger it poses.'

'I don't see what the problem is,' she said. 'Sometimes clients come here with their young children, and they have to be occupied somehow or they get bored. I suppose someone must have come in with a child and he played marbles and left one behind.'

What fatal obtuseness! Surely it doesn't take much imagination to see the damage a marble can cause? I don't count myself particularly gifted, except perhaps in the possession of more than average common sense, but even I could see the possible disastrous consequences of a child's marble in a waiting room.

'Someone could easily tread on it and slip,' I said. 'I'm sure that you have more than your fair share of old people as clients. They are particularly vulnerable, and could fracture their necks of femur. That is often a harbinger of death for them,' I said.

'We've never had an accident in here,' she said.

'You've never died,' I replied, 'but that doesn't mean you're never going to do so.' (Especially if she continues to eat sandwiches like those, I thought to myself). 'And then there are all the people with osteoporosis, brittle bones to you. They are especially likely to fracture their femurs. I suppose that many of your clients smoke?'

'Some of them,' said the receptionist, with the puzzlement that invariably accompanies ignorance.

'Smoking promotes osteoporosis, which increases the risk of fractures,' I said. Compared with her, Dr Watson was a shrewd man.

'It's only a marble,' was all that she could say.

'And how many orifices do you suppose it could get stuck in?' I asked. Of course, there was no point in asking her to think. She probably didn't even know how many orifices the human body had. I saw that I would have to enumerate the dangers for her, though of course this was spoon-feeding her.

'First, there are the ears,' I said. 'Can you imagine how difficult it might be to get an impacted marble out of the external meatus of the ear, assuming of course that it has not been pushed so far in as to damage the eardrum itself?'

Frankly, I don't think she could. She was the kind of person who took her auditory canal and eardrums for granted.

'And then, of course, there is the oesophagus. It could easily get stuck in a child's oesophagus and he would need an operation to remove it. Every operation carries a risk. Furthermore, the marble might be inhaled, and a bronchoscopy would be needed, that is if the person had not already choked to death. I suppose you're trained in the Heimlich manoeuvre?'

'What's that?' she said.

'*What's that?*' I confess that I sneered as I repeated her words. I am a tolerant man, but – like everyone else – I can be pushed too far. 'The Heimlich manoeuvre was invented by Henry Heimlich as a way of saving the lives of the choking. You wrap your arms around the stomach of a choking person from the back and squeeze sharply several times in quick succession.' I illustrated what I meant, but of course it would have been better and more realistic if there had been a dummy, or better still a volunteer, to perform the manoeuvre on.

'Then, of course,' I said, 'there is the rectum. A marble, even several marbles, could easily be insinuated into the rectum via the anus, especially as glass is so smooth.'

'You'd rattle if that happened,' said the receptionist.

'My dear madam,' I said, 'this is no laughing matter. This is not something to make jokes about. Foreign bodies in the rectum are a great nuisance, as every surgeon will attest. Alfred Poulet, in his treatise on foreign bodies in surgical practice, devotes fully forty-nine pages to them. It would, perhaps, be indelicate to mention other places in the human body into which marbles could be insinuated. Kindly, therefore, dispose of this marble in a waste bin from which there is no possibility of its escape. There is surely no point in avoiding danger in one place only to create it in another.'

I handed the marble over to her, and she took it from me rather reluctantly. I sat down again and resumed my reading.

'Mr A... will see you now,' said the receptionist, interrupting my train of thought without the slightest apology.

She pointed to what I suppose Mr A... considered his inner sanctum, entered through a plain deal door.

I went in. There was a smell – no, a veritable fug – of stale cigar smoke, and cheap cigars at that, I should imagine. I coughed immediately, as a matter of principle, just to let Mr A... know that I had noticed, disapproved of and suffered the physiological consequences of his appalling habit.

The room was cluttered: papers, files, old law books. Mr A... sat in a swivel chair behind a desk, and behind him was a grimy, never-washed window with bars to prevent anyone from climbing in. The window gave on to a brick wall about six feet away. Mr A... had not reached the top of his profession.

I took the measure of Mr A... at once. He was enormously fat and would have had breasts the prominence of a woman's had it not been for his vast protuberant belly. He was like Ganesh fallen on hard times and sent out to work.

He wore no jacket and his tie hung loosely around his open collar. This, I have to admit, was sensible if not sartorially elegant for someone in his circumstances, even if those circumstances were self-inflicted. With a neck like his, the size of a sumo-wrestler's thigh, any attempt to do up a shirt collar would have exerted further pressure on the pressure receptors in his carotid arteries. Now these receptors, if chronically stimulated, raise the blood pressure. As Mr A...'s blood pressure was almost certainly raised already, on account of his unhealthy girth, additional pressure from a shirt and tie could have been fatal to him. (I took all this in at a glance.) Not that I suppose that this was the reason he did not do up his collar: it was probably more a matter of comfort than health with him, because most people put the former before the latter, though the latter is the precondition of the former.

Mr A... made a slight movement towards me in his chair, that reminded me of a nature film I saw when I was young (before I realised the dangers of television) about elephant seals. His movement was the best he could do without exhausting himself and getting out of breath. It was clear to me at once that what he needed was surgery: for once you have let yourself go so far, surgery to reduce your capacity to eat and absorb food is the only reliable way to lose weight.

'What can I do for you?' he asked, even those few words causing him to wheeze a little.

'You could give up smoking,' I said. To underline my point, I coughed again.

'That's for me, not you,' he said.

'No man's an island,' I said. 'Your clients have to breathe in your smoke with all its tar and carcinogens. What you do in the privacy of your own home is your own affair, of course, assuming you have no wife and children, but a public place such as your office is another matter.'

Stung by my reproach, he said, 'You don't have to worry, you're not going to be here long enough to suffer any harm.'

'That's not the point,' I said. 'I'm not just speaking on my own behalf. Besides, it has been demonstrated that there is no safe dose of second-hand smoke a person may breathe. And even if the risk to your clients is only a very slight one, it is completely unjustified to make them run it when it could be so easily avoided. First do no harm.'

I think I had established that I was no ordinary client, to be fobbed off with reassurances, but rather a man of forensic precision of mind.

'I presume,' he said, his wheeze getting worse, 'that you haven't come here to complain about the smoke in my room, of whose existence you were unaware until you arrived.'

I confess he had a point, if a small one. Of course, he made it merely to divert the conversation from an uncomfortable course, rather than for any other reason; once again, we see how the search for comfort distracts from the search for health.

'I'm thinking of suing the Department of Work and Pensions for negligence,' I said.

'On what grounds?' he asked.

'It owes me a duty of care,' I said, 'that it has wilfully and maliciously failed to discharge.'

'How so?'

'It has repeatedly sent me unnecessary and vexatious letters that it must have known, or ought to have known, would be deleterious to my health.'

'How?'

'By raising my blood pressure.'

'And?' asked Mr A... 'What else?'

'What do you mean, what else?'

'I mean, what harm have they done to you?'

I suppose that by now I should not be surprised by ignorance of pathophysiology, even in a supposedly educated man, and yet this indifference to the queen of the sciences, the science that after all serves to make all the others possible, continues to amaze and appal me.

'A raised blood pressure is a harm in itself,' I said. 'Even if it is only temporary.'

'Can you explain?' he said, a slight smile of derision playing about his fat lips. Here was not only ignorance, but triumphant ignorance. I was prepared for it, however.

'"The time has come to abandon the high and normal blood pressure dichotomy and to focus on global risk reduction." Do you know what that is a quote from?'

'No,' he said.

'*The Lancet*. I presume you have heard of *The Lancet*?'

My question was rhetorical and even if it wasn't, I had no interest in the answer. 'It's one of the most important medical journals in the world. And what that quote means is that there is no safe blood pressure. Your risk of the conditions that raised blood pressure causes rises with your blood pressure. Therefore, anything that raises your blood pressure even for a short time raises your average blood pressure and, therefore, the chance of suffering from those conditions. I suppose you know what those conditions are?'

'Tell me,' he said.

'Heart attack, stroke, kidney failure and dementia. Not trivial conditions, I think you must agree.'

'But you don't have any of them,' he said, although I could see that he made a possible exception for dementia. Pioneers for the public good have always had to suffer the mulish scepticism and disdain of their opponents and therefore grow adept at understanding what they think.

'Not yet,' I said. 'But the situation is even worse than I have described. The fact is, unfortunately, that Man is a conscious, thinking, reflecting being, and the knowledge that his blood pressure has been put up in the past, and will probably be put up again in the near future, thus increasing his chance of catastrophic complications, is enough to worry him severely, which of course puts up his blood pressure. So it's a vicious circle, and the only way to stop it, other than a fatal stroke or heart attack, is to break it.'

'How?'

'I'm not greedy,' I said. 'I'm not doing this for myself alone. I'm not seeking damages, however justified they would be. No; I'm seeking an injunction against the Department of Work and Pensions to prevent it from sending any further letters that are injurious to my health.'

He put his sausage fingers together: a sign that, at long last, he was thinking.

'Even if such a risk were actionable,' he said, 'which I doubt, you would have to prove that the letters actually did raise your blood pressure.'

'Nothing easier,' I said. 'I have a continuous record of my blood pressure.'

'You might have forged it.'

'Impossible. I have an electronic recording device with time and date, and any electronic engineer would be able to testify that I haven't tampered with it.'

'But how are we to know that the rise in blood pressure coincides with and is caused by the letters you received?'

'I've thought of that, also. I don't want to waste your or anybody else's time. I've installed video cameras in every room in my flat, which of course also record the time and date. So I'm able to prove that there is a perfect correlation between receiving, opening and reading the letters and a rise in my blood pressure.'

'Video evidence is often fuzzy and equivocal,' he said. 'You can show that you opened and read a letter, perhaps, but not that it came from the Department.'

'That's precisely why I installed digitally-controlled tape recorders in my rooms as well. I read out the letter as soon as I opened it, timed and dated. There is no possibility of error.'

He leaned back. 'This is a very unusual case,' he said.

'I'm not bringing it for myself,' I said. 'There must be hundreds of thousands, if not millions of people in exactly the same situation, though without knowing it of course. I'm doing it for them.'

'It would be the first case of its kind.'

He wasn't thinking of my good, of course, but of his own. He was already dreaming of a class action in which he would play the leading part, that would lift him from the bottom to the top of his profession. I could see the plush chambers of his imagination. He forgot that, to adapt the famous lines of Horace slightly, they change their offices, not their souls, who ascend the professional scale.

But it is immature to be disappointed that someone is more interested in his own welfare than your own, especially when life has taught you nothing else. And, as Deng Xiao Ping said, in another context, what does it matter if a cat is black or white, so long as it catches mice? It was therefore essential that, dispassionately, I should strengthen my case as much as possible.

'In the very same edition of *The Lancet*,' I said, 'there were two articles about apical ballooning syndrome. The left auricle suddenly balloons, and the person dies before he's even had a chance to become a patient. And do you know what brings it on?'

'No,' he said. Obviously, he did not keep up to date with the literature.

'Extreme emotional stress,' I said. 'Such as the receipt of a threatening letter from the Department of Work and Pensions.'

He was now writing some notes. He looked up briefly and said that he would have to apply for legal aid funding, and that this might prove a serious hurdle.

I took it that our consultation was now over, but I am not a selfish man, concerned only with his own affairs, and I felt it only right that I should mention something that had been on my mind since the beginning of our brief acquaintance. (Besides, it would not do my case much good if he were to drop dead in the middle of it, quite likely in view of his size. Another lawyer couldn't be expected to master the case halfway through, so it was in my interest to preserve his life.)

'You should read the *New England Journal of Medicine* for the same week,' I said, as I got up to go. 'It has two articles about the survival of obese people after surgery for their obesity. It was much increased, and you fall into precisely the category – the super-obese – who benefited most. Of course, surgery doesn't eliminate your increased chance of death entirely, it is much too late for that.'

He looked up from his desk. His face was so well padded with fat – and when I say well, of course, I mean badly – that it was virtually expressionless. Therefore I saw no gratitude on it such as one might expect of a man who had just received life-saving information. This inability to express himself facially was yet another disadvantage of his obesity.

'You know what the Body Mass Index is, I suppose, BMI for short?' I asked.

He murmured a negative. So fat, and yet so ignorant! Not untypical, though.

'It's your weight divided by your height squared,' I said. 'In kilos and metres, of course. Looking at you, I should say that yours is over forty. Anything over thirty is considered obese. Mine is twenty-two – considered ideal.'

I hope no one will accuse me of the sin of pride when I express a certain satisfaction in my Body Mass Index. I think I should be allowed it because, I need hardly point out, it is not God-given, but is the result of a lifetime of regulation and self-control. (I have been measuring it every week for ten years now, and I am glad to say that the graph I keep of it is an absolutely straight line.) If one is not to be a little proud of one's Body Mass Index – one as stable and healthy as mine – of what is one to be proud?

A little like a life-insurance salesman, but with only his best interests at heart, I wanted to give him a practical illustration of the benefits of surgery.

'In the Swedish study,' I said, 'people like you, that is to say with a Body Mass Index of at least forty-point-eight, had an overall reduction in their death rate of thirty per cent if they had surgery. In the American study it was forty per cent.'

He was looking at me now – I could tell that much from his face.

'Aha!' I hear the attentive reader say at this point. 'Don't give me the relative figures, give me the absolute ones.' Quite right, you've made a good point. And although Mr A… wasn't acute enough to make this point himself, I decided to tell him the figures nonetheless. I didn't want him later to accuse me of concealing relevant facts from him.

'Of two thousand and ten patients from Sweden who had the surgery – and here I must ask you to remember that they included many who belonged to a group who benefited less than maximally because they were not in the fattest group – one hundred and one died. Of two thousand and thirty-seven who did not have surgery, one hundred and twenty-nine died.'

'You seem to have a very good memory for these things,' he said.

'You flatter me,' I said. 'I have an average memory, although I keep my brain in trim by doing mental arithmetic every day. Research shows that it helps to prevent Alzheimer's. No, I remember important facts by clearing my mind of all the rubbish that seems to occupy the minds of other people. I don't bother with anything that is not of vital importance.' Once again, I used the word 'vital' advisedly.

By now, I had backed my way into the door of his office.

'But before you decide to have surgery,' I said, 'I ought to warn you of two things.'

'And what are they?' he asked.

'First, in the American study, although the overall death rate was much reduced, the death rate from suicide increased. Therefore, if you have ever felt suicidal, it would seem an elementary precaution that you should consult a psychiatrist before proceeding to surgery. It's not an absolute contraindication, of course, only a relative one.'

'And the second thing?'

'A very fat man was stabbed by a youth in France recently. He was saved by the fact that he was so fat that the blade couldn't reach his vital organs. If he had been thinner, he probably would have died.'

'I don't think I need worry about that,' he said.

'But more and more youths are carrying knives these days, especially in an area like this. And presumably you meet quite a lot of them.'

'I've never been threatened.'

'You've never died either, but that doesn't mean you'll never die. We have to think ahead, which means assessing the risks. Once these knife-carrying youths realise that there are people too fat to stab to death, they'll start carrying longer blades. It's just like fraud: whatever you do to try to stop it, people will think of new ways to commit it. Be that as it may, if you have the operation and lose a lot of weight, I would recommend that you wear a stab-proof vest.'

Have I already mentioned that I never go out without one? I am, of course, far from suggesting that the youths who stab people in the street are not fully responsible for their actions: but it seems to me nonetheless that those who are stabbed in the chest and heart while away from home, and who were not wearing such vests at the time, are at the least guilty of contributory negligence – as guilty, morally if not legally, as those who are burgled who have failed to lock their houses, especially in areas with a high rate of burglary.

'I'll write to you,' said the lawyer as I left his office.

5

ON THE STREET OUTSIDE, two Moslem women were passing, dressed in those black tent-like robes that leave only a slit for the eyes. Some people find this form of dress offensive, arguing that it implies that all women are temptresses and all men are rapists; but I see it only as a practical and sensible precaution against the ultra-violet rays of the sun. Whoever heard of a woman who wore such a costume getting skin cancer, either basal cell or melanoma? I am sure that this is the true origin of this form of dress. As for the grille over the slit for the eyes, it is surely to prevent flies from landing on the eyes and thus spreading trachoma, just as Jews and Moslems do not eat pork in order to avoid the risk of contamination with the roundworm, Trichinella spiralis, that encysts itself in the muscles and can even cause death. As for there being no trachoma in England, no doubt the women in the black tents were always going back and forth between England and wherever they came from, where trachoma was endemic; and since it is easier for people to adopt a safe habit by performing it every day, even when strictly speaking it isn't necessary, than only when necessary, especially if they are not fully aware of why they are doing it in the first place, the wearing of this costume even where there is not trachoma is fully rational.

Then one of the women said something to the other that really shook me by its sheer irresponsibility.

'Have you got a fag on you, love?'

What, did they smoke inside their tents? I need hardly point out the fire hazard, it is so obvious. Indeed, it is so obvious that one could almost call it attempted arson. But even if they didn't set themselves alight like Buddhist monks protesting at the Vietnam War, there was another important consideration, namely the trapping of the smoke inside their robes that could escape only very slowly through the slit for the eyes. Therefore it would concentrate, and they would re-breathe it many times, with extra carcinogenic effect.

What this demonstrates is that thoughtlessness, negligence and frivolity are not confined to any one human group but are universal, always requiring vigilance to suppress.

Shuddering, I made my way home.

I would not be honest if I did not admit that I awaited Mr A…'s letter with impatience. I knew about the law's delay, of course, but you would think that common humanity would dictate expeditiousness in a case such as mine, which was of such personal and, if I may say so, of such public importance.

Once again I was deceived. It was six weeks before I received a letter – six weeks of health-threatening anxiety. But at last the letter came, and I opened it with all my usual precautions, my eagerness notwithstanding.

Dear Sir [went the letter],
I have to inform you that the Legal Aid Board considered your proposed action against the Department of Work and Pensions frivolous and even vexatious, and therefore declined to fund it.

In the circumstances, there is nothing further I can do. The Board even declines to repay the costs I incurred in writing to them.

Frivolous! Vexatious! Costs incurred by writing! Comment is hardly necessary. We live in a society that is concerned only about money, not about human life. I could live or die for all it cared.

I must now return to my account of the present day, that is to say the day on which I am writing this, not merely to vindicate myself, but to show an example to the world.

It will by now be obvious to the reader of these pages that I woke up this morning. (I could hardly have written these pages if I had not.)

That you woke up this morning, I hear you object, *is completely banal. Get on with it!*

But it is not completely banal, far from it, as I shall now prove. I am afraid your reaction proves your ignorance of cosmology and statistics. In fact, it was practically a miracle that I awoke this morning.

According to the current best guess, the universe existed for ten billion years before my birth. It is half-way through its life (something that I have in common with the universe). That is to say, the universe will have existed twenty billion years without me, and, if I am lucky, eighty years with me. (This is by no means guaranteed, of course. It depends on the care I take of myself.) It follows that the chance of my being alive on any given day in the existence of the universe are approximately two hundred and fifty million to one – against, I need hardly add. Thus the fact of my having woken this morning, far from being banal, was as near a miracle as any event could be, that did not violate the laws of physics.

I pointed this out to the doctor once.

'That is true of all of us,' he said.

'So you admit that it is true,' I pounced. It is amazing how even a supposedly educated man cannot grasp the simple principle that if something is true for everyone, then it must be true of someone in particular, in this case me. And since I was his patient at that moment, he should have been considering me to the exclusion of everyone else.

Before getting out of bed this morning, I checked the time so that I could mark it on my sleep chart. I regret that, as yet, there are no cheap electroencephalographs on the market, because of course a continuous record of brainwaves would provide a much more accurate record of one's sleep, both in quantity and quality, than a crude record of the time you think you're about to drop off and the time you wake. I naturally mark any interruptions to my sleep, if for example I should wake up, using a subdued night light because a brighter light, besides causing visual discomfort, would have the effect of keeping me awake long after it was turned off.

As I have said, this is all very crude and inexact, for obvious but currently unavoidable reasons – one needs to know, for example, whether one is getting sufficient Rapid Eye Movement sleep, because it has been shown that it is the deprivation of this phase of sleep that makes sleep deprivation as a whole dangerous and eventually fatal. Even relative deprivation of Rapid Eye Movement sleep is harmful in its effects, though some such sleep is better than none.

If properly displayed in graphic form, however, even a crude sleep chart enables you to perceive a change in pattern, which no one needs to be told may be the harbinger of more serious or sinister changes.

Even if we did not know from scientific research that disturbed sleep is either a sign or a cause of bad health, we might guess it from the fact that Nature itself has decreed that Man should spend a third of his life – more than twenty-five years, if I live to be eighty – asleep. It follows, I think, that sleep must have an important physiological function, equal in importance to that, say, of the kidneys. Disturbed sleep must therefore be as serious a matter as renal failure.

Of course, most people complain of insomnia to their doctors on only the most superficial of grounds, namely that it makes them feel tired or otherwise unwell. For, feeling well, or well enough, is the acme of health, regardless of what is really going on. Doctors are only too willing to go along with this, because it means less trouble for them. Whoever heard of anyone undergoing a thorough examination for occult cancer (the technical term for a cancer that does not manifest itself openly) because he complained of insomnia? And yet sleeplessness is often the first sign of cancer.

However, my chart demonstrated that I had slept eight hours and twenty-three minutes: a slight overestimate of course, because a little of that time I was merely dozing, which is to say half-asleep. The important thing was, however, that this was near enough the same time as I had slept the night before: eight hours and sixteen minutes. My sleep pattern had not varied by more than nineteen minutes the whole week.

People often blame Nature when they cannot sleep. 'I'm not a good sleeper,' they say. By this means they evade their responsibility for their own health, ascribing it to such generalities as their 'constitution' and 'system'. I am the last to deny the importance of our genetic heritage – I have one myself, and I am no scientific Luddite – but to adapt the words of Shakespeare slightly, the fault lies in ourselves, not in our genes, that we are insomniacs.

By the same token, the reverse is also true. It is no happy accident that someone like me sleeps through the night – to say so would be false modesty. The regularity of my habits and the elimination of factors that might interfere with sleep is an example of how foresight can work in beneficent union with Nature.

I have not exhausted the subject of the connection between sleep and health (one does not capture a third of human life in a couple of paragraphs), and there is much more to be said: but for the sake of brevity, I will move on to the other major events of my day.

After I had woken up and noted the time at which I did so, I rose, levering myself up slowly to avoid giddiness or, worse still, syncope. The number of people who fall out of bed because of dizziness on rising, and break their hips, is startling; and while, of course, it is principally the elderly who suffer this, there is no cut-off age at which this could not happen.

The hazards of getting out of bed safely overcome, I took my pulse to check that there had been no silent cardiac events in the night.

There is a widespread misconception that you must feel a pain in your chest if you have a heart attack, but nothing could be further from the truth. Many heart attacks are silent, from the point of view of pain, and can occur without any symptoms whatsoever: surely, everyone has heard of someone who has died unexpectedly and peacefully in his sleep. Well, what does he think the deceased died of, if not a silent heart attack?

I recognise that taking the pulse intermittently is only of limited value, but limited value is value nonetheless. It would be much better, of course, to be connected permanently to an electronic monitor that could, among other things, shock your heart back into proper activity if it stopped suddenly. But my doctor declined to prescribe such an apparatus for me, on the grounds that there was no evidence that I needed one. But what if the first evidence that I needed one was a cardiac arrest, I asked? It would be a bit late then, wouldn't it? He was refusing only because of my age, I said. Nonsense, he replied; age had nothing to do with it. No matter how young a person was, he would get one if he needed it.

Now on the subject of people younger than I, I confess that I feel some bitterness. (It is only honest to present the reader with an account of my vices as well as my virtues.) Why should the young, merely by virtue of the fact that they were born after me, have a longer life expectancy than I? Why should they be able to take advantage of technical advances, to which they have contributed nothing at all, to prolong their lives? Whenever I see a baby, I cannot help but recall that it will almost certainly live several years, or perhaps even a decade or two, longer than I, and – worse still – that this is so even if it fails to take the kind of precautions to preserve its health that I have taken for so many years, at the expense of so much hard thought and self-denial. For all I know, the baby will eat junk food and lie about all day watching television, yet he will still live longer than I. As it is, I have to work harder to live shorter. Moreover, by the time the baby develops the diabetes that is the inevitable consequence of his lifestyle, in all probability a technique will be by then available to make him like new again, to rescue him from his self-inflicted illness. But if I were to develop the same condition now, through no fault of my own (as can sometimes happen), I could not be cured because there is as yet no means available. To think of this injustice of angers me deeply.

Should I be making this confession or not? The dilemma is this: to hold emotions inwardly, without ever expressing them, is to run the risk that, because they are still present, boiling away inside, they will cause both physical and psychological damage. Perhaps the best example is that of bereaved people who do not express their grief by crying, but rather hold themselves in. This is all very well for a time, but a few months or years later they fall prey to depression or even cancer.

On the other hand, there are those who maintain that to express an emotion is to heighten it and make it chronic. The expression of anger does not assuage your anger, for example, but only kindles it and makes you angrier; eventually, you are furiously angry whereas a little while earlier you were only moderately angry.

The best-known example of the self-reinforcing nature of emotion is the harmfulness of getting people who have gone through a terrible trauma to speak of it. Their fear and horror stay uppermost in their minds if they are encouraged to dwell upon their bad memories.

I think I may say, with all due modesty, that I have managed to extract the best – or the least bad – of both worlds by my confession. I have both acknowledged and expressed my anger at the injustice done me by youth, thus preventing resentment from festering in me like a hidden abscess; but by now dropping the subject (I will not mention it again), I have avoided the pitfalls of mental rehearsal of painful thoughts that lead to chronic outrage and hypertension (raised blood pressure), with its inevitable effect upon life expectancy. This is the best that can be hoped for in the circumstances.

Having quickly checked my blood pressure, which can be either raised or lowered by a heart attack, the latter paradoxically being more sinister, from the point of view of prognosis, than the former, notwithstanding the generally deleterious effects of a raised blood pressure, I concluded that it was safe, or at least not demonstrably unsafe, to proceed to the bathroom.

There, of course, I have developed a routine of examination, that is to say self-examination. (Did not the ancient Greeks advise that you should know yourself?) To this end, I have placed a full-length mirror in my bathroom, for there is much to be learned from a person's general posture, even one's own. When someone suffers from a chronic illness, one can discern at once whether he is better or worse by the way he holds himself or walks into a room; and what, when you think about it, is life if not a chronic illness that can flare up in an exacerbation at any moment?

But while general appearance is important, it is not all-important. The devil is in the detail. It would be a very foolish person who concluded that, simply because he looked and even felt all right in general, that he was all right in particular. Human physiology is very complex; man is a delicate organism in whom millions of processes are in constant interaction. It would be surprising if, at any given moment, some of them at least were not out of kilter, or that none of them could go wrong without rising to consciousness of ill-health, though none the less serious for that, indeed even more sinister for not doing so.

I am neither unduly self-obsessed nor hypochondriacal, when you consider all the possible dysfunctions that can occur in a human body such as mine; and it is simply a moral duty, if you consider human life to be in any sense sacred, for a person to carry out a self-examination every day to prevent preventable death. The unexamined body does not survive long.

I once tried to explain this to my sister. She does not take care of herself at all, and as a result is often ill, which I never am – except potentially.

'You should get a life,' she once said to me, using a locution that I abhor.

'That is precisely what I'm trying to do,' I said. 'But life itself is a precondition of having a life, as you put it.'

'You spend so much time examining yourself and worrying about yourself that you have no time for anything else.'

'You exaggerate, as usual,' I said. 'I spend only twenty minutes in the morning and ten minutes at night quickly going over myself. You exaggerate to excuse your own carelessness.'

'That is a hundred an eighty hours a year,' she said. 'Eight full days a year, or eleven days of waking time. That means that in the last twenty years you've spent more than six months examining yourself. Think what you could've done in six months.'

'What could I have done?' I replied. 'Bear in mind that those six months, as you call them, were divided into fifteen thousand short periods. What've you ever done that is so constructive or important in periods of time like that? Or longer periods, if it comes to that.'

She didn't know what to answer, of course. It wasn't as if her own life was so full of transcendent purpose that she was in a position to criticise even the most empty-headed devotee of completely purposeless activity such as, say, music. If ever there were a case of living for the moment, it was she.

Having cast a practised eye over myself in the long mirror, I approached the magnifying mirror above the sink. Living in northern climes as I do, I have often to get up in the morning when there is no natural light by which to examine myself, and therefore, of course, I have bought myself, at considerable trouble and expense, an electric lamp that imitates natural light in wavelengths as closely as possible. Any other wavelengths, or combination of wavelengths, can easily give misleading impressions, and it is an open question, very difficult to resolve into an answer, whether it is worse to diagnose an illness that you don't have than to miss one that you do. Personally, I incline to the opinion that the latter is worse: you can correct the former error, but the latter often proves fatal.

I do not say that my method of self-examination is the only method, or even the best method: surely self-examination is infinite in its possible permutations and procedures, and it would be the sheerest arrogance to assume that one had alighted on the best and most irreproachable of all methods, especially as medical knowledge changes and advances all the time.

On the other hand, a routine is necessary, even in conditions of uncertainty as to what it should be, because even those with the best memories are inclined to miss out important points if they are not routinely sought for. In short, it is necessary both to have a method and a willingness to alter it in the light of new knowledge. That, perhaps, is the fundamental rule of preserving health, and therefore of life itself.

I approached the mirror: there was nothing striking or unusual about my face at first sight. I stuck out my tongue, not as a rude gesture of course (for who was there to offend but myself?), but as a simple clinical test. If it veered to one side involuntarily, that would mean damage to a cranial nerve, most likely as a result of a stroke; a tumour could not be altogether ruled out, though comparatively rare. Was my tongue excessively dry, indicating that I had become dehydrated overnight, and therefore needed to drink – though not water without electrolytes, I need hardly add. Was it excessively smooth or magenta-coloured, because of Vitamin B deficiency, particularly riboflavin? Were there ulcers or growths that could be cancerous? I knew these things did not happen overnight, but there is always a moment of recognition, the sooner the better. And of course, the white patches of thrush would automatically raise a suspicion of diabetes, my Body Mass Index notwithstanding.

Then the eyes, the windows of the soul as some people call them, but more accurately the barometers of the body. I will not go through all the signs of ill-health that are to be observed in the eyes – this is a work of basic principle, after all, and not a textbook of clinical examination, for there are already many such. But two signs I always look for in particular, that so many readers may overlook when they peer into the mirror, are a drooping eyelid and unequal pupils.

Why, you ask? Two reasons. First, occurring together, they might indicate a tumour of one of the lungs in the upper lobe. Of course, I do not smoke, but I wouldn't like positively to affirm that in my life that I have not breathed in enough of other people's smoke to cause such a tumour, which can occur sporadically in any case, irrespective of tobacco smoke, though not, perhaps, of general atmospheric pollution (regrettably, I have taken to wearing a mask when I go outside only in the last ten years).

If the uneven pupils occur on their own, without a drooping eyelid, that has another signification.

When I was very young, twenty-three years ago, I was almost as careless as the average person (wisdom comes with age, alas). Like most men at that age I was at the mercy of my hormones, and fell prey to the wiles of a woman whom I thought then to be old, but I now understand was young. However, young as she was, she was experienced, indeed over-experienced. With her, it was not so much a profession as a vocation. Suffice it to say that no-one could be surprised to catch something from her, she was that kind of woman, and I was foolish enough to go with her without first demanding to see the results of her latest test.

Let me not be thought neurotic, far from it. All my worries are rational ones. I am not, for example, worried that I might have contracted AIDS from her, for two reasons: first, it was well before the epidemic started, at least in this country; and, second, because it would have manifested itself by now – and it hasn't. Besides, I have been tested several times. As for gonorrhoea, I would have noticed straight away.

But syphilis is another matter altogether. Syphilis bides its time and doesn't let you know that it's there. It can lie in wait patiently for a quarter of a century or more. You have to read the old textbooks to understand what it can do. They tell you that the last and most disastrous stage of syphilis, General Paralysis of the Insane, develops with a frequency inversely proportional to the primary and secondary (that is to say the initial or only slightly delayed) manifestations of the disease – which, of course, I have never had at all, in logic making me, therefore, particularly and peculiarly susceptible to the most severe form.

I have discussed this matter with my doctor several times. He makes light of it, as he makes light of everything except economy. Economy is the reason why he has always refused to arrange a blood test for me, though he dresses it up as a matter of principle, or 'not reinforcing an obsession', as he calls it.

Last time I raised it with him, I pointed out that the test was very cheap, and that, once done, I would never bother him again by asking for it.

'He who pays the Danegeld,' he replied, 'never gets rid of the Dane.'

I found the analogy offensive, and told him so. I am not, after all, some kind of Viking terrorist. However, life is too short for the pursuit of relatively, though only relatively, minor complaints, and so I read him instead an extract from the Government's Patients' Charter, setting down the rights and justified expectations of patients.

'The Charter says that the service always puts the patient first in ways responsive to people's views and needs.'

'Needs,' said the doctor. 'That's the operative word.'

'And views,' I countered. 'In any case, there's no difference between views and needs.'

'Of course there is. There's a fundamental difference.'

'What is it, then?' I asked.

I don't think he was expecting that. He probably expected me to say meekly, 'Yes, doctor,' and leave it at that, while dying of something eminently preventable. I wanted to show him with whom he had to deal.

'A need is what is necessary, a view is what is desire,' he said.

Is this the kind of crude metaphysics they teach in medical school? No wonder people are dying all around us, over half a million a year just in this country alone, though you'd never know it from walking in the street. There is a conspiracy of silence about death that leads to a vicious circle: we don't acknowledge that death exists, therefore we don't look after our health, therefore we die. And the more of us who die, the more death is hidden from us.

'All needs are derivable ultimately from wishes,' I said. 'Would there be any necessities in a universe in which there were no wishes, that is to say beings with desires?'

'Look,' said the doctor. 'I'm not here to discuss the constitution of the universe. I'm here to decide whether or not you need a test for syphilis, and you don't. Besides, knowing the result wouldn't put your mind at rest. You'd simply think of something else to worry about.'

It pains me to admit it, but he was right – though for the wrong reason, of course. He thought I was merely neurotic, when actually I was well-informed.

The fact is that General Paralysis of the Insane can develop in the absence of a positive blood test for syphilis. I discovered this fact from a book entitled *Neurosyphilis*, by a neurologist with the awe-inspiring name of C. Worster-Drought. His book probably did not sell as well as the importance of its subject matter warranted, because it was published in 1940, when people were so easily distracted by outside events. Sad to say, I found the book in a charity shop, marked at £3. So small a sum for such vital information! It just goes to show what value we really place on life.

Having re-read it, I returned to my doctor.

'You were right,' I said, and a complacent smile, mocking and ironical, played upon his lips, as the shadow of a cloud on a sunny day plays upon the ground below. 'I don't need a blood test.' He nodded. 'I need a lumbar puncture.'

He nearly slipped off his chair. I think he must have been astonished by, and unprepared for, the depth of my medical knowledge.

'You are not having a lumbar puncture,' he said.

'Before you refuse,' I said, 'I think you ought to listen to reason. It is a medical fact that the blood test is sometimes negative in tertiary neurosyphilis, but the test in the cerebro-spinal fluid never is. In other words, it is positive in a hundred per cent of cases. Therefore, I ought to have a lumbar puncture to exclude it definitively, before it is too late.'

'There's no reason to think you have neurosyphilis,' he said.

'How can that be so, if you won't do the test?'

'Symptoms and signs,' he said. 'You don't have any of the symptoms or signs.'

'I don't want to have any of the symptoms,' I said. 'I want to avoid getting them. That's why I want the test.'

'A lumbar puncture is contraindicated,' he said, beginning to lose his temper – as well, of course, as the argument.

'Not indicated,' I said, 'rather than *contra*indicated. There is a difference.' You'd think a man with a scientific training, so called, would be careful in his use of words. 'Besides, it isn't strictly true that I have none of the symptoms. I have many of them.'

'Such as?'

'I get tired easily. I'm irritable. I have mood changes. Sometimes I have headaches and I can't concentrate. Classic symptoms, in fact.'

'They're symptoms of a thousand conditions...'

'Test me for those also, then.'

'I was about to say, or of none.'

He had to claim that, of course, to justify his own inactivity in my case. But even if it were true that my symptoms might be indicative of no condition at all, which was very unlikely given my intense rationality, it was surely his job to prove it rather than merely to assume it. Moreover, suffering is suffering, even if it is merely imagined, and it is the doctor's duty to assuage it wherever it comes from.

However, a dying man has above all to be realistic. He cannot afford to spend the rest of the little time left to him banging his head, metaphorically-speaking, against a brick wall. My doctor was the brickest of brick walls, but I don't blame him entirely: his training was partly to blame, and also the government, that wants, solely for reasons of economy, to limit the number of tests performed on potentially ill people, even if it means death from preventable causes. At any rate, I had no confidence that any other doctor would have been different or better.

Thus I was reduced to the expedient each day of examining my eyes for the development of the telltale Argyll-Robertson pupils, as a sign of tertiary syphilis. I recognise, of course, that such pupils develop in only fifty per cent of cases, but what else could I do in the face of the obduracy of the medical profession? A glass half-full is better than a glass completely empty.

I will not go through all the details of my self-examination, though I think it is worth mentioning my simple tests with a tuning fork (in the absence of a proper audiogram – a fortune surely awaits the person who develops a cheap audiometer for home use) to check for deafness, of either the nerve or conductive variety. The problem with conditions such as deafness is that they tend to creep up on you unawares, rather than coming upon you suddenly, unless you test for them specifically; you adapt, without your knowing it, to your loss of sensitivity, for example by turning the volume of your radio up (if you are so foolish as to have one). Once again, we see the wisdom of the old Greek commandment, to know yourself.

Last, but by no means least (far from it), I tested my urine. First I took the sterile plasma bottle and the bottle of test strips from the small refrigerator that I have installed in my bathroom to keep biological specimens at the ideal four degrees Centigrade. (Terrible false confidence can arise from the degradation of specimens and test reagents.) Then I discarded the first flow of my urine, the first flow being notorious for giving false results, and collected enough for bacteriological examination, if such proved necessary. (Before you exclaim that I surely do not have bacteriological facilities in my small flat, let me reply that of course I do not. What I would do if such examination was indicated, either clinically or as a result of tests is the following: I would preserve my urine in the refrigerator until I was ready to take it to the doctor, using my insulated, temperature-controlled, cold chain container to transport it. So far it has never proved necessary to do so. Before I forget, I ought to point out, for readers unfamiliar with proper procedure, that prior to carrying out my urine testing, I washed my hands with chlorhexidine – though recently I have read that alcohol is just as good and rather cheaper. I am not immune to economic arguments, and indeed regard it as a fundamental principle of morality that one should obtain the maximum health benefit for the least possible expenditure, while recognising that this is an invitation to the unscrupulous to cut corners.)

Having carefully dipped the test strip into my urine, I set the stop watch mounted on the wall for exactly the thirty seconds necessary to elapse before reading the result. I confess that this thirty seconds is always a period of mounting tension and excitement, possibly greater than is strictly good for me. I have tried to affect indifference, or to distract myself by looking out of the door of the bathroom, but candour requires that I admit to failure. As Hume said, reason is the slave of the passions.

On this occasion, there was no glucose, bilirubin, protein or blood in my urine, and no ketones either. The pH (a measure of acidity or alkalinity) was satisfactory. But it would be a cardinal error to become complacent, to suppose that, just because my urine had always been free of these contaminants in the past, it would remain so in the future. This would be to commit the error of the domestic fowl (to use the example given by Bertrand Russell to explain the fallacy of induction) who assumes that, because it has hitherto always received food from the hands of the farmer, those same hands will never wring its neck.

This is not the place to describe my examination of my bowel movements, for three reasons. The first is that some squeamish people find it an aesthetically unpleasing subject. Squeamishness is the enemy of health, of course, and is responsible for goodness knows how many deaths. The second is that any description or information that I could give is readily available in any textbook, to which I refer all those who responsible enough to have got thus far in my narrative. The third is that, try as I might, I have never been able to train my bowel to perform exactly on time (the colon has its reasons which reason knows not of), and therefore it would not be strictly chronologically accurate to recount the examination at this point, though in a certain sense it would be logical to do so, or at least satisfying from the point of view of literary unity, and of course for the sake of completeness.

6

HAVING CONFIRMED, TO THE best of my limited ability and within the time constraints imposed by a busy life, that I had not developed any serious illnesses overnight, or any hernias (I stood up, put my finger in each of my inguinal rings in succession, and gave a cough) it was time for my shower. Cleanliness is next to healthiness, indeed it is almost a precondition of it. I know that there are those who attribute the rise of asthma and other allergic conditions to the excessively hygienic conditions in which children are now brought up, but to this I would answer three things. First, the hypothesis is far from proved. Second, even if true, we should remember that, serious as the allergic conditions are, the diseases of dirt are infinitely worse, having cut a swathe through humanity since the earliest times. Life is always a choice between evils, and it is the task of reason to decide between the lesser of them – or rather, the least of them, since there are always more than two evils in any situation to choose between. And third, speaking purely for myself, I have passed the age of childhood. While a certain degree of dirtiness may be salutary for children, it by no means follows that it is so for adults. Once the body has been primed by dirt or infection, it no longer needs them; on the contrary. As with mother's milk, there is (on the hypothesis whose truth I neither assert nor deny) a time and a place for dirt in a human being's life, and it is not at the age of forty.

I think, therefore, that I could take my shower with a clear conscience, indeed with an awareness of performing a virtuous act.

The same could not be said if I had decided to take a bath. I have several times discussed this matter with my sister, who insists, against all my objections, on bathing her children. My objection to baths is not that they are wasteful of water, though they are, or that they are intrinsically unhygienic, though they are (inasmuch as the person who wants to clean himself in a bath must then wallow in the water that he has sullied), as it is that there are so many dangers lurking in them. I know that some people claim to enjoy sitting in the bath, but surely no degree of idle pleasure can outweigh dangers to life itself?

People, you will say, have been taking baths for hundreds, perhaps thousands, of years. Yes, I reply, and they have been dying in baths for the same length of time. I am not speaking now of the death of Marat at the hands of Charlotte Corday, or of the Brides in the Bath case: there is no evidence that, statistically-speaking, people are more likely to be murdered in the bath than elsewhere.

I digress here to point out that kitchens are another matter entirely. Study after study has shown that people are likely to be murdered in the kitchen, especially if they live in close association with other people such as spouses, lovers and children. I do not believe that this is a matter only of the availability of knives and other dangerous implements in kitchens, though no doubt this has something to do with it. But whatever the explanation, it seems to me to be a matter of common sense that people who live in close proximity to others, especially women, should take care to spend as little time in the kitchen as possible, consistent, that is, with the preparation of healthy food. I think every household should have a rule that there is no more than one person in the kitchen at any time.

This precaution might seem too rigorous to some, who would argue (always the same argument!) that murder is a rare event and therefore not worth taking precautions against. I reply with several counter-arguments. You will remember Pascal's wager, to the effect that even if there were only a million to one chance of God's existence, it would still be worth believing in Him because the consequences of not doing so were He actually to exist are so catastrophic, while the consequences of believing in him were He not actually to exist are so slight. The benefits of believing in Him if he did actually exist are, of course, immeasurable.

Now surely it is obvious that the same considerations apply to kitchens and murder, except that the chances of a woman being murdered by the man with whom she lives are considerably greater than those that God exists. So even if a version of Pascal's wager were my only argument for precaution in kitchens, it would be a strong one.

But of course there is another, even stronger argument. One of the problems with people, I find, is that they think statically, not dynamically. But society is a dynamic, not a static, thing. It evolves and changes, and behaviour changes with it. To think statically is to fail to think ahead, and to fail to think ahead is to run many avoidable and unnecessary risks.

The homicide rate has been increasing exponentially. Yes, you reply, but it is still very low. This reply demonstrates your failure to understand the power of exponential increase. It is such that, before very long, we may all die of murder. Kitchens will then be very dangerous places indeed, not only relatively but absolutely.

Moreover, there is a cardinal fact that should not be overlooked: namely that, thanks to improved methods of resuscitation and surgery, four-fifths of the people injured in homicidal attacks who would have died only a few decades ago now survive. This means that, for every murder that you would avoid by preventing couples from associating in the kitchen, you would avoid four homicidal attacks; and there can surely be few things more worth avoiding than homicidal attacks. Of nothing is it more true that prevention is better than cure.

But I return to the bath, reminding you that it is not of murder in the bath that I now speak. The fact is that there are many more frequent, and grislier, ways to die in the bath. I shall mention only one, for reasons of space; but there are, of course, many more, which I am sure the averagely well-informed reader could supply for himself.

How many epileptics have died – and die annually – in the bath! The mechanism is obvious and clear: they have a fit and then drown. If any death is avoidable, such a death is avoidable. Whoever heard of an epileptic who died in the shower? Yet, against all reason, epileptics persist in taking baths, and society lets them do so. The only explanation for their obstinacy that I can think of is brain damage.

What can the rest of us (I mean those of us who persist in taking baths) urge in our own defence? That we are not epileptics? This is completely to misunderstand, and exaggerate, the difference between epileptics and non-epileptics: in fact, there is no such distinction. Everyone, given the right – or perhaps I should say the wrong – conditions for him, is an epileptic. There is no human being alive in whom an epileptic fit cannot be produced if the stimulus to which he is most susceptible is applied. Therefore, the most that anyone can say is that he has never had an epileptic fit – yet. In other words, to adapt a Proverb from the Bible so that it is in accord with modern science, pride goeth before a fit and a haughty spirit before a seizure. (Even to say that one has not had a fit yet is, in reality, to say too much. Many epileptics – for what else can I call them, the crudities of our language being too great to capture the subtleties of clinical phenomena? – have fits only in their sleep. Thus someone can be sure that he has never had a fit only if he has never slept alone; and even if he has not slept alone, the person with whom he sleeps may not have noticed a fit, if she is a heavy sleeper or the convulsion a minor one. Then, of course, there are fits that do not manifest themselves in bodily convulsions at all, but in repetitive behaviours, and are not recognised as epileptic.)

But surely, you say, people who have fits wet themselves, and if, therefore, they wake in a wet bed they would know that they had had a fit in the night?

All they would know from this, however, is that they might have had a fit. People wet the bed for a variety of reasons, especially as they get older; besides, not every fit is accompanied by an involuntary discharge from the bladder, and therefore, though I am not of course against examining one's bed in the morning for wetness, a dry bed is no guarantee of a fitless night.

In short, there is no way for an average man to know whether or not he has ever had an epileptic fit, unless, of course, he has had one in front of credible, that is to say medically informed, witnesses. Neither a normal nor an abnormal electroencephalograph will inform him, what is more, for there are both false positives and false negatives; though of course such an apparatus will accurately record a discharge while he is having a fit. This is yet another reason for the development of a cheap domestic electroencephalograph, for such a machine would allow everyone to assess whether he had had a fit in the night. To provide conclusive evidence of the occurrence of fits, of course, it would have to be used every night; though it must be admitted that non-occurrence is more difficult or impossible to prove, given the unknown events of the future.

One might consider other methods, though. For example, dogs have been trained to recognise when people are about to have a fit. But I am not so unrealistic as to suppose that such a dog could be trained for every household in the country. Among other reasons why not, it would divert much-needed resources from the prevention and detection of other diseases, of which there are so many. There is no point in avoiding death by drowning in the bath only to die of cancer of the thyroid. Besides, dogs bring their own diseases, including worms if they are not properly de-wormed and asthma even if they are.

Nor should I omit to mention the blood test that, if taken soon after a fit, can establish that one has taken place. I discovered this in the public library, where unfortunately medical textbooks are not prominently displayed, unlike works of frivolous distraction that do nothing to preserve the very precondition of the possibility of distraction, namely life itself. The blood level of a hormone called prolactin, secreted by a gland connected to the brain, rises immediately after a fit. Surely it would be possible, and highly beneficial, to develop a strip-test, similar to that employed by diabetics to test their blood for the glucose level, to test the blood for its prolactin level? The potential sales are colossal; I would develop it myself, if I had both the time and the capital.

Of course, the fact that the level of prolactin falls only half an hour after the fit raises a problem; the blood must be taken very soon after a fit, moreover at a time when the sufferer himself may be a little confused. And therefore also, a movement detector, capable of distinguishing between normal tossing and turning in the night and an epileptic seizure, which produced a ringing tone strong or loud enough to alert the neighbours who might then come and take the blood themselves from the epileptic (on condition, no doubt, that this service would be reciprocated by him in the event of need), might overcome the difficulties. I am not an electronic engineer, far from it, but I should have thought that such a piece of equipment would have been of comparatively easy manufacture in these days of technological marvels. Unfortunately, inventors and engineers prefer to expend their energy and ingenuity on trifles that are of no conceivable benefit to human health, quite the reverse in fact.

The fundamental point is this: that you cannot know, when you get into a bath, that you are not going to have a fit and therefore drown in it. Moreover, epileptic fits are only one of many causes of unconsciousness that may lead to drowning. It is impossible to drown in a shower.

Of course, it does not follow from the fact that baths are unsafe that showers are safe, at least in the absolute sense – the sense that we are all interested in. For example, it is possible to slip and fall in a shower, and thereby break a leg or dislocate a hip. (I use these only as examples: it is not that the other bones and joints are immune from damage.) That is why it is so important to exercise, to strengthen the bones and muscles, and thereby render them less susceptible to damage in the case of an accident. I will describe the proper exercise to take in due course, because I do not want to get ahead of myself in my account of my day; but, in any case, it is possible also to avoid accidents in themselves, for example by installing a non-slip surface on the floor of one's shower, as I, as a responsible citizen, have done. I have also installed, at considerable personal expense, and with no help from the public purse although I asked for it, pointing out that I was potentially saving the country a great deal of money in the event of an accident, strong railings on the sides of the shower to which I could clutch if I felt myself slipping.

Before getting into the shower, I made sure that the water-temperature regulator was set at exactly thirty-seven degrees: one does not want any nasty surprises when one steps into the shower, of the kind that can lead to sudden movements that, even without ensuing accidents, can result in pulled muscles. I therefore cannot agree with those who believe in cold showers, I think mainly for puritanical reasons; for surely everyone knows that to emerge suddenly from the warmth into the cold can provoke angina attacks, to say nothing of asthma? Only in the susceptible, you say? Tell me, who exactly are these uniquely susceptible people, divided by a Berlin Wall of vulnerability from the rest of us? Surely I don't have to repeat all that I said about epilepsy, but this time with regard to angina and asthma?

As for the alleged character-building quality of cold showers, show me a man who takes them and I will show you a bully and a sadist.

No; thirty-seven is exactly the right temperature for the water of a shower, that is to say warm but not scalding. It is, of course, precisely the temperature fixed for us by nature. No doubt there are purists among you who will point out that the skin temperature is at least a degree below the body core temperature, but surely a man may be allowed an extra degree of warmth above skin temperature now and again just for his own comfort? Obsessionality is as much to be avoided (and reprehended) as carelessness: and, of course, has its own dangers.

Today was a day for washing my hair. I have long puzzled over the difficult question of how many times a week I should wash it, and I readily confess that, after all my deliberations, I am still not quite sure. It is not that am not phobic about my hair, having no rational cause to be; it is a long time since any physical intimacy put me in danger of contracting lice, nits, fungi, or suchlike. No, the real question is how best to avoid sebhorrheic dermatitis, or dandruff as it is commonly but inaccurately known. I think I may say, without being accused either of boasting or of false modesty, that I am not by nature particularly prone to this condition; yet, I need hardly add, that except for a few conditions that are one hundred per cent genetic in origin, that is to say that the possession of a certain gene or genes is a necessary and sufficient condition for developing them, all conditions can be induced by the right (or perhaps I should say, since I am talking of illness, the wrong) environmental conditions and circumstances.

Too frequent or too infrequent washing would obviously lead to the same result, namely dryness and flaking of the scalp, but that begs the question as to what is too often and not often enough? Unfortunately, this is one of those many questions that cannot be answered with certainty, since there is insufficient information to decide it; but yet it must be answered nonetheless – unless, that is, one is never to wash one's hair, which is a *reductio ad adsurdum*. Thus one is reduced to trial and error of the crudest kind, precisely the kind that leads fools to take patent medicines and write testimonials to them. What is needed, of course, is proper scientific information, but despite extensive searches in libraries and on the internet, I have been quite unable to find any. So I have been forced back on my impression that, at least for me, twice a week is best. (*Nota bene*: I am definitely not claiming that twice a week is best for everyone, and I accept no responsibility if someone follows my practice and then finds not only that it does not suit him or his scalp, but that all his hair falls out.)

Having checked with my hand, only approximately it goes without saying, that the water temperature regulator of the shower was still working, for machines can go wrong no less than human bodies, in fact more often considering their far greater simplicity, I advanced into the shower. It was, I admit, a pleasant sensation to stand under the water, but of course I was not there to idle away my time in self-indulgent pleasure, very far from it; I had my hair to think of and therefore business to conduct.

I reached out for the shampoo. (Did I forget to mention that before getting into the shower I put on my goggles to prevent soap from getting in my eyes? Soap in the eyes is not in itself dangerous, though it can inflame them and therefore give a misleading impression of illness, for example conjunctivitis. It is not as important to avoid thinking you are ill when you are well as to avoid thinking you are well when you are ill, but it is not without importance nonetheless. Could the fact that I had forgotten to mention so important a precaution as goggles in the shower mean that my cognitive function is deteriorating? I am still young for this to happen, except subclinically as a manifestation of the ageing process of course, but it has been known.)

Imagine my absolute horror when I realised that I had bought the wrong shampoo! I had bought Neutrihair instead of Neutrahair. How could such a thing have happened? Normally, I am extremely careful about such matters. Perhaps I had been distracted in the supermarket by an item I had read on the internet the day before, claiming a connection between refined sugar and cancer of the pancreas. It was only as yet an unconfirmed or preliminary report, but if it is confirmed I will have to have regular ultrasound scans of my abdomen, not because I eat a lot of refined sugar now, very far from it, I refuse to buy any product containing such sugar, but because when I was a child, before I reached the age of discretion, my mother gave me sugar lumps to suck as a treat. I do not go so far as to say that she was trying deliberately to harm me, but is it not ironical that those who are supposed to protect you while you are vulnerable actually put you at risk? At any rate, I was worried about how I was going to pay for regular ultrasound scans, for I knew that my doctor would not agree for me to have them on the public system. So on my meagre fixed income, I would have to forgo something else – but what? Everything I bought was already very carefully worked out to achieve the most benefit and least risk. But now, with the need for ultrasound scans, I would have to begin my calculations all over again.

For the moment, however, my problem was the shampoo. Neutrahair is far from perfect, of course, but it contains far fewer chemicals than any other product I have found on the market. Neutrihair, which sounds so similar, is in fact very different. One, Neutrahair, is formulated to do your hair no harm and cause no allergies; the other, Neutrihair, is formulated to nourish your hair and make it grow back with a healthy sheen. I suppose fools can be found to believe any health claim made about any product by any manufacturer: but how, in the name of God, can a product applied externally to hair, which after all is dead matter secreted by cells in the skin, 'nourish' it? As for sheen, you could probably achieve as much with furniture polish. 'Nothing works better than Neutrihair,' says the advertisement: to which my reply is, then use nothing.

Before agreeing, then, to apply Neutrihair irrevocably to my scalp, I decided to investigate its contents. I therefore turned off the shower and stepped out of it. Although I was now very anxious to know the precise contents of the rogue shampoo, I controlled myself and rubbed myself down thoroughly to avoid excessive cooling by evaporation. Although I am aware as the next man that the research at the Common Cold Research Centre has established that changes of ambient temperature do not lead to an increased susceptibility to infections with the viruses that cause colds, nevertheless I find it difficult altogether to dismiss out of hand the wisdom of ages on this subject. How often has it been the case that a popular wisdom about health, long held in contempt and derision by doctors and scientists as being merely a superstition, has turned out to contain, if not the whole truth, at least a grain of truth, to ignore which is to cause unnecessary suffering and perhaps even death itself? From time immemorial the peasants of eastern Europe, for example, used to apply mouldy bread to their wounds. Perhaps if the doctors and scientists had condescended to take serious notice of them and their ways, penicillin would have been discovered in the fifteenth century instead of the twentieth, and millions of lives would have been saved. (On the other hand, of course, they'd all be dead now, and resistance to penicillin would have emerged much earlier than it did, as well as fatal allergy to it.)

In any case, there is no use in crying over spilt milk; we live in the present and it is of our present and our future health that we must think.

I put on my dressing-gown – natural fibre with organic, which is to say non-chemical, dyes – and sat at my computer terminal with the bottle of shampoo in my hand. I had realised that it would soon be necessary to avail myself of the services of the internet.

I looked at the list of ingredients of Neutrihair. It was like peering into the abyss. We cannot stare too long at the sun or death, said La Rochefoucauld; or, he might have added, at the contents of a modern bottle of shampoo.

Here I advise the reader to sit down, grip the arms of his chair, hold on tightly and take a deep breath, before proceeding to the list of ingredients below. It will literally take his breath away.

I give readers one final warning before continuing with the list. I advise those with heart conditions to skip the rest of the page.

Ceteryl alcohol, Quaternium-18, Stearamidopropyl diethylamine, Quaternium-80, Sodium laureth sulfate, Glyceryl stearate, Ascorbic acid, Panthenol, Tocopheryl acetate, Biotin, PVP, Aloe barbadensis leaf juice, Dimethylpabamidopropyl laurdimonium tosylate, Steareth 21, Oleamine oxide, Propylene glycol stearate, Polysorbate 20, Glycerin, Methylisothizolinone, Citric acid, Benzyl salicylate, Hexycinnana, Limonene, Linalol, Parfum, CI 60730 (Extract of violet z) CI 17200 (Red 33).

I decided to take a look at this appalling witches' brew, and went to my pharmacy cupboard (as large as that in which some people keep their clothes; my flat being a small one, not large enough for two such cupboards, I put health before vanity and used it for medicines and medical equipment). I took out a plastic galley pot and returned to the bottle of shampoo. I put on gloves and a mask because it seemed to me likely that some, at least, of the above chemicals were volatile, and I would not want to breathe in any fumes before I knew what they were and that they were safe.

Taking the bottle, I opened its little lid and tipped it upside down. Precisely as I had expected, the liquid was too viscous to come out without squeezing. (Did I mention that plastic bottles such as this contain feminising chemicals which is another reason, as if none already existed, for handling them with extreme care, even if you are already a woman?) I squeezed, and squeezed again: nothing came out. On the third squeeze, however, a gluey mauve blob emerged with a small explosion, like that of a poisonous gas emerging from a volcanic lake (I use the metaphor advisedly, of course).

This mauve blob, of a colour quite unknown to nature, maintained its shape in the galley pot: precisely what the label on the shampoo claimed it would also do for your hair. But who in his right mind would cover any part of himself in this artificially-coloured goo? I took a toothpick – one should not allow particles of food to remain between one's teeth even for a few minutes, for that way caries lies, so they should always be to hand – and poked the blob with it. When I removed the pick it was followed by a sticky thread of shampoo. It was disgusting.

However, none of this was science. No doubt our instincts are often to be trusted, as for example in our fear of snakes; but more than instinct is required to form safe judgements, it requires proper investigation. I could see that I had a formidable task, and a morning's work at least, ahead of me.

Don't get me wrong: I don't enjoy this kind of investigation, on the contrary, I find it extremely tiresome. However, the nature of the modern world imposes the duty on every responsible person. A man who would not care for his health, to paraphrase and update Doctor Johnson slightly, would not care for anything. A man deserves to go bald, or worse, if he takes his shampoo on trust.

I turned on the computer, having first re-adjusted the anti-glare, anti-flicker screen. Even if you are not susceptible to migraine (though, again, whether one is or is not susceptible is a matter of degree rather than of kind), a glaring or flickering screen can give you a headache, and I hardly need return to the subject of epilepsy after all I have said about it. Then, of course, there is cancer, though the connection is not yet proved – or, far more to the point, not yet disproved.

It would not be appropriate in a non-technical work such as this for the general reader to go through everything that I found on the internet relating to the contents of the shampoo. Not only could the interested reader find it for himself if he were sufficiently responsible for his own health, and had the self-respect to do so, but I am much more concerned to lay down general principles than to give detailed information about a particular case, namely my own. Readers, after all, may have bought other brands of shampoo.

Nevertheless, just as one picture is worth a thousand words, so one or two concrete examples are more convincing than any statement of general principle. Therefore, I will give such examples, though I ask the reader to bear in mind that they are but a small sample of what I found.

Sodium laureth sulfate can irritate the skin and give you diarrhoea when swallowed. That is not a problem, you say, because you do not drink shampoo. True, but irrelevant. Can anyone truly say that he has not, wittingly or unwittingly, licked his lips in the shower, or that he has removed all traces of shampoo by the time he steps out of it? To those who say that it is obviously the dose of sodium laureth sulfate that counts, I reply that the intestines of some people might be – indeed, almost certainly are, given the variation between human beings – especially sensitive to its effects.

But I have kept the worst of sodium laureth sulfate for the last: it is carcinogenic! Again, someone might console himself with the thought that he is not in contact with it for long, and surely its carcinogenic properties depend upon prolonged contact with it? I refer him to the end of the above paragraph, in case he has already forgotten it: besides which, contact with it might be much longer than you think, which a little simple arithmetic might prove. Careless thought costs lives.

An average shampooing lasts, shall we say, ten minutes. That is twenty minutes per week, or a thousand and forty minutes per year, which is (more or less) seventeen hours per year. Over an adult lifetime of fifty years, that amounts to more than an entire month in constant contact with the shampoo. Now I ask you: would you be willing to smear a toxic, carcinogenic substance over a part of your body and keep it there for more than a month? Yet this is precisely what the manufacturers of Neutrihair ask you to do.

Then there was tocopherol acetate, commonly known as Vitamin E. It is a very common error to suppose that, because vitamins are necessary for the health, they are actually good for you. Nothing could be further from the truth. They can be, and tocopherol acetate literally is, deadly.

People with diabetes or heart disease who were given tocopherol for four and a half years had a thirty-eight per cent increase in their rate of heart failure compared with those who took a placebo. It follows that tocopherol is cardiotoxic, for how else could it produce heart failure?

This is the least of it, however. A meta-analysis of more than nineteen trials of tocopherol, given to people on precisely the theory that if you need tocopherol then it must be good for you, showed that those who took it had a four per cent higher death rate than those not given it! Four per cent might not sound very much, but when you add it to all the other hazards of life and shampoos, remembering that after all tocopherol is only one of millions of possible contaminants of our environment, the risk rises to well over one hundred per cent. I am the last person to underestimate the health benefits of clean hair, but surely it is not worth dying for. One must get one's priorities right – or suffer the consequences.

I have saved the worst – that is to say, the most typical – example for last. I refer to CI 17200, or Red 33. This is a dye and as such cannot possibly be or do any good for the health or the hair. There is very little information about it to be found, but everyone is agreed: there have been no good health studies on this compound! This, surely, is one of the most terrible sentences ever uttered!

And yet CI 172000, or Red 33, is in widespread use! Could anything better illustrate the connivance of the authorities with profit-making corporations than this, or demonstrate their complete indifference to the well-being – which is to say the health – of the population that they are supposed to protect?

Not that the population in question is itself entirely blameless in the matter. Far from it. It not only fails to demand any serious attention to such matters on the part of its elected representatives, but you have only to observe it purchasing its shampoo regardless to see that it is far more concerned with trivial and entirely secondary considerations, such as colour and smell (or 'Parfum', in the list of ingredients, which itself covers a multitude of sins), and the alleged effect of the shampoo on the appearance of their hair, than with primary and important considerations such as health. Indeed, I would go so far as to say that the great majority of purchasers of shampoo do not even look at the list of ingredients on the bottle before parting with their money. In fact, I know this for a fact because I once, purely out of horrified fascination, spent an hour watching them, and would have spent longer to confirm my observations had I not been worried that to stand rooted to a spot for longer might have added to my chances of developing varicose veins. Not a single one of them so much as glanced at the list of ingredients, though all of them pondered long and hard over the question of whether they should buy a product for dry, greasy or medium hair. For them, appearance is reality.

There is another important aspect of all these chemicals to think about, namely their interactions with one another, and also with any medications the person using them may happen to be taking.

Tocopherol, for example interacts with dapsone, a drug for leprosy. It is true that there are only a few hundred lepers in the country (even that number surprises people, who imagine that leprosy is entirely a disease of the past), but with drug resistance developing daily that could quickly alter. In any case, dapsone is only one of thirty-five drugs with which tocopherol interacts adversely.

Moreover, the number of potential interactions between the ingredients of the shampoo is, for all intents and purposes, infinite. In the list of ingredients as I transcribed it, I did not include aqua, commonly known as water, because to have done so would have made it appear to the reader that I was trying by the sheer length of the list to appal him.

Not that water is just water, of course: was it soft, distilled water, or hard water, or water with organic residues? Hard water is good for the heart, though of course it makes it more difficult to raise lather from soap and therefore to keep clean. People who live in hard water areas have fewer heart attacks than those who live in soft water areas. On the other hand, they might be less clean as a consequence, and therefore suffer more skin diseases, such as infections. I am not sure whether there have been any comparative studies of this important dilemma.

Still, I think most sensible people would agree with me that, in principle, heart attacks are more to be feared than skin infections, and it was for this reason that I approached the Housing Department and asked for a transfer from my current address, where the water supply is soft, to one where the water supply is hard, failing which I wanted, or demanded, that the department install a water-hardening device for at least that part of the water supply that from which I draw my drinking, and cooking, water. (I will drink mineral water, flat or fizzy, but only if it comes in glass not plastic bottles; this, I may tell you, is not easy to find round here, besides being so heavy that it constitutes

a dangerous degree of exercise to bring it home from a long way off.)
I explained to the department that the water that I consumed needed
to be hard, from the prophylactic point of view; but, not surprisingly,
in view of its bureaucratic indifference to the welfare of its tenantry,
it declined to entertain my request, which it even called frivolous. The
man at the department to whom eventually I spoke said that in any
case someone had to live in my flat with its soft water supply and run
the risk, or the additional risk, of a heart attack, and it might as well
be me. Here was an example of the utter lack of imagination of those
set in authority over us, for I was able in an instant to think of an
obvious solution to the problem, namely than no-one was required,
or allowed, to live in a flat with a soft water supply for more than, say,
two years, before being moved to accommodation with a hard water
supply: for, of course, soft water does not effect its baleful influence
on the rate of heart attacks quickly, it would be the purest neurosis to
think that it did.

From the point of view of the consumption of soft water, I said
to the unfeeling bureaucrat, I had paid my debt to society, and now
society owed me something in return. Even this did not convince
him, and he merely said that if I didn't like it I should make my own
arrangements – as if in my state of health and finances I could.

But I had known that I would receive a dusty answer, and had
planned accordingly. I spent the next few days searching the home
appliance stores for a water-hardener, but everywhere met with
the same reply, namely that no such appliance as a water-hardener
existed. This, in turn, proves that people are more concerned with the
state of their pullovers, which they want to be 'nice and fluffy', than
with the state of their hearts, and I hope that I will not be thought
unduly harsh and cruel when I say that such people deserve all the
avoidable death from which they will undoubtedly suffer as a result of
their attitude. The lack of water-hardeners on the market – surely an

opportunity for an inventor desirous both of doing good and making a lot of money – has forced me to add chemical salts to the water in which I boil my food, though this, of course, is not the place to give the precise formula I use, for I repeat that I am not writing a technical manual, but only a rough guide for my fellow-citizens as to how to live. Suffice it to say that the salts contain magnesium, potassium and calcium, and that once a week, that is to say every seventh day, I add trace elements such as molybdenum, vanadium, chromium and selenium. (The difficulties I have had in obtaining the latter salts could be the subject of another book; you would have thought I was trying to obtain thallium to decimate the countryside, the way the pharmacists looked at me when I asked for them. I would have thought the fact that trace elements are necessary for health, though of course not good for you in the larger sense, would have been sufficient to convince them of my *bona fides*.)

Incidentally, I intend to write to my Member of Parliament to ask him what his position is on CI 17200, or Red 33. I want to start another red scare, only this time a real, and fully justified, one.

Even discounting water of unspecified quality, however, the shampoo known as Neutrihair contained twenty-seven ingredients, which means that there were twenty-seven raised to the twenty-sixth power possibilities for interactions between them. I cannot be sure, having forgotten the chemistry I learnt as a schoolboy, but I suspect that this number is larger than the number of atoms, or maybe just molecules, in the universe. At any rate, it is a very large number, and it beggars belief to suppose that the company that manufactures the shampoo has tested all those combinations for possible harmful interactions. Yet it feels no shame in pronouncing its own product not only safe but positively health-giving.

It will not surprise readers to learn that my preliminary enquiries into the safety of Neutrihair took me some considerable time, and I was horrified to discover that, having completed the first and simplest stage of the investigation, it was already nine-fifty. Normally, I try to lie down from twenty-to-ten until ten-to-eleven, because Spanish research has shown that the most common time for people to have a heart attack is ten-past-ten in the morning, and while no controlled trials have yet been conducted to establish whether lying down at that time reduces either the rate or seriousness of heart attacks at that time, it stands to reason that it should. After all, heart attacks happen when not enough blood reaches the heart muscle, and the harder and faster it beats, the more blood it needs. Therefore, resting, when the heart beats comparatively slowly, should help to get us through this most hazardous time of day. Let us not forget that even now, at a time of admittedly declining incidence, heart attacks are responsible for a quarter of all deaths. The good, which is to say healthy, life is a matter of putting two and two together.

However, my plans for a rest – well-earned, I might say – were somewhat disturbed by what I saw as I moved to turn off my computer. (I turn off my computer as a matter of social responsibility: wastage of energy contributes to climate change, and there is little doubt that climate change is in turn contributing to the epidemic of skin cancer that has overtaken the west – climate change, that is, and the irresponsible habit of exposing skin to the carcinogenic rays of the sun.) I saw an advertisement for an on-line dating agency, whose procedures I decided to investigate: not that I was searching for someone with whom to share my life, far from it, for illness shared is illness doubled, so that it would not only be foolish and dangerous for me to live in close association with someone else, but unethical, too. I am not so lacking in self-awareness that I believe myself incapable of communicating a disease to another person.

But I was appalled at the laxity of the agency's procedures. Purely out of concern for the public health, I looked at the electronic form its prospective clients were asked to fill in, and while there were scores of irrelevant questions concerning such matters as interests and hobbies, there was not a single elementary question about health, for example about hepatitis status, medication taken, and so on and so forth.

Just think about it! Suppose two insulin-dependent diabetics got together (I use this example at random, not from any animus against diabetics, and I am sure that the reader could supply scores, if not hundreds, of examples of his own), and both happened to have hypoglycaemic attacks at the same time. Both would be unconscious and neither would be able to come to the assistance of the other. There could therefore be two perfectly preventable deaths, simply because of a lack of proper precaution and co-ordination of illnesses. The incorrigible habit that humans have of associating with one another is quite dangerous enough without added dangers caused by suicidal insouciance.

I know what I would do if I were in power (unfortunately my state of health precludes me from seeking, let alone attaining, it). If people continued to insist on intimate physical contact with one another, all official advice to the contrary notwithstanding, I would not go so far as to outlaw it. This, it seems to me, would be unduly dictatorial, however laudable the outcome would be, and there must be some concession to human weakness and irresponsibility. However, risks to the rational man are what entities were to William of Ockham: they are not be multiplied unnecessarily. Therefore, agencies such as the one whose procedures I investigated and that are casual to the point of criminal negligence should by law be required to demand a full disclosure of medical records by their clients, and to perform standard laboratory and other tests (for example, for the presence of measles antibodies) on them before registering them. And it seems to me only a matter of elementary human rights, as well as practical prudence, that the person who wishes to make contact with another should have the right to demand further examinations or tests before continuing, and that all clients should make an undertaking to undergo any tests that may be required by the other party without reserve, protest or demur. The obligation would, of course, be mutual.

To those who object that such a manner of proceeding might or would indefinitely postpone many a potential love affair, I can only answer, So much the better! After all, a lot of suicides follow love affairs.

In fact, when you think about it, what has love brought mankind? Venereal disease and jealousy, that's all. I don't suppose I need say more about venereal disease, it is so self-evident and obvious; but without love there would be no jealousy, and without jealousy there would be no domestic violence, or at any rate much less. Murder in the household – whether in the kitchen, the bathroom or elsewhere – would almost disappear. In short, countless lives would be saved, and would be much calmer, if there were no love. The frustration and despair that love – which always fails in the end, indeed usually after a few months at most – brings is responsible, according to neuropsychoimmunolgists, for countless diseases. Therefore, all objections that detailed health questionnaires, checks and examinations would preclude love are frivolous, and are really arguments in favour of them.

Irritation that such obvious considerations had been completely overlooked by successive governments of all political stripes was not propitious to the rest and calm that I so badly needed to reduce my chances of a heart attack, besides which there was another concern that arose as a consequence of my investigation of the safety, or should I say the dangers, of Neutrihair and its ingredients. I had not yet had breakfast, and research has shown that to consume three meals a day, frugal as they ought to be, is best from the point of view of preserving health, or rather of avoiding illness, since health, strictly speaking, cannot be preserved. In other words, I would be retiring to rest on an empty stomach, and as everyone knows, the physiological output of hydrochloric acid in the stomach increases during recumbency. With nothing to neutralise the acid, I risked aggravating a peptic ulcer, if I had one, and thereby provoking a perforation, with consequent peritonitis.

As if this were not bad enough in itself, it would occur precisely at a time when, the incidence of such perforations having declined greatly, surgeons were less skilled than they used to be at treating them. Moreover, it is possible that the perforation itself would produce such physiological shock that in any case I should not be able to summon help by telephone (the ability for another to do so on one's behalf is one of the few advantages of living in close association with someone else, though it by no means cancels out, far from it, the dangers of doing so). I have investigated thoroughly the possibility of an alarm system such as is frequently employed by elderly people, who carry a radio-operated bell around their necks which they can press if they fall; but again I met with a brick wall of indifference or obtuseness by those charged with my welfare. The last time I telephoned my doctor about it, and he told me not to be neurotic, I nearly lost my temper – much to my own detriment, of course. Each time you lose your temper, it has been estimated, you shorten your life by five minutes.

Eventually, I decided that, if the public authorities did not want to save my life by this means, I would have to pay for it myself. I called an alarm company which, alarmingly, did not answer for quite some time.

'Lucky I'm not dying,' I said when finally someone answered. 'At least, not acutely.'

The woman on the other end was not quick on the uptake. She asked me my age.

'Forty,' I replied with my customary truthfulness.

'Forty?' she said. 'Did you say *forty*?'

'Yes,' I replied. 'What of it?'

'I'm sorry,' she said. 'But the youngest age at which we provide a service is sixty-five, except in exceptional circumstances.'

'All circumstances are exceptional,' I said.

'No they're not,' she said. 'How can they be?'

'So you deny that each man is unique?' I asked.

'No, of course not.'

'Well, then,' I said, 'all circumstances are exceptional.'

Like someone who had been trained to recite a magical incantation without understanding it, she repeated that her company provided peace of mind for the elderly by means of the latest technology.

'Why only the elderly?' I asked.

'Because that's what we do,' she said, apparently under the impression that she had answered me satisfactorily.

'But why do you do what you do?' I continued.

'Because it's what we're paid to do.'

She seemed to think that I was enquiring after her personal motives. It is astonishing how wrapped up in their own situation many people are nowadays, how unable they are to think in general terms or about anyone but themselves.

'What I meant,' I said, speaking very clearly so that there should be no mistake, 'was, Why do you provide your service only to old people?'

'Because they're at risk,' she said.

'We're all at risk,' I replied.

'Well, they're most at risk.'

'Ha! So, you admit, then, that we're all at risk?' I pounced.

'I didn't say that,' she said defensively, as if accused of something beyond her comprehension.

'Yes you did, even if you don't realise it.' Why do people not think of the logical implications, let alone the health implications, of what they say before they speak? 'If the old are most at risk, it must follow that others are at some risk, because zero multiplied by zero is still zero.'

'I don't know what you're talking about,' she said, part pertly, part unhappily.

I could tell it was pointless to try to get her to understand. I changed tack slightly, to something I thought she would be able to understand.

'Why should you want to save only old people?' I asked. 'Are their lives worth more than those of the young or middle-aged?' I added 'middle-aged', because from the sound of her voice she was still young enough to consider forty a good age.

'No, of course not,' she said.

'If anything, they're less valuable. They consume but they do not produce, and never will produce, at least the vast majority of them. If you save an old person's life, the chances are that it is only for a short time, perhaps only a few months or even less. But if you save a younger person's life, someone of my age, for example, you save it for a long time. Which is more worthwhile, and a better use of effort and resources?'

As if she were a chicken whose head had been cut off but who continued to race round the run, she repeated that her company provided peace of mind for the elderly by means of the latest technology. I knew then that I wouldn't get my alarm: my safety was not of sufficient concern to her that she might depart from her script.

I therefore had to decide for myself, with no one to guide or advise me, whether, even without an alarm, and even with added acid secretion on an empty stomach, it was safer to lie down for the sake of my heart, or to get on with my day, for example by eating breakfast.

I decided to lie down.

7

NO DOUBT THERE ARE those who will blame me, who will claim that I made the wrong decision. But I ask people to believe me when I tell them that at least I thought about the decision seriously, for at least five minutes, perhaps even longer; and to remember that, man being a fallen creature, and his powers of reasoning being fallible, they should extend to me their indulgence, compassion and understanding if I chose and did wrong. Is there anyone who always makes the right choice with regard to his health, on each and every occasion he has to make one?

As soon as I lay down, there was another important, indeed vital, question to be answered: since the period of my rest before ten o'clock had been truncated, should I extend the period of my rest after ten-past-ten to compensate for it, especially as the truncation had been brought about by a particularly stressful, I might even say traumatic, investigation of the ingredients of Neutrihair? I decided that it was probably wise to do so, though before settling down I set the alarm clock just in case I should fall asleep. A prolonged sleep during the day would naturally affect adversely my sleep at night, and, as I think I have already mentioned, insomnia is both a sign and a cause of ill-health of many different causes.

There was still the problem of the missed meal. Now I had missed one, how was I now to make up for it?

If it were simply a matter of calories, nothing could have been easier: it would simply have been to unite what I would have eaten for breakfast with what I was going to eat for lunch. But the idea that proper nutrition is a mere matter of calories, or indeed of the other constituents of food, is so crude that it may, indeed must, be dismissed out of hand.

Why not, you ask, take a late breakfast and then a late lunch? Because that would mean the postponement of my dinner; and since it is quite wrong, both from the point of view of digestion and sleep, to go to bed on a full stomach (though of course a completely empty one is also to be avoided), it would mean a disastrous departure from my health-preserving routine that would have knock-on effects for days, or weeks, or even months to come. I would have to go to bed much later than usual, which would result in one of two effects: either I would sleep badly, in the sense of not enough, by waking at my normal time, or I would sleep well, in the sense of long enough, but wake up late. Neither of these alternatives was attractive, which is, of course, to say healthy.

I turned the alternatives over and over in my mind until, quite frankly, I grew bored with them – a very dangerous state of mind, because it leads to impulsive and irrational decisions, not for the sake of choosing the better alternative, but for the sake of disencumbering oneself of the necessity to think any more about the problem.

On the other hand, one has to recognise that some dilemmas are, in the present state of knowledge, insoluble. I therefore decided on a compromise that should partly satisfy both schools of thought (assuming there to be only two on a question of such complexity). I think my compromise was sensible. Which elements of breakfast were, nutritionally-speaking, the most important? It was this question, easily answered, that enabled me to overcome the *impasse*. It was obvious to me that the vital nutritional elements of breakfast were the Vitamin C from my fruit juice, and the dietary fibre, commonly known as roughage, from my organic muesli with extra sunflower seeds and dried kale. I would take enough of these nutrients – if roughage can properly be called a nutrient, but I won't quibble over technicalities in what is, after all, not a technical work – to meet my essential needs without having to postpone my lunch by more than a quarter of an hour, thus not upsetting my normal routine by very much.

This matter settled, I was able to enjoy a few moments' peace of mind: but long, as Shakespeare puts it, it could not be. Disturbing thoughts of the dangers I would soon have to face crowded in on me. The fact is that the modern world is one in which it is impossible to relax or lower one's guard, for it will not allow you to do so: danger will come to you if you do not go to it. No one escapes danger for long, if at all.

The reader will have remembered that I had received in the early morning a summons to attend a medical examination, so called, at the Department of Work and Pensions, by implication expressing scepticism about my inability to work for reasons of health.

This, of course, was completely illogical, indeed self-contradictory, as I can demonstrate with such ease that the very obviousness of it raises questions about the good faith of the Department. I do not claim that the Department is staffed by intellectual giants, far from it, but the staff are not so stupid that they could not follow the argument, or even think of it themselves.

There are three possibilities with regard to my state of ill-health. First, that I am really ill. This speaks for itself. Second, that I am fabricating my ill-health, in short lying. Third, that I genuinely believe myself to suffer from illness when in fact I do not. It is the logical consequences of the latter two possibilities that I now consider.

If I am making up my illness out of whole cloth, I am suffering from factitious illness. Those who suffer from factitious illnesses over a prolonged period are recognised both by the *Diagnostic and Statistical Manual of the American Psychiatric Association*, and by the World Health Organisation's *International Classification of Diseases* to be suffering from a *bona fide* medical condition. If they were not, after all, they would not appear in either of these two systems of diagnosis. And for people to have a medical diagnosis, they must first be ill.

The alert reader, if any such there be, will already have divined that precisely the same argument must apply to those who genuinely believe themselves to be ill but are not. They too have a *bona fide* medical condition according to the DSM IV and the ICD 10, as they are affectionately known throughout the medical world.

In other words, I am ill even if I am not ill: therefore I am ill. This is the inescapable conclusion to be reached from a correct understanding of those two authoritative volumes. If Descartes were alive today (and incidentally he died of Sweden's harsh climate), he might have come to a rather more important conclusion than *cogito ergo sum*, one with profound practical consequences: I think I am ill, therefore I am ill. I don't think anyone can refute this, certainly not the kind of doctor employed by the Department to examine people like me.

The last time I was examined at the Department, it was by a doctor in his late fifties. He had that cadaverous look that chain-smoking often gives, at least when not accompanied by excess consumption of the most fattening of all alcoholic drinks (unsuitable for coeliacs, of whom there are more and more because of the over-refinement of our food), namely beer. I could also see by the way that he breathed that the cigarettes had affected his lungs: bronchitis or emphysema, or both. I told him straight away that I thought he was setting a very poor example, and indeed that he was in no moral position to judge the right of other people to social security payments.

With an expression on his face that I can only describe as a rictus, he asked me how I had come to that conclusion. Why is it that you have to spell everything out to some people?

'Simple,' I said, 'and obvious. With your lung condition, which is progressive even if you stopped smoking immediately, which I think is unlikely in your case anyway, you will not be able to continue your work for very much longer. Therefore you will have to retire early.'

'And so?' he asked sardonically.

'Well,' I continued, 'you will retire early on medical grounds, which means that you will receive your full pension. And who will pay for this? The taxpayers, of course, or the other contributors if you have a private pension.'

'That is in the nature of insurance,' he said.

'I am not talking of legalities,' I said, 'but of morality. There is a difference. Not everything that is right or wrong is laid down in pension scheme rulebooks.'

'We are not here to…' he began, employing the old diversionary tactic of changing the subject.

But I was prepared, and raised my voice. It was easy to overpower his voice because his breath was so short, and he probably wouldn't have been able to finish his sentence anyway without catching his breath. I noticed that his lips were a little blue, or bluish, which meant that, despite being thin, he was more a blue bloater than a pink puffer, to use the expressions that doctors employ colloquially when speaking of the two kinds of chronic obstructive pulmonary disease (though the two kinds are not absolutely distinct, of course).

'The fact is,' I said, 'that you have knowingly and with carelessness aforethought – if I may be permitted an expression that appears paradoxical but that in reality is not, for as a doctor you must surely have known the possible and even likely effects of smoking heavily for many years – with carelessness aforethought, then, you have brought this condition upon yourself. And as a result you have not only made yourself unfit for work, and will ask others to pay for your enforced idleness, the entirely foreseeable result of your own bad habits, and will almost certainly consume vast medical resources in attempts to ameliorate your condition, but you presume to judge the fitness for work of others who, as I do, suffer from conditions not of their own choosing, that have simply happened to them by a stroke of ill-fortune, and that they could have done nothing to avoid.'

The doctor coughed. Although his case was chronic, like mine, I could not bring myself to feel sorry for him.

'Indeed,' I continued, 'I think I may fairly say, for false modesty is precisely what it says it is, namely false, that I have gone to exceptional lengths, above and beyond the call of duty, to preserve and recover my health so as not to require the support of the public purse, grudging and financially limited as it is, and return to work. Alas, it was not to be, but that is hardly my fault.'

'Nobody is saying…' said the doctor.

'I have done all that a citizen could reasonably have done to keep himself healthy,' I said. 'More, in fact. I have controlled my weight, eaten healthily and denied myself everything delicious but dangerous, I have checked my temperature regularly, heart rate, blood pressure, body mass index, sleeping pattern, urine for blood, bilirubin, ketones, protein and glucose – not necessarily in that order, of course – and in general have behaved with great responsibility. With all due respect, I don't think the same thing can be said of you, and it is certainly not my fault and none of my choosing that I find myself in a state of chronic ill-health.'

I don't know whether he was suddenly struck by a guilty conscience at his own irresponsible conduct over the years, but with a wave of his hand he dismissed me, or tried to do so.

'All right,' he said. 'We'll continue your benefits.'

'You're not even going to do a physical examination?' I asked.

'No,' he said. 'Your problem's elsewhere.'

I didn't like that. Was he implying that there was something wrong with me mentally? The unbiased reader of these pages would surely agree that I could hardly have written them had there been anything wrong with me in that sense.

And to tell the truth – for there is little point in writing anything else – I was a little disappointed that he did not want to examine me. I know that he was unlikely to be a very good doctor (or else why would he have been doing that job?) but even a poor doctor may sometimes come across something that others have missed or has developed since the last examination.

Of course, I wasn't really a patient of his: social security doctors don't have patients. I wasn't a client, either, since I wasn't there voluntarily: victim, or specimen, perhaps.

At any rate, even a doctor at the Department of Work and Pensions might have been able to feel a mass in the abdomen overlooked by even the most skilful and assiduous of self-examiners, such as I prided (and pride) myself on being. In the case of self-examination, familiarity does not so much breed contempt as a lack of comparative standard. Besides, most processes such as enlargement of the liver are gradual, so that one may easily come to accept the abnormal as normal. There is therefore nothing like an examination by an outsider, even if he is one of the lesser lights of his profession.

I need hardly point out that the need to examine one's abdomen regularly is yet another reason to remain slim: for how is one to palpate an enlarged organ through a mound of blubber? And some organs are much easier to feel than others, the liver by comparison with the spleen for example. This is despite the fact that enlargement of the spleen is even more sinister than that of the liver: nature rarely makes things easy for us.

I hesitate to describe my method of examining my abdomen, in case I should be thought to be putting myself immodestly forward as an exemplar to be followed, or as prescribing a method to be followed in a rigid way. Once again, I deny this: my method is only one among hundreds. But when I consider the ignorance of the general population of the disposition of the organs in the abdominal cavity, and that some people are even unaware of the existence of separate organs within it, believing the contents of the abdominal cavity to be an undifferentiated and presumably semi-liquid mush, I do not think it is entirely superfluous to describe the way in which, twice a day, on waking and retiring to bed, I carry out my examination.

I begin with the liver because it is the easiest. I move my hand, which I have previously warmed to prevent any unpleasant cold shock, palm downwards, at the level of my *umbilicus* and parallel to the ribs the right side, my fingers being at right angles to the vertical axis of my body. (It is surprising how difficult it is to put these things into words. A video demonstration would work much better, and I even once proposed the making of such a video to a production company, but it replied that it thought there would be an insufficient market for it to justify the expense of making it. I suspect that it did not want to upset the medical lobby, which wants to maintain a monopoly on physical examination. Of course, the dangers of watching a video might more than cancel out the benefits of self-examination – only detailed further research could answer the question.) I breathe in and out deeply, each time moving my fingers slightly in the direction of the ribs.

I will not here go into the subtleties of the enlarged liver, and the different significance of a rough or smooth or tender or painless edge. This can be found in any textbook. Rather, I will move on to the spleen, which is enlarged in so many conditions, none of them less than serious.

I place my right hand in my right *iliac fossa*, digging it inwards gently but firmly, and then, as with the examination for the liver, breathe in deeply. In the event of not feeling the spleen (and so far, I have never felt it) I move my hand diagonally towards the left upper quadrant of my abdomen about half an inch at a time, breathing in and out deeply and slowly each time, repeating the process until I reach very near the left bottom edge of my ribcage. It is necessary to do all this slowly, not only in order not to miss anything, but because if you breathe in and out too quickly you can feel a little dizzy, with all the consequences that dizziness can bring with it.

The various forms of palpability of the small and large bowel are so numerous that there is not the space for an enumeration in a schematic work such as this. Suffice it to say that inflammation or tumour of the bowel, and even severe constipation, must eventually make itself palpable through the abdominal wall – provided, as I have already mentioned, that it is not too fat.

Of all the major organs, perhaps the kidneys, because of their anatomical position, are the most difficult to palpate, and although I have developed a technique of such palpation, I think beginners might safely omit this without incurring the charge of carelessness – provided, of course, that they test their urine thoroughly and regularly.

However careful one is, the fact remains that it is always possible to overlook something detectable by someone else, and therefore no opportunity for examination by a third party ought to be missed, the dangers of contagion notwithstanding. The great advantage, incidentally, of being examined by second-rate doctors (the only one) is that, when they find something, the person they have examined can be sure it is pretty far-advanced, or they would not have found it.

I had no faith, however, or any great hopes, that any future doctor employed by the Department of Work and Pensions would so much as lay a finger on me by way of examination. It has recently been announced that such doctors are to be paid according to the number of people from whom they withdraw benefits and return to work, an open invitation to callousness and indifference to suffering such as mine.

8

THE LETTER STATED that my appointment at the Department was for the afternoon, and therefore, before departure, I had to take lunch (although I had partaken of my reduced breakfast, nothing on earth would induce me to miss two meals in succession). Of course, a meal always brings one face to face with the most fundamental question of human life, namely what to eat.

All flesh is grass, but not all grass is, or ought to be, flesh. Take cheese as an example: it is more or less a direct product of grass itself, give or take bacteria. People eat it just because they like it, without heeding the consequences. What a way to eat! Anyone would think that eating served no biological purpose, and therefore carried no dangers, that Nature endowed us with an appetite merely so that we could enjoy ourselves and derive pleasure from putting things in our mouths and swallowing them. It is hardly surprising that, with so frivolous an attitude to the most serious problem of human existence, people die; and not merely die, but die young and often.

This cheese question is important. Not only is cheese fattening in itself, and fat people have higher death rates from practically all known diseases, at least those of developed societies, but the levels of low density cholesterol of those who eat cheese are extremely high. There is therefore nothing to be said in favour of cheese, especially as all the nutrients it contains – and candour demands that I admit that it is proteinaceous – are obtainable in other ways that, if not entirely safe, are much less damaging.

This is not the place, however, to elucidate fully the reasons behind my choice of nutrients for lunch. Man's pursuit of the balanced diet is eternal, and the last time I looked there were 3,470,000 internet websites devoted to this cardinal subject. (Not all websites are created equal, however, and some are distinctly misleading. Moreover, I was appalled to discover that there were two million more websites devoted to Mick Jagger than to a balanced diet. Is it any wonder that, with such a sense of priorities, people continue to suffer from cancer of the bowel?)

An absolute account of my decision would necessarily include a recent dietary history: for how can a diet continue to be balanced without reference to what has lately been consumed? In the interest of brevity, I will merely remark that I had reason to be concerned about my recent intake of selenium, a low level of which in the blood is associated with cancer of the prostate and has been associated in the past with heart attacks. Indeed, there is a form of cardiac muscle degeneration called Keshan disease that is caused by low selenium levels. It occurs principally in Keshan province in North Eastern China, where there is no selenium in the soil, and results in chest pain, breathlessness, bilious vomiting and death, though it can be prevented by selenium supplementation of the diet. It has since also appeared in Finland and New Zealand, and while it has never been reported here this may be more because it has not been recognised than because it has not occurred. It is best, therefore, to keep the selenium levels up.

I decided on boiled fillet of fish (I advise cod because it is an ocean fish, and therefore less likely to be contaminated with heavy metals released into seawater as industrial waste) with raw broccoli and grated brazil nuts. All three contain selenium, of course, but in addition broccoli contains sulforophane, a chemical that, in mice, has shown to have a synergistic protective effect against the development of cancer when combined with selenium. Of course, I decided on raw broccoli to preserve its Vitamin C content, washing it in chlorhexidine first and then rinsing it thoroughly. As to the fish, first I examined it for bones with a magnifying glass, because although it was alleged to be a fillet, one never knows. Fishmongers are careless, and don't much worry if their customers choke to death on unexpected bones. Then I boiled it, in distilled water, of course, without added salt. The harmful effects of salt are too well-established and too well-known to need rehearsal here. And the boiling must be thorough (I recommend thirty minutes as a minimum), to avoid infestation with fish tapeworm, Diphyllobothrium latum, which can cause Pernicious anaemia and can live in the human gut for twenty years.

Upon completion of the cooking, I opened a drawer to procure eating utensils. Here, in parenthesis, I must enter a protest at the laxity of the authorities. It is well-known that knives are the principal instrument of murder in this country, to say nothing of near-fatal and less serious injuries. Knife crime, we read constantly, is increasing. We have already discussed the issue of murder in the kitchen, and yet there is no effort to control or licence the possession and use of knives in this most deadly of rooms. There is not a kitchen in the country that is without an instrument, or a whole armoury of instruments, of murder; anyone, no matter how unstable, unsuitable or irresponsible, can buy one. Is it not time that we introduced a system of licensing and inspection of these objects? If we can do it for guns, why not for knives?

I sat down to eat this nutritious, balanced and healthful meal.

Once it was over I had, of course, to decide how I was going to the Department, which is a large concrete office block about four miles away, next to a roundabout with a pedestrian underpass notorious for the muggings that take place in it. There is no source of fresh air in the building, which is ventilated artificially, and therefore puts all who enter it at risk of Legionnaire's disease: for who can believe that the government looks after the ventilation systems of its buildings better than it looks after anything else?

What appals me most, however, is that a visitor to the building is not allowed to wear a surgical mask to protect himself from the risk. I

111

have once tried to wear one in the building, but such is the surveillance by closed circuit television there that no sooner had I donned such a mask than I was approached by at least two men in grubby uniforms who told me, in the rudest way possible, almost shouting in fact, to take the mask off at once. I complied, of course, for fear of injury in any scuffle, but I asked them why I should not wear a mask. They answered as if I had been stupid.

'Where do you live?' they said. 'The South Pole? Don't you know there are terrorist attacks going on?'

'Terrorists don't wear surgical masks,' I replied. 'They wear balaclavas and baseball caps. You'd be better off attending to them.'

'Masks are not allowed in the building.'

A Moslem woman in a niqab, that black, tent-like garment with only a slit for the eyes, glided by.

'You're not stopping her, I notice,' I said. 'She could have anything in there, a Kalashnikov, a hand grenade, anything.'

I have noticed that nothing infuriates petty officialdom as much as logic.

One of the security men, almost beside himself with rage, obtruded his face close to mine. He bared his teeth, mottled and stained, as he snarled at me.

'Don't you get lippy with me, sunshine,' he said. I noticed that he had gingivitis, and halitosis. 'Or I'll throw you out.'

'You should spend more time at the dentist and less in the pub,' I said, also noticing that he had the kind of solidity often possessed of beer-drinkers who nevertheless do some exercise. 'Your teeth are terrible – and your gums.'

'If you don't button it, you won't have no teeth in a minute.'

'All right,' I said. 'But for your information, so you know next time, I wear a mask not because I'm a terrorist, but so as not to breathe in the organisms that give you Legionnaire's disease. And if you take my advice, you'd do the same. After all, you're here eight hours a day, and I'm only a visitor, so you're even more at risk than I am. And by the way, if I catch Legionnaire's disease, I'll hold you personally responsible, because now that I've told you, you won't be able to say "We didn't know." So I'll see you in court.'

If it ever came to that, of course, their defence would be that they were only obeying orders. Thus the mentality that produced the Holocaust lives on, and people are still dying because of it.

Face masks remain forbidden in the confines of the building (though perhaps only for the moment, as I have written to the Secretary of State, enclosing a stamped addressed envelope so that he cannot refuse to reply on the grounds of expense, outlining my powerful arguments as to why they should be permitted, with a subtle hint that they should be made compulsory at some time in the future).

The reader will be interested, no doubt, to know the precise nature of the arguments I presented to the Secretary of State. Since he was, first and foremost, a politician, I presented him first with the economic arguments, for these days money is more precious than life itself, especially the lives of others. It is not that I like or approve of arguing in this fashion, but one has sometimes to compromise one's principles to achieve a practical end. To win an argument and have the last word is no doubt gratifying, but for those who, like me, want to change the world for the better, it is not enough.

Legionnaire's disease is expensive. First, it occurs in epidemics; second, it usually takes a prolonged stay in hospital before anyone thinks of the diagnosis, costly investigations and useless treatments having been carried out in the meantime. And of course it kills people, up to a quarter of those infected.

I didn't mention in the letter that the old and the chronically ill are particularly susceptible for two reasons: first, it would have been a rhetorical own-goal, as it were, in so far as the old and chronically

113

ill are a financial liability rather than an asset from the government's point of view, which is that of cost-benefit analysis; and, second, the special susceptibility of the old and chronically ill emphatically does not mean that others may not contract and die of it. A heavy innoculum of bacteria of a causative organism can overcome any degree of fitness or immunity. Nor do I overlook the fact that, in any case and almost by definition, of those who enter the Department, a far larger proportion than might be expected by chance are unwell to start with, and therefore have a right to expect especial care in the maintenance of the ventilation system of any public building which they are obliged to frequent.

There is no case of Legionnaire's disease without blame and (which is related but not identical) culpability, for it is entirely a man-made disease, not in the sense that he, man, created the causative organism, but in the sense that he created the conditions in which it flourishes and can cause fatal pneumonia. Thus every outbreak is followed by expensive litigation, and since almost all such outbreaks occur in publicly-owned buildings, and since the litigants themselves are funded by public money, the cost to the taxpayer is enormous. And this is without counting the loss of production that results.

All this, as I informed the Secretary of State, could easily be avoided. If at the entrance to every public building there were a supply of surgical masks, Legionnaire's disease would soon be a thing of the past like leprosy, at least in this country, a forgotten nightmare (apart from those few hundred cases to which I alluded earlier).

Of course, the masks would have to be like education, free and compulsory. It is a complete myth that people are the best judges of their own interests. If they were, they would be wearing faces masks already and would not have to be forced to do so; they would not still die in hecatombs of entirely preventable diseases, to say nothing of accidents, so called (in reality, there is no such thing as an accident).

Oh, I already hear in my mind's ear the objections of those who have always stood in the way of the public health, namely the expense of it and the supposed loss of freedom it entails. They even objected to clean water on those grounds in Victorian times.

As to the expense, the masks would cost very little, probably less than the annual maintenance of one death-dealing military aircraft. (Every year, one or two crash in residential areas. It is always worth glancing skywards at frequent intervals just to check, though I admit that it might not be easy to take avoiding action. And while looking upwards, of course, it is vital to stop walking, in case of holes in the ground.) In any case, the expense would not be all loss: it would stimulate the surgical mask industry.

As to the supposed loss of freedom entailed in the compulsion to wear masks, what freedom, I ask you, is there in lying in a hospital bed with an undiagnosed pneumonia that is likely to kill you? In short, what freedom is there in death? Is not life the precondition of freedom? Hence, when viewed in the correct light, the compulsion to wear masks – or denying entry to those who refuse to wear them – is an extension of freedom in the real sense of the word.

I pointed all this out to the Secretary of State, but so far have not had a reply. In this country, people who think are treated as cranks.

However, I must not let my anger get in the way of my rational preparations for going out. These depend upon my proposed mode of transport, of course; to travel on a bus does not present the same spectrum of hazards as to travel on a train, or by bicycle.

In general, I am opposed to buses and bicycles. One is enclosed in a bus in a confined space with large numbers of people, of the condition of whose respiratory system one knows nothing, rebreathing air that they have rebreathed from others before them: a real recipe for disaster.

If you propose bicycles as the answer to the problem of buses, I can only reply that you know little of modern traffic and the diffusion of the gases such traffic emits. The concentration of a gaseous contaminant is inversely proportional to the square of the distance from its source. Hence a bicyclist, who prides himself on the healthy exercise he is taking, is so close to the exhaust of the vehicles that spew out carbon monoxide (to say nothing of carcinogens) that he is many times more at risk of harm than a pedestrian who confines himself for the most part, except when crossing the road, as of course, regrettably, he sometimes must, to the pavement. No one, as far as I am aware, has carried out a study of the pulmonary consequences of urban bicycling, and I have searched the internet many times for one, but common sense dictates that they must be severe. The choice between bus and bicycle boils down to that between infection and suffocation or cancer, Scylla and Charybdis, the devil and the deep blue sea.

I refuse to make such a choice, especially when an alternative is available. I mean walking, of course, though I am very far from complacently suggesting that it is without dangers of its own. For example, if you walk too far, especially on hard ground such as is found in towns and cities, none harder in fact, you risk a fracture – called a march fracture – of one or more of the bones in your feet. This may not sound terribly serious, but I once had a neighbour who had such a fracture and found it so painful to walk thereafter, even with a plaster cast, that he retired to bed where, remaining immobile, he got a pulmonary embolus and died. There are few places more dangerous, in fact, than bed.

But, you say, one death doesn't make a holocaust, and here I am glad to agree with you for once. As I have said, life is a matter of weighing the greater against the lesser dangers, although I must point out that a march fracture is not the only risk of walking, far from it.

That is why I always wear my pedestrian helmet when I walk in town. (The size of the city being what it is, I cannot reach the countryside without undertaking a long and therefore proportionately dangerous journey, and therefore the question of whether such a helmet is necessary for walking in the countryside does not arise.)

I confess that I get some strange looks as I walk in the street with my helmet, the same kind of looks that Columbus no doubt got when he proposed to sail across the Atlantic. But why should I get such looks? After all, the pedestrian helmet is only the same as cyclists wear, and are not pedestrians liable, even if a little less liable, to the same head injuries that afflict cyclists? Moreover, there are some injuries to which they are even more liable than cyclists. One is constantly reading in the newspapers of groups of youths who strike a pedestrian in the street, who bangs his head on the kerbside as he falls, and then dies in hospital a few hours or days later.

I hope I shall not be suspected of sympathy for such youths when I say that those who die in this fashion do so in part by contributory negligence if they are not wearing a helmet at the time of the attack. Many who are dead would still be living (admittedly in a brain-damaged state, perhaps) if they had worn a helmet. Such helmets don't cost much, and are light to wear: therefore there is no excuse for failing to wear one. Thoughtlessness kills.

Here, I think, is another ground for liberating compulsion. If the government were at all concerned for the safety of its electorate, it would surely by now have enforced the wearing of pedestrian helmets in the same way as it has enforced the wearing of seat-belts in motor vehicles. And yet, when I wear my helmet, people look at me as if I were mad instead of a pioneer.

No doubt for some my appearance is all the stranger because of the tinted goggles I wear. These, of course, should be both closely-fitting and filter out the ultra-violet light, or else they lose their point.

Thanks to them, I can honestly claim, hand on heart, never to have caught an eye infection or suffered an eye injury while out walking in the street, and furthermore I believe that I have delayed senile degeneration of the retina by protecting it from glare.

The stab-proof vest I think I have already mentioned. There is regrettably little, in the present state of manufacture, that one can do to protect one's abdomen or limbs, especially legs, beyond ensuring that one's clothes are of a suitable thickness and toughness, though at the same time they should not be made of any fibre than can give rise to allergies, of course. Metal of any kind should be abjured for fear of contact dermatitis; though insistence on plastic zips, I have found, severely limits one's choice of garments, unless one is a do-it-yourself tailor.

It is worth, for a moment, examining the issue of clothing in greater detail, specifically as to the dyes used in colouring it. Information regarding the properties of said dyes should be sought on the internet; as yet the clothing companies do not provide even the limited information about their products that the food companies have been forced to provide about theirs. This is an anomaly to which I have repeatedly drawn the attention of the authorities and the press by means of letters, not a single one of which has yet been published – such is the influence of the clothing industry, which of course is responsible for much of the press's advertising revenue. The arm of commerce is long and without scruple.

On the subject of proper, that is to say safe, footwear, I shall be very brief. It has long seemed to me to be the perfect negation of hygiene to enclose one's feet, that are endowed with so many sweat glands, and are potentially prey to so many infections, in those hermetic, airless vessels known as shoes. They promote fungal growth between the toes and in the nails which, while not life threatening, are unsightly and necessarily reduce the quality of life, and – because fungal infections are contagious – provide one of many very good reasons for people not to live in close proximity to one another. What people should wear – and here again I see good reason for compulsion – are sandals, though whether with or without socks depends upon climatic conditions. I never leave the house without consulting the weather forecast on this question.

It goes without saying that, before leaving the building, I apply sun-screening cream to the areas of my skin exposed to sunlight. People are inclined to believe, because it is convenient for them to believe, that they can be harmed by the sun's rays only when the sun is shining brightly, but nothing could be further from the truth. Indeed, cloudy weather, by lulling people into a false sense of security, could be considered the most dangerous kind of weather (from the skin's point of view), inasmuch as it does most harm because people take no precautions against the less powerful rays which, however, are greater in aggregate than those received on overtly sunny days, our climate being what it is. Cancer of the skin could be virtually eliminated if people took but a few elementary precautions.

9

I WILL NOT GO INTO the question of whether, after the age of thirty, everyone should go out with a portable defibrillator attached to him. I think the evidence is not yet strong enough to recommend it fully, and I admit that my practice is somewhat inconsistent: sometimes I do, and sometimes I don't. On this occasion, I decided to risk an hour or two without it.

Here the manuscript ends. Unfortunately, the author, on his way to his medical appointment, was knocked over as he crossed the road. The driver of the vehicle, who remarked on the strange apparel the victim was wearing, claims that the victim appeared to be preoccupied by the flight of a helicopter overhead, since he was looking intently upwards as he crossed the road, disregarding the traffic.

I append extracts from his medical file. I have omitted all the technical details, including figures, but have included what seem to me to be the salient points.

EXTRACTS FROM THE MEDICAL NOTES OF MR A.H.

13.40 40-year-old Caucasian man brought to hospital by ambulance. Knocked over in street by car.

Wearing helmet, goggles, stab-proof vest (difficult to remove), shin pads and sandals. Exposed areas of skin covered in cream.

General condition: Weak but fully conscious. Answers questions. Orientated to time and place. Has full memory of events. Pale and sweaty. Tachycardia. Blood pressure low and declining. In surgical shock.

Injuries: Superficial lacerations, corneal abrasion caused by splintered goggle. No sign of fractures. Abdominal injury: guarding left upper quadrant. In view of history, signs and symptoms, ruptured spleen likely. Urgent surgical opinion required.

Attempted to set up intravenous infusion. Patient demanded to know our rate of infection at injection sites by comparison with other hospitals. Demands written evidence on this. Informed that it does not exist and that there is no time in any case: his condition is grave. He needs urgent blood transfusion. Demanding to know rate of transfusion errors. Also wants to know our procedures for preventing transmission on hepatitis C and other new forms of hepatitis. Asking for latest research on these forms of hepatitis. Says I am not an expert (true) and demands to see the hepatologist.

Informed that without transfusion he will bleed to death. Demands evidence of this, including latest papers.

13.54: On call surgeon. Thank you. Probable ruptured spleen. Needs urgent laparotomy. Demanding to know my personal results for this operation by comparison with others. Wants evidence that ruptured spleen never heals spontaneously. Also demanding to know consequences of splenectomy. Will it interfere with his life? How often will he need immunisation against pneumococcus and what are the side effects of the immunisation? What are death rates from splenectomy compared with death rates of untreated ruptured spleen (demands recent controlled trials and demands to know how, in absence of any, I know that operation is necessary). Demanding to know about rates of herniation through scar, both in his case and in general. What are the anaesthetic risks? Do we anticoagulate against deep vein thrombosis?

Explained that operation is essential. Says 'Prove it.'

13.58 General condition deteriorating fast. Pulse undetectable. Very weak. Words can only just be made out. Says that would agree to transfusion and operation if someone would demonstrate convincingly that it was necessary, and safer than alternatives.

14.03 Certified dead. RIP.

So Little Done

1

YOU HYPOCRITES! You pretend (not only to others but even to yourselves) that you're reading this for a higher purpose, such as understanding the mind of a so-called serial killer like me.

But why are you interested in the mind of a serial killer in the first place, may I ask? And what good would your understanding do you, even supposing it were attainable from reading what I have written? Would it prevent the emergence of a single such killer in the future, or facilitate his detection? No, it's not enlightenment you're after, but salacious entertainment; you'd be much more profitably employed on learning something of practical value, such as how to repair your central heating system. Go to the immersion heater, thou sluggard; consider its ways and be wise. (I have adapted very slightly a verse from *Proverbs* in the Bible, Chapter 6, verse 6, I believe, though it isn't easy to check in my present circumstances: I mention this only because I consider it the height of bad manners to make a literary allusion without disclosing its source to the reader.)

Cheap thrills and a frisson of excitement: that's what art is all about, when you strip it of its pretensions. It's prurience, after all, that keeps the cinema, the newspapers and literature going. The world has a lot to thank murderers for, when you come to think of it. Not that I expect gratitude, though my activities have stimulated something of a tourist boom in Eastham, a dismal town hitherto devoid of attractions, even (or perhaps especially) for its inhabitants. I understand I have provided employment for the manufacturers of souvenirs: for I am reliably informed that T-shirts with the legend *I visited Graham Underwood's house and survived* are on sale everywhere in the town.

According to the Italian newspapers, I am *Il Mostro di Eastham*: the Monster of Eastham. I'm learning Italian in prison, a beautiful and poetic language, and have managed to force the Prison Department to deliver *La Repubblica* to me every day, though it arrives a few days late for no good reason that I can detect.

My feat of interring fifteen people in an urban garden hardly bigger than a graveyard plot – my life has been full of ironies – without having been found out by my self-righteous neighbours has caused wonderment throughout the world, and added immeasurably to the gaiety of the nation. People imagine they are being witty when they call me 'Graham Underground', and suppose they are the first to have thought of the joke. But how much greater would their admiration for me have been had it been generally known that I have successfully eliminated seven others – so successfully, in fact, that even after I had provided the police with the fullest possible details, it proved quite impossible to trace them.

Not that the police tried very hard, except to prevent knowledge of my subsidiary confession from leaking to the public, and thereby becoming a reproach to their negligence and incompetence. They pretended to believe, when I made my confession, that I was trying to mislead them at a time when the resources of their forensic laboratory were already overstretched by the fifteen cases whose bodies had already been found; besides, I overheard one police officer remark to another that the kind of person I had killed was the kind of person nobody missed, on whom it was hardly worth wasting a lot of time and effort. And these, ladies and gentlemen, are the men who present themselves as the guardians of public safety and morals, and who presume to stand in judgment over me!

I need hardly add that this was not the only instance of hypocrisy of which I was, and am, the victim. Two weeks after my arrest, a journalist, dressed in a sharp double-breasted olive green suit and posing as a long-lost cousin, succeeded in visiting me in prison and offered me £1 million for the exclusive rights to my story. Naturally, he represented one of those cheap and sordid newspapers which campaign regularly for the execution of people such as I (I am punctilious in my insistence on the correct grammatical use of I and me, by the way): but only after they have written their memoirs to boost the flagging circulations of tabloid newspapers, of course.

As for the prisoners, they felt at liberty, indeed at a moral compulsion, to attack me whenever they could, usually in packs of at least three, just in case it should turn out that I was a karate champion. I was initiated into the ways of my fellow inmates when five of them set upon me in the showers which the prison authorities, in the belief that everyone under arrest must also be infested with lice, have decreed that everyone remanded into their tender care from the courts should take on reception into it. 'You fucking nonce,' they – my fellow-inmates – repeated a hundred times (verbal invention not being a strong point of the criminal classes), as they kicked me black and blue while I lay defenceless on the shower room floor. The warders (or screws) turned a blind eye to these proceedings, because they approved of them. A nonce, I discovered soon enough, is a sex offender; and in the moral hierarchy of the prisoner (if moral is quite the word I seek), even a cockroach is higher than a nonce. The authorities are delighted that the prisoners, or cons as they call them, have a hierarchy of their own – it helps them run the prisons, and I do not exaggerate when I say that there's no one lazier in the world than a screw. So long as men have someone whom they can call their inferior, they are happy.

And why did the other prisoners consider me a nonce, I who have been described by several psychiatrists as completely lacking in sexual drive, indeed as entirely asexual? Because, in their impoverished imagination, the only reason anyone could have for killing fifteen people was to enjoy that momentary orgasmic gratification which played so large a part in their own miserable lives (and, I am led to believe, in the lives of almost everyone else). How many hours did they dream in their cells of this fleeting moment of sexual pleasure, how many hours did they pass speaking about it among themselves! They could not conceive of someone, such as I, who lived on an altogether higher, more intellectual, less instinctual plane.

But let us suppose for the sake of argument that it was for sexual reasons that I killed. Let us suppose also that, at the moment of death of my so-called 'victims', I experienced that sudden release from desire which is the absurd and self-contradictory object of all desire. Would that have made me worthy of my fellow-prisoners' scorn, and given them the right to beat me up *ad libitum*? Would it not, rather, have exonerated me from all possible blame? Which of us knows from where his sexual proclivities come, how they develop, how they are formed, what nourishes and sustains them? How, then, can anyone be held accountable for what excites him? And in any case, is not the proscription of certain sexual acts merely a matter of social convention? Homosexuality – for centuries vilified, condemned, outlawed and severely punished – was suddenly declared by fiat of parliament to be not so terrible after all, and rendered legally permissible at a stroke. But bestiality and necrophilia remain beyond the pale. Who suffers from these latter acts, however? The chickens, the corpses? No, they are forbidden still because someone in authority is personally repelled by them – which is usually a sign of secret attraction. Those who protest loudest are always unsure of themselves. There are parts of the world, after all, in which bestiality is so common as to be perfectly normal. And what about the incest taboo? What rational grounds can there be against incest in these times of a hundred different methods of contraception? The taboo is biologically necessary, we are told, to prevent the birth of the monstrous offspring of consanguinous parents: but what force does such an argument hold when a simple operation, much safer than any pregnancy and parturition itself, is available to rectify the failures of contraception? What is permitted and forbidden, ladies and gentlemen, is fundamentally a matter of taste – and power, of course.

Let us take these prisoners – the majority – who are so outraged by the crimes of nonces that they cannot refrain from assaulting them repeatedly. Let us compare them with, say, an imaginary man who is sexually aroused by the strangulation of old ladies in their nineties, and who has gratified himself in that direction on three separate occasions. Please note that it is not their crimes which we are now comparing, but the harm done by their respective sexual behaviour. Which of them is worse, the average prisoner or the strangler of old ladies?

The average prisoner, in case you don't know it, is an avid procreator of the species. But the care he takes of those whom he fathers is exiguous, both by choice and circumstance. Generally, he sees the mere fact of paternity as a proof of his potency, though his sperm count is something which is scarcely under his control. He has usually fathered children by at least two mothers, the more the better. He abandons such mothers with scarcely a thought, or beats them at will, or sometimes both. It would never occur to him, not if he were to live to be a thousand years, to provide any of them with the necessities of life. And even if by some strange mischance he concerns himself with the fate of his children, he nevertheless commits acts which are certain to lead to prolonged separation from them.

As for the women he selects, they are as fit for motherhood as fish for flight. You see them – those few who maintain contact with their so-called lovers – on their way to prison at visiting times, tarts all of them, tottering along on their absurd high heels, dressed in cheap and flimsy finery despite the cold, or in body-hugging lycra and multicoloured shell suits, their hair badly dyed with the roots showing their true colour, their faces vivid with a surfeit of cheap makeup, their figures kept unhealthily slender by the smoking of sixty cigarettes a day, or fattened by the incessant consumption of junk food. They drag their little children after them, smudge-faced and resisting, the girls prematurely slatterns, and the boys already fixed at the age of three with an expression of determined criminality upon their faces.

What is the future of these children, in all conscience? A life of pointless crises brought about by themselves, of cheap and damp lodgings whose furniture is impregnated with urine, of evictions and bailiffs, of domestic arguments and assaults, of drunkenness and nights in police cells, of poverty and a circle of misery spreading outwards from them like the ripples in a pond after a stone has been thrown into it.

All this is known – or, at least, is knowable – in advance, yet the average prisoner not only has several children, but thinks he has done something fine and worthy in having them, and thirsts for more. He is the willing progenitor of lifetimes of torment.

Contrast this with the strangler of old ladies in their nineties. It is more than likely that the 'victims' are stricken with arthritis, unable to walk or even to rise from a chair unassisted, incontinent, partially blind and half-deaf. What value, then, does their life have for them? Probably they have begged their doctors many times to put them out of their misery. They are alive only because they cannot die by willpower alone. Death comes to them not as an enemy, but as a friend, long-awaited and heartily welcomed.

I am not so foolish as to deny that strangulation causes them some temporary fear and discomfort. I wish to be completely open and honest in this brief essay, unlike the defenders of the law and others who stand in authority over us. But few indeed are the modes of death which are completely without their moments of terror and discomfort. It is unlikely, therefore, that the old ladies would have shuffled off this mortal coil (*Hamlet*) entirely free of pain or discomfort; and strangulation is therefore not worse than what they would eventually have experienced in any case.

And so, if we draw up a balance sheet of the predictable suffering caused by the sexual activities of the average prisoner and the 'pervert' who derives pleasure from strangling old ladies, we must conclude that the suffering caused by the former is incomparably the greater than that caused by the latter. Indeed, the strangler might be said to be a benefactor of mankind, insofar as he reduces the sum of misery in it. The prisoner, of course, is to misery what compound interest is to money. But how do the law and conventional morality distinguish between them? I need hardly ask you to imagine the fulminations in the press of which such a strangler would be the occasion. But the press passes over the procreative activities of the average prisoner in complete silence; and the law treats his right to recreate mayhem around him as absolutely sacrosanct, while condemning the strangler's proclivities in the strongest possible fashion.

2

YOU WILL HAVE noticed by now that I can quote literature with facility, though I am not what you, with your conventional ideas, would probably call an educated man. I haven't been to university or any other institution of so-called higher learning, though that doesn't mean that I cannot think for myself. On the contrary.

It wasn't that I lacked the necessary ability for higher learning: only the opportunity. I am what is contemptuously known by those more favourably placed at birth as an autodidact, which is why (they allege) I take pleasure in long words and convoluted arguments. I have never been able, or rather allowed, to live up to my natural abilities: my voice has a nasal, suburban whine, and is too high-pitched. I grant that I am no Adonis and my posture leaves much to be desired, but above all my vowels are wrong. A man could be a genius in this country, but if he mispronounces his vowels he has no hope of success. It is speech which distinguishes Man from the animals, after all, and to be told that you don't speak properly is to be told something deeply wounding.

My father was a Scotsman. How or why he came to England I never discovered. The child may be father to the man, but we must not forget that the father is nevertheless the father to the child. And my father was violent, in or out of drink: my earliest memory is of him beating my mother, and then giving me a swipe – *en passant*, as it were, which hurled me across the room and into the wall – when I began to cry.

Then suddenly, when I was seven, he deserted us, and it is a measure of the confusion his desertion caused that I still cannot decide whether this was a good or a bad thing. At any rate, it meant that my mother had to provide for me, since there was no question of my father doing so. She went out to work, but having no skills to speak of she could take only menial employment. She worked for several years as an assistant in the kitchens of a local school (not even achieving the rank of cook), and there conceived such a strong dislike of children that she never spoke to me in anything but an exasperated shriek. I think she blamed me for my own existence, as if I had called myself into being without any participation on her part, and whenever she touched me, which was as few times as possible, it was as if she were handling something – some object – which was deeply distasteful and uncleanably dirty. Her inability or unwillingness to form any physical intimacy with me has affected me down to this day: I have never liked to be touched, and associate the sensation of two human skins in contact not with affection or pleasure, but with rejection and humiliation. I remember the violence with which she would seize my hand after I returned from school and try to remove the deeply ingrained blue ink from my fingers with a rough pumice stone. She said it was to keep me clean and respectable, but I think it was to inflict pain upon me for my unpardonable crime of having drawn breath.

She received no help from anybody, and we lived – hating one another – in a dismal, dark and damp little flat above a shop. The landlord, who was the greengrocer below, would shout abuse at us if the rent was as much as an hour overdue. She pretended that if it weren't for me, and my constant need for food, she would have been living a life of ease and luxury. When my shoes wore out because my feet had grown, and I needed a new pair, the sour look on her face told me that she blamed me for my perverse tendency to grow while her income remained the same. I wasn't allowed to ask my contemporaries at school to come home to play with me, in case they asked for something to eat. Not that I would have wished to subject any of them to my mother's embittered hospitality.

Whether or not I was solitary by nature, I soon enough became so. One grows into one's circumstances, as it were. If I found myself alone in the company of another child, I had nothing to say to him. The harder I thought of something to say, the less anything occurred to me. I was teased as an oddity, as someone who held himself aloof by choice, did not participate in games, and did not share in the adventure of smoking in the school bomb shelters (it was a full decade after the end of the War, but still they were not demolished). More than one child gained his spurs as a warrior by attacking me, usually at the instigation of a group of jeering bystanders. Even as a victim, however, I was contemptible, because I did not fight back in the expected way, which would have justified retrospectively the initial, unprovoked attack upon me. It is surprising how exhausting it is to hit an unresisting person (just as the body of a man feels heavier once the life has gone out of it), and my attackers soon gave up, slinking away unsatisfied by, and even disgusted with, my inertness. I did not alight upon this tactic by cunning or by deep reflection: it came to me naturally. I was no Christ figure, turning the other cheek (*Matthew*, chapter 5, verse 39), loving my enemies and doing good to those who hated me (*Luke*, chapter 6, verse 27). On the contrary, I conceived an absolute contempt for my tormentors who, it seemed to me, could do nothing of their own volition but had always to act in concert. Even my teachers, who should have been my protectors, sided with the other children because of my oddity, and made jokes about me in front of the whole class.

My pastimes were solitary, therefore: for a while I collected the numbers of buses or trains, spending long hours on bridges over roads or railway tracks and deriving real excitement from spying a locomotive or a bus which I had not previously seen. I wrote down the numbers in a little book which I have still (I admit that I am something of a hoarder). I had by then come to the conclusion that Man's artefacts were more to be relied upon, and were definitely more admirable, than Man (or rather Boy) himself, and I spent as much time as possible away from human company. I avoided my mother, also, and she was happy enough for me to do so, though she pretended otherwise: her bitterness, her unceasing and unsparing criticism of me, the ill-grace with which she provided what little I had, encouraged me to lock myself away from her, a habit which then became the grounds for further criticism of me. 'You're becoming just like your father,' she would say 'Why don't you speak to me? Or do you think I'm here just to provide your meals whenever you want them? Isn't it enough that I've ruined my life for you, without you being so sullen? Speak, child!' And she would hit me on the ear, as if conversation were money to be shaken out of a money box.

An ill-used or maltreated child dreams of his revenge upon the world, but his means are limited by his size and weakness. Friendless and alone, what could I have done to right the wrongs I suffered? It was at the age of eight that I discovered the joys of inflicting pain upon other living creatures. And who dare blame a child of that age for his cruelty, who not only lacks the capacity to understand the wellsprings of his actions, but has no one who cares about him sufficiently to correct him?

I caught flies and removed their wings for the pleasure of seeing their frantic but hopeless and unavailing struggles. The faint crisp sound made by their wings as I picked them off gave me an inexplicable thrill. It never occurred to me that the nervous systems of these insects were too lowly on the evolutionary scale for them to suffer in any intelligible sense, but if such a thought had occurred to me it would have destroyed the purpose of the game. The arbitrariness and whimsicality of my actions (occasionally I would let a captured fly go) was what pleased me, and the exercise of power over another living being, which was a new experience for me. I found beetles and turned them onto their backs, watching their legs kick to the point of exhaustion and immobility in their attempts to right themselves, which I ensured would not succeed. Then, using my finger-nails as pincers, I picked off their legs one by one, thereafter turning the beetles right way up to 'discover' (as if I were conducting a scientific experiment in search of knowledge) how many legs a beetle needed to drag itself along. What an exquisite pleasure it was to watch the maimed insects trying to drag themselves to safety, in the knowledge that I could resume my 'experiment' at any moment I chose. That the beetle knew neither the cause nor the reason for what I supposed was its suffering was, of course, an additional joy to me.

I experimented in other ways. I immersed worms in water, but finding that, after an initial frenzy of squirming, they settled down and seemed content enough, and in any case survived longer in their new environment than my patience would bear, I added various substances such as salt or bleach to the water to make them lively again and finally disintegrate into vermicular slime. Quite often I persuaded myself that I acted from curiosity and not from cruelty: the faculties of self-deception and dishonesty being among the first of the human mind to develop. But could my self-imputed curiosity explain why I laughed for joy as I observed with minute attention the death-throes of my captives?

No living creature that came within my power was safe from my experiments. I put vinegar or acetone in fish-bowls: how frenziedly fish die! Table salt placed on a frog's moist skin was a superb experience. Ants were a constant source of delight: how easy it was to imagine that they were pests, and that, by pouring boiling water into the cracks in the ground from which they seemed to emanate in such numbers, one was actually performing a useful function!

One day I discovered by chance that warm eggs taken from birds' nests would hatch if kept warm in a jar filled with cotton wool. The fledgling suffocated: thenceforth I was not interested in the cold eggs of abandoned nests, beautiful as I found them, but only in the warm eggs of brooding birds which I frightened off their nests. Older now, my patience had increased, and I would watch my little jar for hours on end, in anticipation of the birth of the hapless fledgling, which would struggle blindly for air and then – slowly – expire.

I should have liked to progress to cats and dogs, for I was becoming aware of the deficiencies of the lower animals as subjects for torture. But I realised also the difficulties involved: my mother had always refused to keep such an animal because of the unnecessary expense involved, and their capture was likely to prove difficult. They could bite and scratch: in short, fight back. I was not interested in a contest – my instincts were not at all sporting – but rather in the sure infliction of suffering without the least chance of escape. I knew that with cats and dogs the pleasures were in proportion to the risks, but I have never been a taker of risks. My one success with a cat was with an old, scarred and arthritic tom belonging to our neighbour, which would not have lived long in any case. I doused him in kerosene and set him alight. Old as he was, but impelled by the flames, he discovered reserves of both energy and agility. I had never seen such frenzy before, nor have I seen it since.

For the most part, however, I had to content myself – where cats and dogs were concerned – with the fights which arose between them spontaneously, the lure of which I never could resist. I loved to see the arched back of a cornered cat, its fur bristling; or to hear at night the unearthly screeches of two cats in dispute over their territory; or to see a large dog in the local park grip a smaller one by the throat with its teeth and shake it like a rat. But in the last analysis, these fights always disappointed me: firstly, because the owners of the dogs would separate them, or the cats would desist before killing one another, but secondly, and more importantly, because they did not fall within my power. There was no revenge upon the world, no assuaging of my humiliation, in suffering and injury not inflicted by the exercise of my own will.

I mention my childish cruelties in the interests of truth: I do not wish to present myself as a born saint. But you will still condemn me: a monster, you will exclaim in a rush of self-righteousness, a congenital pervert! But I repeat, my cruelty was the natural, indeed the inevitable, outcome of my upbringing, which I did nothing to choose for myself. And even if cruelty were part of my essential nature, which it needed only a certain environment to germinate, who would be to blame for it? A man is born into this world as helpless as the fledgling in my bottle.

Look to yourselves, I say! Are you quite sure you do not countenance cruelty on a vastly greater scale than ever mine was, and all the more reprehensible because you could put an end to it if you so wished? I see that a puzzled expression spreads over your face, a look of offended innocence. You grow angry: how dare he compare himself with us, who love our pets and send donations to the RSPCA! Has he no shame? But, ladies and gentlemen, you eat meat, you drink milk, you consume eggs. It does not matter whether or not you know how these commodities are produced: for if you do not know, your ignorance is wilful and therefore culpable. I am not speaking now of the comparative handful of lower animals which – as I now realise – were incapable of the suffering which I attributed to them, but rather I am speaking of the untold millions of sentient beings which are maintained in unspeakable conditions, just so that you might afford their meat or other produce. Am I mistaken in recalling that at the time of my childhood, chicken was still a luxury food, which my mother put on the table but once or twice a year, and then only to demonstrate the extent of her martyrdom? Who now remembers the days, which after all were not so very long ago, when to eat chicken once a week was a sign of prosperity?

And what, I ask, do you suppose has brought about the transformation of chicken from a luxury food into the meat of the masses? Cruelty, of course. I do not mean that the principal object of the modern chicken farmer (a profession to which Himmler gave a bad name) is the deliberate maltreatment of these foolish and in some ways unattractive, but nonetheless sentient, birds. By all means let us not overstate the case by falsely claiming that these creatures are capable of the highest processes of thought or the most refined of sentiments. But I still maintain that for avian flesh to be so widely available, within the budget of all, cruel means of raising it are imperative. And who wishes the end wishes the (inescapable) means.

I presume I do not have to describe in any detail a modern battery chicken farm to establish my point. Let me mention merely the tiny cages in which the unfortunate creatures spend their entire lives, so small indeed that there is not enough room in them for the birds to turn round or move in any direction whatever; and let me mention also that the birds are so immobile that their feet grow round the wire mesh below them, and become so intrinsic a part of the cage itself that when the time comes for the removal of the birds from their cages their feet have to be cut from under them while they are still alive. Needless to add, the separation of a chicken from its feet is performed without anaesthetic: you wouldn't like contaminated flesh, and in any case the government wouldn't permit it.

The other meat which you so thoughtlessly consume every day is likewise the product of cruelty. Only your desire to continue dining in peace of mind prevents you from enquiring into the conditions of your local abattoir, conditions which you would pharisaically claim to horrify you if you were presented with inescapable evidence of their existence, and which you dimly apprehend but from which you delicately avert your gaze. You are the Pontius Pilates of meat-eating.

At least as a child I had the courage of my cruelty. Unlike you, I did not depute it to others to commit on my behalf, that I might claim to be an animal lover. I did what I had to do myself, and never imagined that suffering inflicted behind a veil of secrecy ceased to be suffering.

I have renounced completely my former cruelty to animals, and have become a strict vegetarian. I also wear plastic shoes, though I permit myself wool because it does not necessitate the slaughter of sheep which, moreover, are still kept in fields. When sheep are factory-farmed I shall renounce the use of wool.

In this respect, I am vastly your moral superior. I no longer form part of that self-satisfied majority at whose implicit and silent, but nevertheless imperious, behest numberless atrocities against defenceless animals are committed throughout the land – a land of people who burst into tears at the sight of a puppy with its paw in plaster, and who give large sums of money to support a trauma unit for injured hedgehogs!

I need hardly add that the screws – men who personify roast beef and plenty of beer, and who for the most part did not join the prison service from the love of their fellow men – found my vegan diet and convictions a matter for derision. (Eggs and milk are produced in this society under conditions which are not acceptable to me.) The screws and other prisoners considered it funny to hide meat in my vegetables, and when I protested they replied, 'Sorry, we thought you was a cannibal, Underwood!' And I had to threaten court action to obtain the vitamin supplements which the atrocious diet provided for vegans in prison makes a matter of necessity, not mere preference. The prison authorities thought that, if they half-starved me, I should give up my diet and become a normal meat-eater again. They little knew with whom they had to deal, or what it is to have fixed moral principles.

But why, you may ask, did they try so hard to reconvert me to a carnivorous existence? The provision of a complete vegan diet for me was not, after all, a difficult matter. I know the answer, however: because they themselves knew in their heart of hearts that I was right and they were wrong. And how could these pillars of the law allow themselves to be the moral inferiors of *Il Mostro di Eastham*?

3

NO, LADIES AND GENTLEMEN, I am not a cruel man. The police found no signs of torture on the bodies of what both you and they are pleased to call my 'victims'. Of course, they lost no time in explaining this mysterious and to them incomprehensible absence by the advanced state of decomposition of the cadavers. But with such paltry arguments they could have proved anything they liked: and I need hardly allude to the growing propensity of the police to concoct their evidence, and not just their arguments. If it were not for the fact that I freely admit to my 'crimes', indeed that I proudly avow them, you would not be absolutely certain that I was the author of them, insofar as the administration of our so-called justice system has come to such a pass that any verdict of guilty arouses (quite rightly) as many doubts as it settles. And it should be borne in mind that even so I am guilty only in the formal, or juridical, sense of the word, not in the much more important moral sense, which so very few in our society understand.

Another thing which puzzled the police, with their defective and impoverished imaginations, was the fact that my 'victims' (it would be tiresome not to use the accepted, if entirely misconceived, designation) were of both sexes and of many, if not quite all, ages. In the past, killers of more than one person – who is usually the wife – specialised, as it were: that is to say, they killed only prostitutes, young children or homosexual lovers. The sexual motive of the killings has generally been obvious, even to the slow understanding of the police. And therefore in my case the police, assuming that whatever was the motive in the past must be the motive in the present and the future, have publicly stated that I was 'a polymorphously perverse sadist' (one can just imagine how proud the semi-literates of the force were of that polysyllabic and grandiloquent phrase). Naturally, I took immediate steps to defend my reputation: I instructed my lawyer to file a suit for libel. But it wasn't only my reputation I was concerned to protect: there was an important matter of principle at stake, namely that the authorities should not be at liberty gratuitously to denigrate citizens. The case did not even reach the courts, however, because the police climbed down, issued a public apology and offered me a payment which I donated to charity. I have always acted in the public interest.

Then they sent in the psychiatrists, to pluck out the heart of my mystery, as Hamlet remarked to Guildenstern (or was it Rosencrantz? You will understand that it is not always easy to check one's sources in my present circumstances.). There were four of them, two for the prosecution and two for the defence. Convinced of my own sanity, I had not asked for any such examinations, but my lawyer persuaded me that, since I was defended at public expense, I had nothing to lose by such examinations and no stone should remain unturned. We did not have to disclose the reports of the psychiatrists hired to defend me, should they prove unfavourable to my case, and therefore it was best to cooperate with them.

Nothing to lose, said my lawyer: oh, but there was, there was. It had always been my intention to write an explanation and defence of my activities, which are so easily misunderstood, and I flatter myself that my story is not without points of interest. But I found that I had to repeat my life history, in precisely the same form, to four psychiatrists in quick succession, and there is nothing quite like repetition for removing the freshness from a narrative.

And of what does the supposed science of psychiatry consist, in any case? At best it is the mutton of platitude dressed up as the lamb of profundity. In its parlance, a man does the things he does because of his character. And how does it know what kind of character a man has? Because of the things he does. This, in a nutshell, is the whole science of psychiatry.

Judges listen to this nonsense, of course, and accord it deep respect. Knowing nothing of life, indeed protected from it by the elaborate and pompous ceremonial with which they are surrounded, they are perfect fools: that is, when they are not perverts themselves, like a Lord Chief Justice of the recent past who was reputed to have had an orgasm each time he passed the death sentence.

It is well-known that psychiatrists are not the most balanced of people themselves, yet they presume to judge the sanity of others. And what a procession of the intellectually halt, limping and lame passed before me in the name of psychiatric science! One of them, dressed in a corduroy jacket and open necked shirt (very unprofessional) spoke in exaggeratedly dulcet tones, as if to imply that he would understand anything I said to him, and that his understanding was a form of infallible absolution. I had the distinct impression that another of them, younger than the rest but already balding, was excited, and perhaps even honoured, to be called upon to examine a personage as notorious as I, whose conduct had preoccupied the newspapers for days on end. He looked at me as though he were searching for visible signs of wickedness upon my countenance, but he asked the same foolish questions as all the others, that I might fit into the procrustean psychiatric moral and diagnostic schemata. In particular, they were interested in whether I heard voices.

'Of course I hear voices,' I said. 'I'm not deaf. Don't you hear voices?'

'I mean, do you hear voices when you're on your own?'

It was clear from this question that these psychiatric gentlemen had no conception of what prison life is like. You are never alone in prison. Even a celebrated professor (you could tell his academic rank from the electric blue bow tie he wore, which no one else would have dared to wear), who had devoted his entire life to the study of criminals and prisoners, asked this inane question.

'At night,' I replied, 'when I am alone in my cell, I hear hundreds of voices. They keep me awake, in fact. Prisoners are very noisy.'

'No,' said the psychiatrists, one and all. 'I mean when there is no one there.'

'If I heard voices, I'd assume there was somebody there, wouldn't I?'

'Well, have you ever heard voices and been surprised to discover that there wasn't anyone there?'

'Unfortunately; my present circumstances are not conducive to an extensive search for the source of the noises which I hear.'

They expressed a consistent interest also in whether I thought there was anyone against me.

'The five million readers – if that is quite the word for them – of *The Sun* newspaper, for a start,' I replied. 'It has run a campaign protesting against the luxurious conditions in which it alleges I am held. I hear there has been an impressive postal response to its campaign, unprecedented in fact, suggesting a variety of punishments for me, mostly involving surgery without anaesthetic. Yes, I think there are people against me.'

All the psychiatrists said that they had meant whether I thought there was anyone in *particular* against me, any individual as such.

'The crown prosecutor,' I suggested.

They hadn't meant him, either. They meant, did I consider that there was a plot against me? Lord, what fools these mortals be! (*A Midsummer Night's Dream*, Act 3, scene 2.) I had merely relayed to them what was common knowledge, obtainable from any newspaper: namely, that the dossiers on my case – or more properly, cases – were so extensive that they filled five rooms, that ten prosecutors, aided by two clerks each, were engaged full time upon them, and that for the time being the police forensic laboratories of an eighth of the entire country were accepting no work on cases other than mine. And if that did not constitute a plot against me, I didn't know what would have done so.

No, it wasn't *that* kind of plot the psychiatrists were talking about either, they said. One of them lost his temper and began to play the outraged citizen: how could I call it a plot against me, when all they were trying to do was discover the truth about the bodies in my back garden? He even suspected that I was being flippant, on a subject upon which humour was not only deeply misplaced but profoundly distasteful.

Well, I replied, the July plot against Hitler may have been fully justified, but it was still a plot.

And didn't I realise, asked the psychiatrist, who by now had turned the shade of purple which I suppose writers of letters to *The Daily Telegraph* turn as they pen their immortal thoughts on how criminals ought to be more severely punished, that I had cost the taxpayer not thousands, not tens of thousands, but hundreds of thousands and possibly even millions of pounds? The orchid in his buttonhole (he was the flamboyant type in a green tweed suit) fairly shook with indignation as he thought of it.

On the contrary, I replied. It was not I who had asked the police to dig about in my garden, or to instigate an investigation at such huge public expense. It was therefore the police who had put the public to it, not I: for was it not a time-honoured principle of English law that each man is deemed to be the author of his own acts and therefore responsible for their foreseeable consequences? Besides, the financial balance of my activities was clearly to the advantage of the taxpayer – but that is a question into which I shall go more deeply at a later stage.

In one of the reports written by these charlatans, there appears the following sentence:

Mr Underwood [with what unctuous pedantry they all prefaced my name by Mr, to maintain the fiction that a man is presumed innocent until proven guilty, and to differentiate themselves from the whole penal apparatus, from which, however, they derived a handsome income] compensates for his deep sense of inferiority by insisting upon winning verbal victories.

I suppose, then, that the learned author of these words compensates for his deep sense of superiority by insisting on suffering verbal defeats!

But at least all the psychiatrists recognised my intelligence, I'll say that for them, though they couldn't quite bring themselves to admit that I was not merely intelligent, but highly intelligent. No, the best they could manage was *Mr Underwood appears to be of at least average intelligence*, which is damning with faint praise to say the least of it, when one considers what average intelligence is like.

And they conceded also – at my insistence – that I had never been employed in a capacity commensurate with my talents and abilities, though they took back with one hand what they granted with the other, through the use of the condescending phrase *Mr Underwood feels that*, as if the injustice under which I have laboured all my life were a matter of mere opinion and not of palpable fact, and as if I were incapable of distinguishing between fantasy and reality. Did not my mother say to me in flesh and blood reality, not in my overheated or psychotic imagination, that I was not to dream of continuing my education beyond the age at which it might legally cease, however good my results at school might be, because she was not prepared to support me after the age at which it was possible for me to find a job, and because she had already sacrificed more than enough years of her life to my welfare? I was fourteen years old at the time, my native intelligence had overcome the effects of an unhappy home life, I was top of my class and thinking of a career in a learned profession to which I would have been very well-suited. Yet on mature reflection, can one really blame her for her narrowness of mind when she worked for such meagre wages while others lived off the fat of the land? Why were her wages so small? Because those of others were so large, and she knew it. Thus was the injustice of our society transmitted to me via my mother: while some succeeded in life merely by virtue of having been born into the right families, others – such as I – were denied all opportunity and thus condemned to perform menial tasks for the rest of our lives.

But why, I hear some of you ask in your plummy and complacent middle-class voices, why couldn't he have gone to evening classes or to a college of further education, if he wanted to better himself and find more satisfying work? To which I reply: do you know of a single person who has used this route to success, among all your friends and acquaintances for example? No, you who have gone through life like a hot knife through butter don't understand, and don't wish to understand, how difficult it is to recover after failing – or rather, being failed – at the first hurdle of life's race. To return after a day's work to the miserable accommodation which society provides for such as I (in a neighbourhood in which the most ruthlessly antisocial person sets the tone and rules the roost, if I may be allowed for once to mix my metaphors) is not conducive to strenuous efforts at self-improvement: on the contrary, it is a standing invitation to go to seed.

Nevertheless, I *did* improve myself, though not in ways of which this materialistic and diploma-crazed society would approve, or for which it would reward me financially. I spent every hour available to me in the public library, reading philosophy, history and literature – matters which lead nowhere as far as a career in this philistine country is concerned, but knowledge of which is essential to a cultured man.

But if you had energy for that, I hear some of you asking again, why not for accountancy or computing, which would have opened up real career prospects to you?

To which I reply: can a man help being interested in those things which interest him (in my case, the Truth)? Does a man say to himself, henceforth I shall be interested in accountancy, and lo! henceforth he is interested in it? No, ladies and gentlemen, when a man has to struggle just to keep himself fed, housed and clothed, as I have had to do all my life, he cannot afford to use the fraction of energy remaining to him to study what is repugnant to him: and I am not a man, in any case, to compromise on matters of principle.

The psychiatrists admitted as much in their reports about me, but as usual made a vice of a virtue. They claimed that what they delicately called my 'activities' were the result of a confluence of three circumstances or conditions: first, that I was consumed with resentment because of my upbringing and the subsequent course of my life; second, that I was an autodidact and therefore not trained or able to discern the validity of an argument, with a tendency to accept uncritically what I had read; and third, that the rigidity of my character led me actually to act upon the principles which I came to accept.

To the charge of resentment, I plead justification.

As to my supposed inability to discern the validity or otherwise of an argument, an inability which supposedly derives from my lack of formal education, it so absurd a charge as to require no refutation. Do they suppose, these psychiatrists and so-called experts on the mind, that I read nothing in the public library with which I did not agree, or accept as true and valid? I read the materialists and the idealists, the Utilitarians and the Marxists, the divines and the atheists: how could I accept them all without making a choice between them when their arguments were so opposed to one another? A logical impossibility, even for such a one as I, who am untrained in argument. But these gentlemen with so many degrees and diplomas that they cannot sign themselves on a single line imagine that a plain contradiction is invisible to anyone lacking such an alphabet soup after his name: otherwise, they might have to admit to themselves that they had wasted their lives in pointless and arid academic exercises. Did Shakespeare have any of their precious degrees, I ask you? Would anyone dare to say of him that, being an autodidact, he was neither trained nor able to discern the validity of an argument? Would he have been a greater writer had he been William Shakespeare M.D., Ph.D?

And finally to the most serious of all the charges against me, namely that I acted upon my principles. It isn't difficult to imagine that these psychiatrists would have written had I acted against my professed principles, or upon no principles at all: that I was a conscienceless psychopath (though such a description would have explained nothing, except to their satisfaction). Yet so hypocritical is the world they inhabit that they find it deeply disturbing when a man like me acts upon his principles in defiance of convention. Indeed, it becomes a matter of pathology for them.

Supposing I had acted in accordance with the dictates of convention, and allowed my fifteen (or twenty-two) 'victims' to continue living. How could I have reconciled such inactivity on my part with my conscience? I could not have quieted it by telling myself that I was only obeying the law: that argument was successfully disposed of at Nuremberg, albeit with the usual inconsistencies which characterise the behaviour of constituted authority Every man must work out for himself how he should act: he cannot hide behind laws, social conventions or the orders of others. The denial of personal responsibility leads to the most terrible consequences, as the history of our century has all too clearly demonstrated. But the law which I broke, you protest, was a good law, a law necessary for the proper ordering of society. Moreover, it is one of the Ten Commandments (the sixth, in fact, being found in *Exodus* Chapter 20, verse 1): Thou shalt not kill.

And with this argument, you assume that the matter is now settled: I am guilty and should therefore be punished with such rigour as the law prescribes. But the matter is not settled, far from it: and I have much to say that will discomfit you, providing that you are not utterly incapable of overcoming those prejudices which the majority of mankind mistakes for principles.

I shall do you the honour of presuming that you are not a Tolstoyan pacifist, for surely it is an evil policy not to resist evil: in the contest between non-resistance and evil itself, the latter always emerges victorious. And, as I have said before, who wills the means, wills the end.

So I may take it that you have conceded that violence, including the taking of life, may sometimes be justified. There is such a thing, after all, as a just war. The last great world conflagration was precisely such a war: and had I been alive to see it, I should have been both honoured to fight and willing to sacrifice my life. And if I had killed fifteen (or twenty-two) then, rather than now, I should have been accounted a hero rather than a villain. Even if I had killed twenty-two thousand, by dropping bombs on German cities and immolating the innocent along with the guilty, I should not have been reproached, or expected to reproach myself, as a criminal.

How, I ask, is a person transformed from a citizen with the normal legal obligations into a licensed killer – a killer, moreover, who is praised in proportion to the number of fellow beings whom he kills? The transformation cannot be effected merely by the fiat of the government of the country in which he happens to live, which declares war and orders him to kill: for that way Nuremberg lies.

Nor can it be because the government which declares war is democratically elected, or is so popular that it embodies the general will of the people. Did not the Nazi government fulfil both these criteria? Yet if Nuremberg erred, who can doubt that it was on the side of leniency, and because a third of the judges represented a regime and jurisdiction as steeped in blood as that of the Nazis?

There remains one possibility alone, therefore, to explain the legitimacy of the transformation of normal citizen into approved killer: that one may legitimately become such a killer when, and only when, one judges it right to do so. And this being the case, one may reasonably ask why it is right to kill only in war and not at other times: does an act become permissible merely because of its prevalence at the time? The fact that in wartime one acts with the imprimatur, as it were, of a government neither adds to nor detracts from one's personal responsibility for one's acts, as I have demonstrated. Neither can the fact that in war one's 'victims' are entirely foreigners alter the case, unless human life is to be valued according to its country of origin, a view which mankind has at long last, after centuries of immolation, rejected.

No, ladies and gentlemen, the conclusion is inescapable: one may be an ethical murderer. And I was one such.

4

I COME NOW TO yet another instance of the hypocrisy by which we are surrounded in this society as much as we are surrounded by oxygen in the atmosphere, though it would take a moral Lavoisier to discern it (I have read in the history of the sciences as well as in political and social history). It is this hypocrisy which has given rise to the excessive public interest in my case to which I have already alluded, an excess all the more striking when one considers that this same public has been unaware until now of nearly a third of my fatalities.

Shouldn't the interest a rational man expresses in a subject be proportional to the importance of that subject? Is this not a moral as well as an intellectual imperative? So that even if my activities were reprehensible in themselves (an hypothesis I entertain temporarily only for the sake of argument, and therefore not to be taken as an admission of blameworthiness), they were of no account, they were trivial even, set against the frightful events from around the world of which we receive news every day of the year, without fail.

But these events are very distant, you protest, and affect us not at all. To which I reply:

i) The moral significance of events is not proportional to their proximity to us, or inversely proportional to their distance.

ii) No man is an island (a hackneyed quotation, perhaps, from Donne's *Meditation XVII* from his *Devotions upon Emergent Occasions*, but appropriate to my argument nonetheless). Therefore, send not to seek in whom the blame lies: it lies in thee.

iii) You were not in any case directly affected by my activities.

But I am getting ahead of myself. It is essential to establish certain important points, such as that the first three of my fifteen killings now known to the public took place so long ago – more than twenty years, in fact – that I have even forgotten the names of the so-called 'victims'. These the police are now making every effort to discover. But to what purpose, I ask? I selected my 'victims' with some care, as I shall in due course relate, but even supposing I made some mistakes in the selection process, and chose persons who were highly esteemed or even loved by their relatives, who have long wondered what became of them, it surely cannot serve anyone's interest that the names of these three now be revealed. Why open old wounds?

When I remarked to the detective who first interrogated me after the unlucky discovery of the human remains in my garden (if that is the right word for the mere handkerchief of land behind the terraced house which, on my miserable salary, it was formerly my life's work to purchase) that it was not worth his while to enquire after the oldest of the remains because the events which led up to their deposition were now so long ago, he was outraged – or at least, he affected outrage. I should not have said he was a man of deep or quick sensibility: he had that kind of solid fatness (common to plain clothes policemen and prison warders, though between the two professions no love is lost, each regarding the other as a form of low life) which is indicative of great strength in short bursts, such as is necessary for the beating up of a suspect, while it results in breathlessness, much sweating and even a heart attack when exertion over longer period is required.

For the most part, however, the detective adopted that tone of sweet, even sickly, reasonableness which fundamentally cruel, aggressive and cynical people adopt when they are trying to be (or rather, to appear) kind. He pretended that we were equals, engaged upon an exciting voyage of discovery into the past, striving for academic reasons to uncover the truth of what happened. He did not mention the life sentence (in the absence of the death penalty) which he hoped would be my reward for my cooperation, and he called me by my first name immediately on meeting me, insisting that I also call him Bob. One could almost hear the police manual of interrogation speaking through him. When he offered me sandwiches, for example, he asked what filling I should like.

Is this the moment to ask who exactly was harmed by my activities? It is, of course, the philosophical, not the practical, question which I ask.

I have already implied that my 'victims' (though I should have preferred the word beneficiaries, had not the use of such a word in this context risked so alienating readers that they would refuse to read any further) were without relatives or friends to mourn the loss. I did my pre-event research thoroughly: one or two of the 'victims', it is true, may have had relatives still living, but such were their relations with them that their deaths (or disappearances, as it appeared at the time) were a cause more for celebration than for sorrow. One or two were the mothers of babies, but they were too young to mourn. Moreover, coming from that particular social *milieu*, which I shall in due course describe, the babies were destined for a life of such utter misery that, prevention being better than cure, I extinguished their lives also. No, the relatives of my 'victims' decidedly did not suffer from their deaths.

Who, then, suffered? The rest of society? I shall prove that this was far from having been the case: indeed, the exact opposite was nearer the truth. For the moment, I ask merely that you believe me, or rather suspend your disbelief, as the Athenian philosopher Aristotle (384-322 BC) put it: for have I not so far proved many things to you which you would not previously have believed?

This leaves but one candidate for the person or persons who were supposedly harmed by my activities: the 'victims' themselves. No doubt this is perfectly obvious to those of you, my readers, who have never read any philosophy. A great wrong, you all too easily suppose, must be done to his subject by a murderer.

But philosophy is the systematic examination of our unthinking prejudices. Let us, therefore, examine the question a little more closely. There is a long tradition of welcoming death as a positive good: call no man happy, said the lawgiver Solon, till he dies, he is at best fortunate. (In any case, my 'victims' were not even fortunate.) And Francis Bacon, who achieved more philosophical detachment in his *Essays* than in his shady financial dealings, wrote famously of the absurdity of the fear of death. 'Men fear death as children fear to go in the dark,' he said. Not for nothing, ladies and gentlemen, did I spend the evenings (and the Saturdays) of twenty years of my life in the public library.

But it is not to the Ancients that I look to justify myself, excellent though they may have been. I look to the moderns: there is, after all, such a thing as progress, even in philosophy.

And it is the unanimous conclusion of all the best modern philosophers that the fear of death is at best a confusion, at worst a logical impossibility and therefore literally meaningless. Please note that I am not here appealing to authority to establish my conclusion: I am most emphatically not saying that something is so because those philosophers who are generally deemed by their colleagues, by *cognoscenti* and prizegivers etc., to be the best in the field have said it is so. On the contrary, I have read them myself and come to the conclusion, by my own ratiocination, that their arguments are conclusive.

And what they, and I, have to say about the fear of death is this: assuming that Man is possessed of no eternal soul which survives beyond his earthly end, his death is but oblivion or rather non-being: his consciousness is utterly extinguished. Now when people say they

fear dea...
endless, dark n... So Little Done
perhaps, frustrated b... ve in their minds is that of a long, indeed
with those they have love they imagine themselves buried alive,
senses, but with a continuation speak or otherwise communicate
after death there is no consciousn... them a deprivation of the
experience, such as having breakfast or rec... iousness. But of course,
for alleged misconduct in the office (of which written warning
though I succeeded in having them withdrawn, and on tw... ived several,
extracted written apologies from my accusers, which had fr... casions
and placed upon my desk). Thus to fear death is to fall into complete
incoherence: you literally do not know what you are talking about,
and it makes no more sense to ask what death is like than to ask what
it was like before birth (or conception, if you prefer). Non-being is not
an experience, and therefore cannot be feared.

But, you object, whether the notion is incoherent or not, fear
of death is almost universal, except among the truly suicidal. No,
I reply, it isn't death which is feared, but dying – the process itself.
Everyone knows of people whose dissolution has come about in an
undignified and painful way And since death is inevitable, surely it is
a consummation devoutly to be wished (*Hamlet* again) that we should
die suddenly, and very nearly painlessly?

With these incontestable arguments in our minds, let us now turn
to the alleged harm done to my 'victims'. Being dead cannot be a loss
to them, since there is no one who exists who could be the subject
of that supposed loss. I agree that the process of strangulation was a
harm done them, but only a very slight one because they were destined
(as are we all) to die anyway. Even had I tortured them to death, which
I emphatically deny having done, I could hardly have done so for very
long, indeed for only an insignificant portion of their lives (compare
this with the ravages of chronic disease). In fact, I disposed of them

humanely, more humanely than ... peacefully and I strangled
course. I spiked their drinks, t... ...ring, and it was a death such
them. They knew neither ...
as I could have wished ... myself their benefactor. Most of them
Indeed, I justly ... at least some of whom would have contracted
were heavy smok... ally, or the other painful and debilitating diseases
lung cancer ... natural consequence of that disgusting and antisocial
which are ...
habit ... ch, incidentally (but not coincidentally), is universal amongst
my fellow-prisoners. Others of my 'victims' – I am referring now
especially to the women – had led notoriously promiscuous lives since
an early age and would probably have died of one of the cancers
associated with that way of life: another painful and lingering death.
Yet others of my 'victims' were drunks, their livers already rotted so
that one day they would have vomited blood like a dark red fountain
(medicine was another interest of mine, and unlike most doctors,
including my own, I have read one of the large textbooks – *Cecil and
Loeb*, one thousand seven hundred and twenty three pages in the
seventeenth edition, excluding the index – from cover to cover). From
all these terrible deaths I preserved my 'victims'.

Our non-being lasts an eternity, literally an infinity of time. Hence,
to bring it forward by a few years is not to increase its length: infinity
plus one still being infinity.

I have reduced you now to the arguments of desperation, the
kind of argument in which our less cerebral newspapers frequently
indulge, in order to produce a pleasant *frisson* of outrage in their
readers: namely, that I not only killed my 'victims' but 'desecrated'
their bodies. I cut them up and put them without ceremony into a
common fossa.

How else, I ask you, was I supposed to dispose of them? My
garden, as I have already informed you, was not exactly an estate.

Some dismemberment was inevitable, in the circumstances. I derived no satisfaction from it, let alone thrill or sexual gratification: it was a job to be done, and an unpleasant one at that.

But this is not to go to the philosophical heart of the question. Again I ask: who was harmed by the so-called 'desecration' of the bodies? I blunted several knives beyond possibility of resharpening, for the human body is tough (a fact which has saved many a doctor from the consequences of his own incompetence), especially after death; but though several knives can said to have been harmed in the process, this is not a harm which counts in the moral sense. Yet the bodies were objects as inanimate as the knives themselves. It was no longer possible to harm the persons to whom they once belonged, the temple of whose souls they once were, or however else you might wish to put it. And since no one claimed the bodies either, since my 'victims' were selected precisely for their lack of close contact with others, I damaged no one's property. The alleged 'desecration' therefore turns out, on philosophical examination, to be nothing more serious than a breach of what you consider good taste. But again I say, *De gustibus non est disputandum*: (Surely it isn't necessary to translate?)

If, then, we look at my actions from the purely rational standpoint, it can be seen that they were wholly without ill-effects. I explained as much to the interrogating detective, who was utterly baffled and unable to answer me on the philosophical plane, because he had spent his evenings in the pub chatting inconsequentially with his mates rather than in the public library. To much of what I said he replied not a word, so beyond dispute was its truth. I advised him to devote his working hours and such talents as he possessed to the solution of crimes whose victims (without the need this time for inverted commas) were still living and therefore capable of suffering from the effects of the offences committed against them. Was he not aware, I asked him, that only a third of all crimes were reported to the police, and that this was because so few criminals were caught that the average citizen no longer considered it worthwhile even to report the crimes committed against him? Instead of wasting his time on me, therefore, he would be better employed elsewhere: that is, if he had any compassion at all for the real, the true victims of crime.

5

I REALISE THAT I HAVE strayed slightly from what I had intended to say.

The interest excited by my case (though I find it difficult to think of myself as a mere case, as surely anyone would), not only in this country but around the world, seemed to me excessive, to say the least. Some commentators have even suggested that I acted as I did specifically to court publicity, a fatuous suggestion which goes against the most elementary reasoning, when you consider that I concealed the material results of my activities for many years: a fact which other commentators, slightly more perspicaciously, have taken as evidence of my extreme cleverness, or 'cunning' as they disparagingly put it. No, ladies and gentlemen, I have never been a publicity-seeker, and would have been content to carryon my work for ever in private, without acknowledgement.

Your work! you exclaim. I shall explain further when the time comes, for now I must ask you to have a little patience.

No sooner were the remains discovered quite by accident – my neighbour's sewer had flooded and the work to repair it strayed into my garden, without my permission I hasten to add, and I'm thinking of suing the water board – than an entire circus descended on Mandela Road (the council had changed its name from Waterloo Road only the month before). Floodlights blazed by night and the neighbours complained that they could get no sleep: they did not see the urgency of the work in any case, considering that many of the 'victims' had been dead for decades and were hardly to be resurrected. The digging went on twenty-four hours a day, while around the corner large vehicles containing generators for the arc lights needed by the television cameras made a continuous low grinding noise (so

I am told: I wasn't there to hear it). Bulletins were issued every hour throughout the day, read to the press by a policewoman who tried to sound well-educated, or at least well-spoken, but who stumbled over long words, dropped her aitches and inserted them where they did not belong. Whom was she trying to fool? Everyone knows that the police are uncouth and ungifted intellectually, and the use of a few long words will not change matters.

Reporters besieged the entire neighbourhood. They stood vigil outside the homes of my neighbours, or of anyone who they thought might have some knowledge of me, however slight or inconsequential. Those who did not wish to speak to them (very few, considering the poverty of the neighbourhood and the blandishments which the gentlemen of the press were able to offer) were chased down the road whenever they ventured forth. A few stalwarts tried to escape the attentions of the fourth estate by leaving their houses via their back gardens: but the public guardians of truth soon caught on, and staked out the rear of the houses as well as their front.

In general, however, the neighbours were only too eager to oblige, if necessary with pure fiction. Mr Aziz, the owner of the nearby corner shop, who until then had been only too happy to accept my custom, pretended that he had known all along that I was a criminal, and alleged that I had been a shoplifter (the worst crime of which his avaricious *petit bourgeois* soul was able to conceive) as well as a multiple murderer. This was the rankest ingratitude, since the turnover of his miserable little shop tripled after my arrest, at least for a while. And then a kind of informal competition emerged in my street, to discover – for the benefit of reporters – who had discerned the most disgusting traits in my character, and who had discerned them earliest and therefore most presciently. My neighbours thought (probably not without reason) that the more extreme their allegations and supposed memories, the more they would be paid. Even their children joined in (they were paid in chocolate and other proletarian tooth-rot), and were induced to allege that they always used to cross the road whenever they passed my house, because they sensed that there was something wrong with – or rather, in – it. And who can argue with the intuitive wisdom of a child?

What discernment, what extraordinary foresight, the whole neighbourhood displayed - strictly in retrospect, of course. Looking back on it, everyone had known from the day I moved into number 17 that something strange was going on there. The house was too often in shadow, the curtains too often drawn, for all to have been well. But the whole neighbourhood was also too dim, and too blinded by the hope of gain, to realise that this vaunted intuition of theirs turned them into my accomplices, morally if not legally. For they had never voiced their misgivings, not once in all those years.

But how eagerly they informed upon me, once it was safe to do so! I don't suppose there was a house in the neighbourhood (except mine) which did not contain a stolen video or microwave oven: my neighbours were all happy enough to receive stolen goods, providing it was at the right price. They couldn't hang their washing out in their back gardens for fear of theft by their neighbours, and burglaries were as frequent as visits by the postman. Because of their dishonesty they hated and feared the police, whom they regarded as their oppressors. But as soon as they were on the right side of the law (for once in their lives), and as soon as they were convinced that the police were not in the slightest interested in the criminally-acquired goods in their homes, they sang like birds, making it all up as they went along but almost coming to believe their inventions to be the truth.

Yes, ladies and gentleman, Man is a born informer – or perhaps I should say *mis*informer. He loves to land his neighbours deep in trouble, even if he has to tell the most outrageous and transparent lies in order to do so, and even if his own conscience is not at all clear even before he bears false witness (I suppose it is necessary, in these times of mass ignorance, to point out that I allude here to one of the Ten Commandments, the ninth of them to be exact). Man, natural slave that he is, likes nothing more than to tell tales to the very authorities which he has previously affected to despise. If there is one characteristic which distinguishes Man from the lower animals (lower, that is, in intellectual, not moral, terms) it is not his speech, his erect gait, his ability to oppose his thumb and forefinger, his supposed rationality or his use of tools, but his secret burning desire to act the secret policeman.

So the world was treated for a time to the gratifying spectacle of the moral outrage of people who beat their wives regularly, neglected their children, not only coveted but actually stole their neighbour's goods, drank to excess, cheated the Social Security, shoplifted and were proud of it, refused as a matter of the highest principle to work and in general behaved without the slightest regard for the welfare or interests of others. And the reporters behaved towards them − admittedly not sincerely, but with their eye firmly fixed as always on the main chance − as if they were all Daniels come to judgment (as Antonio exclaims of Portia in *The Merchant of Venice*, Act 4, scene 1, a flawed masterpiece in my opinion, since Shylock is clearly the wronged party in the play, and deserves exoneration rather than castigation).

I feel that I am beginning to digress again: I was speaking of the excessive interest in my case and what it signified.

Now I take it that a rational and moral man interests himself in subjects according to their intrinsic importance. To immerse oneself in trivialities is not only an intellectual, but a moral, weakness. So what transcendent importance did my case possess that it should have driven from the minds of men all other subjects of public concern for several weeks, indeed months?

The answer is, none.

Let me briefly remind you of the kind of world in which we have the honour to live. By the time you finish reading this page, ten children will have died throughout the world of diseases which are easily prevented or cheaply treated. By the time you finish reading all that I have to say, a thousand children will have died in this fashion – while you, with your tender so-called conscience, will have munched distractedly on more calories and other nutrients in the form of peanuts or chocolate (for who can sit long these days without eating?) than these children would have consumed in a week (had they survived). The total cost of saving these lives would have been negligible: less by far than that of your DVD machine, for example. But when you bought that machine, did you give so much as a moment's thought to the thousand lives which might have been saved had you spent the money differently? A visit to any store which sells such goods would settle the question beyond doubt: it is interest-free credit which animates the soul of modern man, not the fate of the world's children.

Ignorance of these facts is something which you cannot plead, not unless you are blind and deaf and mentally retarded into the bargain. Information about the state of the world is literally inescapable nowadays. If you don't know about the latest epidemic in South America, the latest famine in Africa, the latest earthquake in Central Asia, or the latest civil war anywhere in the world, it is because you choose to remain in ignorance. And whether you like it or not, if you have done less than was within your power to save the lives of all the people who died in any of the above ways, you are as responsible for their deaths as if you had plunged an obsidian knife into their chests and torn out their still palpitating hearts (I quote, admittedly from memory, from Prescott's *The Conquest of Mexico*).

This is the latest and irrefutable conclusion of philosophy: that there is no moral difference between an act and an omission where the deleterious results of the act or omission are entirely predictable. It makes murderers of you all, ladies and gentlemen – and on an industrial scale, one might almost say.

No doubt my unwanted and unwonted disruption of your complacency has caused you by now to throw my book at the wall, figuratively if not quite literally. You are angry, with that thoroughly enjoyable anger to which the self-righteous are so priggishly prone. Preposterous, you exclaim, that this man should accuse us of being no better than he, and possibly even worse. Is it we, after all, who have been found guilty on fifteen counts of murder without extenuating circumstances?

Legally, I grant you, there may be a difference between us; but morally speaking (the plane on which I am moving in this short work), the difference between us is not at all to your advantage. For what is law but the institutionalised hypocrisy of society, backed by force?

Let us once again examine matters a little more closely. The distinction between us upon which you preen yourselves is that, while I killed by acts of commission, you killed and kill merely by acts of omission. You imagine this difference to be one of vital moral significance; but as I have said, not only I, but all modern philosophers of note dispute and refute this.

Doctors, for example, have long allowed their patients to die of pneumonia when, if they were to recover after treatment, they would lead a life only of suffering and further misery; and such doctors have been applauded for their humanity and wisdom. Yet those same doctors throw up their hands in horror at the very thought of actively intervening to procure the death of their patients, their happy release from useless suffering, by the injection of potassium for example. They cite the very same sanctity of life as the cause of their horror at the very idea of killing which they had entirely forgotten in the case of the old hemiplegic or dement whom they let die of pneumonia. It isn't life, therefore, which is sacrosanct, but life which partakes of certain qualities, the lack of which renders such life at best meaningless, at worst harmful to self and others.

This is a truth admitted by anyone of any philosophical or moral sensibility at all.

Well then, the doctor who does not leave to chance the release of his patients (and their relatives) from unbearable suffering, but who intervenes directly, not only decreases the sum of suffering in the world but increases the sum of justice. For can it be just that one person should suffer years of pain and misery because of a certain incurable medical condition, while another person with exactly the same medical condition escapes that suffering merely because he happens to contract pneumonia in the course of it – and all of this when the remedy lies close at hand, but is unused merely because of a certain hypocritical and self-regarding fastidiousness on the part of the doctor?

The doctor who actively performs euthanasia is thus the moral superior of one who leaves his patients to die at nature's cruel whim, and the latter is in grave error (no pun intended, it would be out of place) if he imagines that his unwillingness to apply the *coup de grace* is a point in his favour. On the contrary, he is a coward, nothing more.

By now it must be clear, even to the least intellectually alert among you, where my argument is leading. I am your moral superior because, like the doctor who practises active euthanasia, I do not do my killing at random: I choose who is to die by my own hand, according to rational and humane criteria. By contrast, your acts of omission, which are responsible for vastly greater numbers of deaths than the numbers which I have ever aspired to bring about, strike the just and the unjust alike: you kill like the madman who enters a supermarket and mows down the customers until he is overpowered or himself shot dead.

But, you will object, happy at last to have found an argument to refute one of mine, you are just as guilty as we of the acts of omission with which you reproach us, in addition to which you have actively ended the lives of fifteen others (or twenty-two, depending on how you look at it). Therefore, having been responsible for more deaths than we, you still deserve the condemnation and punishment to which you have been subjected.

I like a good discussion and, as the psychiatrists said, for once not missing their mark (they say so much that, by the laws of chance, some of what they say must be true), I like to win. Easy victories, however, do not greatly please or interest me. It is the intellectual contest which appeals to me. Therefore, while I applaud your attempt to refute me, honesty compels me to protest at the extreme feebleness of your argument, which partakes of empirical and logical error in equal measure.

But let us suppose for the moment that a part of what you say is accurate: that in addition to having caused as many deaths as you by acts of omission, I have caused fifteen (or twenty-two) deaths by acts of commission. Does this prove that I deserve to be imprisoned for the rest of my life and never released?

Not at all. For the fact is that our mutual acts of omission – the mutuality of which is merely momentarily hypothesised, be it remembered – have caused so many deaths, adding up to thousands if not tens of thousands over a lifetime, that the addition of a mere fifteen (no, let me put your argument at its strongest, let me say the addition of a mere twenty-two) deaths cannot weigh significantly in the balance. For if I were to ask you which man was worse, the man who was responsible in his lifetime for the deaths of 10,739 people, or the one who was responsible for 10,761, you would look at me in puzzlement and no doubt conclude that anyone who could ask such a question was himself morally perverse. It is obvious, you would say when you had recovered from the strangeness of the question, that there is and can be nothing to choose between them, and that, on the contrary, to make such pettifogging distinctions is psychologically to condone at least one of the perpetrators ('At least,' the former will be able to say of the latter, 'I am not as bad as he'), and to miss entirely the monstrousness of the situation as a whole. Was Auschwitz worse – morally worse, I mean, not empirically worse – than Treblinka?

But in any case, I do not even grant you the initial premise of your argument, that your and my acts of omission were in any way comparable. You who read this are likely to be much more comfortably placed than ever I was: and thus to allay the hunger of the starving millions and to cure the equally large numbers of sick of their eminently curable diseases was much more within your power than it ever was within mine. For how much did I ever earn as a minor functionary of local government, denied promotion by a combination of prejudice against my small stature and suburban whine, and a typically bureaucratic dislike of my habits of independent thought, my refusal to toe the line and my devastatingly ironical criticism of the semi-literate circulars which descended on us regularly from on high? I earned a mere pittance, nothing more.

I see a sneer spread over your face. You, who have at your disposal larger sums of money for luxuries than I ever had for necessities! (In general, and from the literary point of view, I despise exclamation marks, but I think the preceding sentence merits one.) In short, you accuse me of special pleading, though nothing could be further from the truth.

I never received more than a thousand pounds a month for my work at the Housing Department, and often less. Of this, I spent a third on food and electricity, a further third on the repayment of my mortgage, and rather more than an eighth on the maintenance of my car, the cheapest possible vehicle which actually ran. This left me with less than two hundred pounds a month for everything else: clothes, holidays, entertainment, furnishings and saving for my old age. Not exactly a life of opulence, I think you are forced to admit.

On what could I have economised to make charitable donations? I did not eat extravagantly, though I admit that a balanced vegan diet involves expenditure not incurred by those who consume less ethical diets. I had to consider the welfare of factory farm animals, however, and as I have already mentioned, I am not a man who is prepared to compromise on principles.

But did you really need a car, you ask? Your question demonstrates that you have never been dependent on public transport for your mobility. In this society, arranged as it is purely for the convenience of the rich, a person without a car is nothing, indeed is regarded with suspicion, almost as a criminal. Not to own a car is taken as a moral failing, rather like a lack of cleanliness or drunkenness. Oh yes, I *could* have lived (I suppose) without a car, if I had been resigned to count my house as a prison, never to go out at times convenient to myself, slowly to develop the agoraphobia which afflicted so many of the housewives around me. For agoraphobia starts as a habit and ends up as a disease.

Well then, you continue, there was always your mortgage. Did a man in your position have to buy his own house, rather than rent one? Yes, more than any other kind of man, in fact. There was no one from whom I should eventually have inherited a house or its equivalent in ready money: on the contrary, I shall inherit from my mother only the expenses of her funeral. To throw oneself on the mercy of the Housing Department (as I am in a position to know better than anyone) is like seeking comfort in a torture chamber, besides which the Department disposes of no accommodation of a standard appropriate to the needs of one such as I. As for private landlords, they are all bloodsuckers, preying unmercifully on the unfortunates who have no place to call their own.

No, ladies and gentlemen, my mortgage was not so much an extravagance, as an elementary form of self-defence, a sheer necessity.

Whichever way you look at it, I had little money to spare, unlike those of you with your Persian carpets, works of art and other luxurious baubles and gewgaws. It is you – the heartless rich – who should be locked up as mass murderers, not me (I pondered here long and hard over whether to write 'I' or 'me', and decided finally on 'me' because it gives a more natural and spontaneous effect, though I know 'I' to be grammatically correct. I do not wish, however, to be dismissed as a mere pedantic autodidact.). If I had been paid what I was worth by the Department, or even half of what I was worth, instead of the gross overpayment of footballers who can hardly string sufficient words together to form a coherent sentence, or of philistine businessmen whose creed is greed, perhaps matters would have been different, and I might have been as guilty as you of murderous acts of omission: as it was, however, it was you, not I, who were (and still are) guilty of them. And in apportioning moral responsibility, it is necessary to stick to the facts, not promiscuously to invent mere might-have-beens.

The inescapable conclusion, then, is that you have more blood on your hands than I. Your righteous indignation stands revealed as a bluff. No amount of protestation on your part will wash off the blood: your hands are more indelibly bloodstained than Lady Macbeth's (*Macbeth*, Act 5, scene 1).

And I haven't finished my indictment of your selective morality yet, not by a long way. Consider for a moment the numbers of people who are killed and tortured every day around the world in wars and by oppressive or repressive regimes. But what has this to do with either us or the matter in hand, you exclaim, and why do you bring it up now? Aren't you just trying to divert our attention from the horrible crimes you yourself committed?

On the contrary, I am only trying to be morally consistent, for without consistency there can be no morality. And ever since Socrates, the best method of achieving consistency has been to unmask its opposite.

The question, therefore, which I now want to ask you is the following: From where do you suppose that the armaments to pursue these wars and to uphold these oppressive and repressive regimes originate? And the answer, of course, is from the country in which you (among others, admittedly) happen to live, and whose authorities have seen fit to pass judgment on me.

We can't help that, you say. We are not arms salesmen; we are not involved in the manufacture of armaments; we are insurance salesmen, car dealers, gastroenterologists, or whatever else it may be. We have nothing to do with the arms trade.

Oh but you do, ladies and gentlemen, you do, whether you acknowledge it or not. Every time you purchase or use foreign goods (and that is every day of the week), you benefit from precisely that trade: for were it not for the export of arms, our balance of payments would be worse than it already is. And this in turn would mean that our currency would depreciate, perhaps to such an extent that the foreign goods to which you have become so accustomed would be placed beyond your financial reach. So rather than go without your German car, your French cheese and wine, your Greek yoghurt, your Italian salami and your Japanese cameras and televisions, you close your eyes to the evident fact that their purchase is possible only through sales of arms to despots who slaughter the peasants of the world and bring about famines to further their own ends. By insisting on your foreign luxuries, you make the torture chambers safe for autocracy. So once again, you are an accessory to murder: moreover, murder on a vast scale. And an accessory to murder is, morally speaking, a murderer.

You retort, naturally enough (for there is no one angrier than the justly-accused), that I go too far with my argument. For once again you accuse me of living in the same society as you, and therefore of having benefited to the same extent as you from the arms trade. Besides which, you add, a man who lives in a society of many millions can hardly be deemed responsible for everything which goes on within it, or is done in its name by its government. There is no responsibility without power.

I grant a certain superficial plausibility to your arguments, ladies and gentlemen, though these arguments are meretricious rather than meritorious. On closer analysis, of course, they dissolve like morning mist in the sunlight, and vanish without trace. For I am not claiming that you are solely or even largely responsible for your country's wholehearted participation in the iniquitous trade; but you are responsible to the extent that you benefit from it and do nothing to stop it. I claim only that you share in the general blame, which being incalculably vast, leaves each individual so great a portion that he cannot point the finger at me with any moral authority whatever – even if my activities were reprehensible, which I deny and shall in due course prove.

I do not wish to boast, or make myself out to be better than I am, but I think I may fairly claim to have done all that was within my limited power to bring a halt to this commercialised iniquity; the arms trade. I have written on innumerable occasions to Members of Parliament and government ministers, to protest against some particularly egregious (but profitable) contract to supply arms to foreign despots. Only two weeks before my arrest, in fact, I wrote to the Minister of Overseas Development to declare my total opposition to, repudiation of and disgust with the sale of twenty-six jet trainers to the government of the Republic of Ngombia. I cannot do better, I think, than to reproduce my letter:

Dear Mr Jones,

I am writing to you once again to draw your attention to agreement to supply twenty-six jet trainers to the repressive military government of the Republic of Ngombia.

As you know, the government of that country has been engaged now for more than a decade upon a war of extermination against the aboriginal peoples who inhabit the country's remaining rain forests.

The government of Ngombia states that the jets will be used for training purposes only. Lies! They are all too easily adapted for dropping napalm, cluster, anti-personnel and phosphorus bombs, and also for the mounting of rockets, as you very well know.

In any case, for what purpose does Ngombia need trained pilots, if not for these activities? She has no external enemies from whom she needs to defend herself.

The guarantees given by the government of Ngombia with regard to the so-call pacific use of the trainers are therefore not worth the paper they are written on. On three separate occasions that government has broken a ceasefire with the rebels.

There is only one possible conclusion: that an export licence for the jets has been granted to serve the interests a) of arms manufacturers and dealers and b) of the international logging companies, on whose behalf the genocide of the aboriginals is being committed. Moreover, the savage destruction of the rainforests puts the ecological balance of the entire planet at risk, will damage the ozone layer beyond repair, and lead to an exponential increase in the rate of fatal skin cancer.

Those who fail to oppose this cynical sale of sophisticated weaponry to a brutal and repressive government, or even worse support it, are guilty beyond all question of a) murder by skin

cancer and b) genocide against innocent and harmless people.
They will have committed crimes against humanity
Yours in indignation,
Graham Underwood

A powerful letter, I flatter myself.

And what did I receive-in return? The following, not written by the great man himself, oh dear no, he is far too busy to attend to mere constituents like me, but by someone (a young sprig from Oxford, no doubt, with political ambitions of his own) calling himself Jones's parliamentary private secretary:

Dear Mr Underwood,
I have been asked by the Minister, the Rt Hon. Mr Sopwith Jones MP, to reply on his behalf to your letter of the 7th ult. He asks me to make the following points:

i) There is no evidence of genocidal intent by the Government of Ngombia, with whom Her Majesty's Government enjoys excellent political, economic and diplomatic relations.

ii) The competition in the field of supply of jet trainers is fierce, and if we had not agreed to supply them, then one of our competitors most certainly would have done so.

iii) The order represents a considerable boost to our exports and therefore to our balance of payments, and secures thousands of jobs for the foreseeable future at a time of high unemployment.
Yours sincerely;
Herbert Robinson, Parliamentary Private Secretary to the Rt Hon Mr Sopwith Jones MP

Not even an apology for the delay in replying! (I think a further exclamation mark is more than justified in the circumstances.) And what weasel words, immaculately typed on thick-woven cream-coloured paper with an embossed green crest, all paid for by the taxpayer, I need hardly add.

If we don't sell them, someone else will: what kind of argument is that, from the moral point of view? Does it excuse *Topf und Sobn*, the suppliers of gas ovens to the SS? Can a burglar argue that if it hadn't been he, someone else would have burgled the house, because burglary is so common these days? What would Mr Sopwith Jones have replied if I had argued successfully in court that had I not killed my 'victims', they would have died of a heart attack or of cancer anyway?

Of course, it is well-known that Mr Sopwith Jones would support government policy to the portals of hell and beyond, if he thought it would preserve his seat in Parliament at the next election. As for the so-called opposition in our so-called democracy, it speaks vociferously of morality while it is out of office, but as soon as it is elected to office it becomes just as amoral as the outgoing government. And this, ladies and gentlemen, is the calibre of the men who make decisions affecting the lives and deaths of millions of people, supposedly on our behalf.

Writing to my Member of Parliament was not the only method by which I tried (unsuccessfully, it is true, but the virtue is in the effort) to bring about an end to this merchandising of the means of mass death. When our local council declared the borough a nuclear-free zone (a small step, but one in the right direction), I organised a meeting in the Housing Department to pressure the council to declare the borough an arms industry-free zone as well. My superior in the department tried to reprimand me for having arranged the meeting during working hours: but I fought him all the way, rulebook in hand. It was a blatant attempt, I said, to suppress freedom of speech and association: and I pointed out that under our terms and conditions of service, staff had the right to hold a reasonable number of meetings which directly affected their interests. And what could have been of greater interest to them than the moral climate of the borough in which, and for which, they worked? My superior deeply resented my victory over him, and has (or rather had) been seeking revenge ever since; but I have (or had) been too clever for him. He never succeeded in his aim of having me dismissed.

The motion at the meeting was passed by an overwhelming majority; but the council did nothing, arguing that there were no arms factories in the borough in any case. But when I wrote to the leader of the council to point out that there were no nuclear installations in the borough either, but that that had not deterred the council from declaring the borough a nuclear-free zone, he wrote back to tell me (not in so many words, of course) that it was none of my business: none of my business, I being merely a citizen and elector!

I wrote to the newspapers as well. In all, I had seven letters published, of a total of one hundred and eighty-six written. And it is pretended that the press is free in this country! Of the seven which were published, six were in the local newspapers, and only one in a national, though the ratio of letters addressed to each was precisely the reverse. Whether you agree with my views or not, I think I have demonstrated sufficiently that I can argue cogently and coherently. The failure of the national newspapers to publish my letters therefore puzzled me at first, especially when I compared what I had written with what was published in the correspondence columns, which was frequently trivial and inconsequential. But then I realised that letters were published not according to merit or the intrinsic interest of their contents, but according to who the editor supposed the correspondent was. And this he guessed by the address from which the letters were sent: unless, of course, the correspondent happened to be a public figure of note, in which case publication was automatic, without reference to the address.

I had to be satisfied with occasional successes in the *Eastham Evening Telegraph* (incorporating the *Evening Messenger*) and latterly with the *Eastham Free Press*, one of those weekly newspapers consisting mainly of small ads which is pushed through your letterbox whether you want it or not. The correspondence columns of such publications, indeed the publications in their entirety, are of course more concerned with trivial local matters than with the great issues of the day, but one has regrettably to start somewhere. No one with an important message is heard straight away. (The strongest man in the world is the man who stands most alone: Ibsen, *An Enemy of the People*.)

I could, of course, give you further examples. It is not by guns alone that Man kills his fellow Man. For it is beyond question that the smoking of cigarettes is now the greatest cause of preventable death among adults in the world. And it should come as no surprise to you that some of the largest tobacco companies in the world are owned, and have their headquarters, in your own capital city.

And what of it, you ask? What has this to do with us?

Well, ladies and gentlemen, cigarette sales have been falling in countries where the harmful effects of smoking have been widely publicised (no thanks to the companies, of course, quite the reverse). And what do you suppose the tobacco companies have done to protect their profits, to maintain the flow of dividends not only to the pockets of individual shareholders but to the institutional buyers of their shares? They have tried to increase their sales of cigarettes in countries where the authorities are too weak and poor to resist their bribes, and where the people are pathetically susceptible to anything which gives them the impression they are partaking of the rich lifestyle of Europe and America.

Still you don't see, of course, what any of this has to do with you. Again you remind me of Pilate, who refused to make a choice as to which of the Palestinian prisoners should be released, on the grounds that it was none of his business.

But answer me this: who are the shareholders in the tobacco companies? Before you point the finger at others, I will answer for you: *you* are the shareholders. But we have no share certificates, you protest; we receive no dividends. Not directly, I grant you; but all of you have pension funds, or contribute to pension schemes, and – as is well-known – they are the largest investors by far in the stock market. And such is the size and profitability of the tobacco companies that no pension fund could afford to be without a block of shares in them.

Perhaps you feel a little less smug after my demonstration, but the really important question relates not to your feelings but to your deeds. Now that you know beyond doubt that you are investing in Third World lung cancer, bronchitis and heart disease, what are you going to do about it? Are you willing to forgo the security of your old age so that the poor will not die of the diseases of the rich? Will you demand of your pension fund managers that they divest the fund of shares whose value increases in proportion to the numbers of deaths caused?

It isn't only the tobacco companies of which I speak, however: it is the whole iniquitous system by which pharmaceutical companies, for example, profit from suffering, and export to other countries drugs which are deemed too dangerous for sale in their home country; and food companies which deliberately create a taste for their expensive junk products of no nutritional value in countries in which the people do not have money enough to feed themselves properly. Neither are the oil companies to be excluded, which are destroying the remaining wildernesses of the world, only that you may travel cheaply (but meaninglessly) between A and B, in the process destroying not only whole peoples and cultures, but entire species of animals and plants. (Species, in fact, are dying out at the rate of one a day.)

If shares in all the death-dealing companies and industries were excluded from the portfolios of the pension funds, nothing would remain; but I do not think I should be wrong in assuming that you have done nothing to protest against this global iniquity, your security being more important to you than the survival of the planet and its biosphere. I, on the other hand, bought a single share in many such companies to embarrass their chairmen at the annual general meeting by asking difficult questions. Their anger in reply was more than sufficient proof of their guilt.

Thus, I think you will concede that I have done all within my unfortunately limited power to bring about the end of our country's complicity in indiscriminate slaughter. I ask you now to look into your own hearts and ask whether you can say as much for yourselves: you with your connections to the powerful, with your money and your leisure. And if the answer is no, which of us is the truly guilty party?

I have mentioned already my disdain for psychiatrists, a mongrel breed if ever there was one – claiming to be scientists and yet humanists at the same time, when in reality they are officially-licensed and highly-paid gossips. But one among them once wrote something true and important (though naturally he was despised for it by his professional colleagues, who conspired to ruin his career by withdrawing his right to practise). I refer to R.D.Laing, who wrote:

> We are all murderers and prostitutes – no matter to what culture, society, class, nation one belongs, no matter how normal, moral or mature one takes oneself to be.

The unvarnished truth, ladies and gentlemen, whether you like it or not. But at least I have tried, consistently and without fail, to escape this condition. Are you able to say the same? And if not, should we not be changing places?

6

BUT STILL I FEEL THAT I have not quite said what I set out to say (your objections having obstructed the flow of my argument). I intended to answer definitively the question of why my case should have aroused so much interest around the world.

First, of course, I had to establish beyond dispute the statistical insignificance of what I did, compared with so many other acts and omissions of the Twentieth Century. For without such a clear demonstration, my puzzlement at my own notoriety might have seemed strange and even pathological to you, brought up as you are in a consumer society not to look behind appearances. No, for you as for the great majority of Mankind, all that glisters really is gold; and, by a logically faulty process of reasoning, you and it (the majority) believe the reverse to be the case also, namely that all that falls to glister is dross of no value. This law, if I may call it such, holds sway in every sphere, but particularly in the moral. You expect your heroes and your villains to be visibly and obviously such; many times I have caught people peering hard into my face as if expecting to perceive there the mark of Cain (*Genesis*, Chapter 4, verse 15).

Second, in proving that you are responsible for many more deaths than I, I have uncovered a likely motive for your obsessive interest in my case: a desire to conceal your own guilt by projecting it (as the Freudians put it in their obscurantist language) on to me.

But even this, I venture to suggest, does not adequately explain why nine authors to my certain knowledge (which may, in this instance be incomplete) have been commissioned by publishers to write books about me and my life, which until now has been one of the utmost obscurity, of no particular interest even to myself. Publishers, after all, are not philanthropists, and would not have signed such contracts unless they thought it were profitable to have done so; and need I point out that publishers' profits derive from sales of their books to the public? A film company is also said to be interested in my story.

No, ladies and gentlemen, in answering the question as to why my activities have been and are of such great interest to so many, we are inevitably dealing with human psychology's equivalent of the dark side of the moon, not with matters which are so transparent that they require no analysis or elucidation.

Let me first point out that I am by no means what is known as a common murderer. This is not to say that one can learn nothing by the study of the latter: and indeed, since the public has insisted upon subsuming me under that category, but writ very much larger, and since it is the mentality of the public which we are now investigating, a few observations on common murderers may not be entirely out of place.

You will not be surprised to hear that I have now met many of this species in my peregrinations through the English *gulag*. They each of them spend their first few days of incarceration in the prison hospital, as if murder were an illness and not a natural act which has survived all attempts down the ages to suppress it, and which must therefore be considered a perfectly normal and universal part of human behaviour. (And should what is normal, I ask, be liable to punishment?) The reason murderers are treated thus on their arrival in prison, however, is that they are thought to be susceptible to suicide, an event which would cause the prison authorities much embarrassment, thanks to the eternal vigilance of our press, which is constantly on the alert for any opportunity to make pointless trouble and thus increase circulation, though the suicide of a murderer would save the taxpayer much expense in the long (and even the short) run. And if there's one thing the warders hate more than a live prisoner, it's a dead one: not because of any humanitarian sentiment, of which they are entirely innocent, but because of all the forms they have to fill in after a prisoner's death. (Most of the warders, I have observed, stick their tongues out with the effort of writing longhand.)

On his arrival in prison, therefore, a murderer (or *suspected* murderer, according to the hypocritical pretence that a man is innocent until proven guilty) is stripped even of normal prison clothes and dressed in shorts and a T-shirt of tough and shiny man-made fibre, the colour of loose faeces. He is placed in a cell completely devoid of furniture or other possible appurtenances of suicide. And there he is left to rot for a few days until, despairing of the alternative, he agrees to go on living.

This ritual, carried out in the name of humanity – that is to say, the welfare of the murderer – has for its true purpose the establishment of who is to be master, that's all. In prison, a man is not the possessor of his own life: which is another reason why the warders hate a suicide: as far as they are concerned, it is a kind of robbery.

How sordid, uncomplicated and lacking in philosophical content are the motives of the common murderer, even when, purely for form's sake, he denies his guilt! It is absurd and grossly unjust to place me in the same category. On the very day I was arrested and taken to prison, for example, a doctor accused of murdering his wife was among my fellow-inductees into the institution, or 'freshmen of the University of Crime', as one screw jocularly put it, imagining he was being both witty and erudite.

The doctor's wife had died of an injection into the veins of her right arm. From the fact that, during life, she was right-handed, even our less-than-intellectually-gifted constabulary was able to deduce that something suspicious had occurred. And with a doctor in the house, the search for a suspect was not a prolonged one.

I grew intimate with the doctor, who until his arrest had been the epitome of complacent and snobbish prosperity. He was glad of the opportunity to talk to someone of intelligence and culture once his period of solitary confinement was over, but he was a perfect monster of egotism, precisely as I would have expected of a man of his class and social standing who had fallen on hard times. He talked only of himself, and evinced no interest in either me or my case. He told me that the police were absurd, incompetent, unable to detect the most obvious contradictions in their so-called evidence against him, that his lawyer had told him that after his release, which would happen at the latest within two weeks, there being no case to answer, he would file suit for wrongful arrest and imprisonment, since anyone should have realised that there could not possibly have been a motive for him to kill his wife − especially when he had so much to lose by doing so, since he was the local representative of the British Medical Association, among other important positions.

This doctor, this scion of the so-called self-regulating and ethical profession of medicine, also informed me that his wife had just discovered that he was having an affair with his receptionist, twenty years his junior. She threatened him at once with divorce proceedings, unless he immediately and unconditionally cease all contact with the receptionist, in short sacked her and promised never even to think of her again. The silly fool thought he was in love with her, and even worse, that she was in love with him: so he told his wife that though he loved her still, it was in a different way from the way in which he loved the receptionist. There never was a clearer case of wanting your cake and eating it.

His wife, of course, would have none of it, and sued for divorce. Because of the divorce laws, he faced the prospect not only of parting with half his possessions, but of supporting her with much of his income for the rest of his days. This was more than he could bear: his house, he told me, was an Elizabethan manor, with three acres of gardens, and it was not difficult to guess what exchanging it for an ordinary dwelling (still a hundred times better and more comfortable than mine) would have meant to him. Priding himself on his technical knowledge of poisons, by means of which he thought to evade the law, he killed her, though he was so naive and lacking in elementary technique (or perhaps so overexcited by his task), that he could scarcely have made his guilt plainer than if he had phoned the police himself and confessed on the spot.

Here, symbolically, you see represented the injustice of our society. I possessed no university diploma, nor even school certificate, and was therefore never able to raise myself above the level of humble clerk: whenever I applied for something better, the first question was, Where are your qualifications? My natural abilities counted for nothing. Whereas this man, this doctor, who had jumped a hundred scholastic hurdles and who could have used his diplomas as wallpaper if he had had a mind to do so, lived in a luxury of which it would have been pointless even for me to dream. Yet he was caught at once, within twenty-four hours, whereas I was caught only after twenty-four years (to round up the figure slightly for rhetorical effect), after twenty-two cases, seven of which still remain to be elucidated and perhaps never will be; and caught, moreover, only by the unluckiest of chances.

Which of us, I ask you, ladies and gentlemen, displayed the more native talent, the more intelligence, and which of us, in a genuine meritocracy, would have risen higher in the social scale?

But of course, we do not live in a meritocracy.

Now it is true that the doctor went through a suicidal stage, like all the other common murderers of my acquaintance. The naive among you – that is to say, the vast majority – might suppose that this stage had something to do with remorse, and all that Raskolnikov kind of crap. (Here, I believe, I have artfully combined two disparate literary references and melded them into a convincing whole: J.D.Salinger's *The Catcher in the Rye* and Dostoyevsky's *Crime and Punishment*. Without wishing to appear boastful, I ask you whether you think that a man of ordinary capacities could have combined such references in this fashion? Is it not socially wasteful that such a man should be condemned to languish in prison, and likewise that he was formerly condemned to languish in the lower reaches of a local government bureaucracy? Such, ladies and gentlemen, is the society in which we live.) No, it is not remorse that leads a man like the medical uxoricide to consider death: his own, this time. It is sorrow and bitterness at the realisation of all he has lost, and will never have again: wealth, social position and so forth. He is in mourning for his life – this time I adapt from Chekhov, ironically in this context. (My adaptation is from the answer Masha gives in *The Seagull*, Act 1, to Medvedenko's question as to why she always wears black.)

The suicidal phase soon passes, unless there is a special reason why it should not: and then it becomes the pseudosuicidal phase. The purpose of this phase is to keep the murderer in the prison hospital as long as possible, because it is more comfortable there than in the rest of the prison. There is a snooker table, and the television is on all the time: home from home for most people, in fact. And some prisoners use the hospital as a refuge from other prisoners. I knew a young man accused of a murder of which he was genuinely innocent (though he wasn't innocent *tout court*, of course – I should perhaps explain that I am not opposed to the use of foreign phrases when they are used not as a display of erudition but to express something for which there is no equivalent in English). The young man had lived all his life in a criminal environment and was a small-time recipient of stolen goods (the only work which he had ever done), for which he had already served several short sentences. One day he took delivery of a consignment from his usual suppliers of stolen goods, wrapped in a thick plastic bag which they asked him to look after for a while, until they came to fetch it again. Then the police arrived: the consignment was a body and he had been well and truly set up. The young man knew with whom he was dealing: that is to say, he knew better than to tell the police the truth about the body, for the killers would not have hesitated to kill again, using the same method of disposal. It was safer for him to admit to the crime which he never committed.

Unfortunately for him, the murdered man had belonged to a gang which was the rival of that which killed him. One of its members was already in the prison, and was under the impression that the young man accused of the murder was a full participant in the killing of his colleague. A severe beating was easily arranged: but a revenge killing would take a little longer to organise, though it was inevitable sooner or later. A dunking in the boiling vats in the prison kitchens, where many prisoners worked, or a slash in the throat with a razor made from prison materials, or even a hanging: all could be arranged in the long run. The young man lived in fear, starting at his own shadow; though he was relatively safe in the hospital wing. But only relatively, mind you: a hit man could easily enough fake his way into the hospital, bluffing his way past the doctor whose only interest in whether his patients lived or died was bureaucratic (it was more trouble if they died), and kill him there. Hence he greeted each new arrival in the hospital with apprehension: was this to be his executioner? And he knew that he would have to live in fear all the rest of his days. Criminals, ladies and gentlemen, are just like you: they have short memories for the harm they do, but long ones for the harm which they imagine has been done to them.

Nevertheless, the hospital wing was the young man's best chance of survival in the circumstances, and every time it was suggested that he should leave it, he scratched his wrists with any piece of metal which came to hand, as a warning to the screws that he would kill himself if he were moved. Brutal but nonetheless sticklers for bureaucratic form, the screws never dared call his bluff: they were terrified of the

Chief Inspector of Prisons, a retired woman judge who dressed in tweeds and smoked a cheroot, who thought that the prisons should be run like Montessori schools, and who fulminated in public every time a prisoner succeeded in killing himself. She called for a public enquiry whenever this happened, instead of calling for research into how this laudable and highly economical activity might be increased among the involuntary guests of the government.

Like most bullies, the screws were also cowards: the very name of the retired judge struck terror into their hearts, and they could only say what they really thought of her when they had drunk (or *sunk*, as they put it so elegantly among themselves) several pints of beer – that is to say, every night.

This is the atmosphere in which I, who could and should have been an artist, and would have been had there been any justice in the world, am obliged to live.

Now the whole point of my story about the young man is that the behaviour of the man falsely accused of murder, but unable to defend himself, and that of the real (common) murderer, is in every way identical and indistinguishable. And the screws, not without reason, treated them exactly the same.

And this, ladies and gentlemen, is another irrefutable proof, if a further one is needed, of my assertion that, when it comes to murder, guilt and innocence represent a distinction without a difference: an error rightly condemned by all philosophers.

7

NOT BEING A PROFESSIONAL writer, I have begun to lose my thread again. If I had been born in the right circumstances, perhaps I might have contributed to literature: for I flatter myself that I possess some natural talent in that direction, and only the overwhelmingly urgent need to earn a living prevented me from doing so.

Besides, conditions in prison are hardly conducive to the creation of works of literary perfection. Whoever designed prisons knew that a vital component of hell was continual noise, so he built them of materials that not only transmitted the faintest sound, but amplified it by a hundred times. Outside its walls, we are told, not a sparrow falls but our Heavenly Father takes cognizance of the fact (*Matthew*, Chapter 11, verse 29); inside its walls, not a prisoner farts (to use the vernacular for a moment) but the building vibrates on the Richter scale. And when a real commotion breaks out – a whistle alarm, say – Armageddon (*Revelation*, Chapter 16, verse 16) would be like a Zen garden by comparison.

There was precisely such an alarm on my landing only ten minutes before I wrote this, for example. I am still trembling slightly. The cell of one of my neighbours, a common criminal, was searched by two screws for illicit radio parts (what is not permitted in prison is forbidden). They came across a blackish substance stuffed into the mattress, for which the prisoner made a grab in an attempt to swallow the evidence. Can you wonder that the law is so despised when it is punishable to possess a substance which it is not illegal actually to have taken? If I were trying to devise a system worthy of the contempt of every intelligent person, I could think of no better.

Anyway, the screws tried to stop the con (the coarsening of my language is a product of my environment, ladies and gentlemen) by force. He resisted and punched one of the screws. The other blew his whistle. Those who have never heard a prison whistle would not credit how loud a single blast of such a puny instrument can be, especially in a confined space: enough to make hear the dead who were deaf in life. This overture was swiftly followed by the symphonic sound of the boots of twenty screws on the Victorian ironwork stairs which lead to our landing. They came like children rushing for a treat. The next thing I heard was a scream of 'Fuck you, you pig!' – another three days' remission lost, on the charge 'That you did use insulting language to Officer Bryden while he was carrying out his lawful duties, namely that you did say "Fuck you, you fucking pig" to him.' (Prison officers, like policemen, are never content to confine themselves merely to the evidence.) Then came the sound of a man being subdued by having his arms twisted behind him, to a chorus of 'Don't move, keep still, you dumb shit!' And, finally, the retreat of the screws, carrying the prisoner with them as he protested in a scream that they were breaking his arms, back down the ironwork stairs to the solitary confinement cells beneath: and all this taking place in the auditory equivalent of a hall of mirrors.

I ask you, ladies and gentlemen, how is a man – especially of my nervous disposition – supposed to develop an argument, and express it in an elegant prose style, when he is subject to such commotions which, moreover, can break out at any time of the day or night, and which, when they happen at night, leave him exhausted and anxious the next day for lack of sleep? What could anyone have done to deserve such an experience as this?

But I started several pages ago to try to explain the excessive, and indeed unhealthy, public interest in my case, and now I shall disclose my explanation to you without further digression, in case another commotion breaks out on my landing and makes me lose my thread once more: *I have only done what you, in your heart of hearts, have always wanted to do.*

Of course, you cannot acknowledge it, even to yourself, and therefore you transform me from hero to villain, a villain so villainous indeed that you pretend you cannot even understand me. This is what the Freudians call *reaction formation*, though of course I do not hold completely with their psychological system, which is burdened with a great deal of implausible elaboration.

Nor do I expect you to accept what I say without protest. Indeed, the very vehemence of your reaction demonstrates that I have touched a raw nerve with you. It is bad enough that I should have proved to your satisfaction that you are morally worse than I; but you find it intolerable that I should now go on to demonstrate that I have in any case only carried out in practice your innermost desires, upon which you were too cowardly to act yourself.

But many famous authors have recognised the truth of what I say, ladies and gentlemen. You will find in them a frank avowal of the most murderous desires, usually – but not always – in conjunction with sadistic fantasies, from which I have never suffered, at least not as an adult. On the contrary, I consider myself an idealist and a humanitarian. I go to the authors, ladies and gentlemen, precisely because they have penetrated into the deepest recesses of the human mind, where others fear to think. They ruthlessly tear away the flimsy facades which you so easily erect to hide your true nature from others and from yourselves. And I am modest enough to believe that I have something to learn from the sages of the past. They knew a thing or two.

Let us start with the Marquis de Sade, accused by some of being a tedious and even talentless writer: but this is surely the jealousy of those disappointed authors who are as likely to have an *ism* named after them as they are to sprout wings and ascend directly to heaven from somewhere in Jerusalem. I had to read him in a semi-clandestine fashion even now, two centuries later, so subversive of good order and discipline (as they call it in the prison) is he considered: I did not want the librarian to know what I was reading in case he would one day use this information to testify against me:

> We are going to describe crime [the Marquis means murder] as it is, that is to say always triumphant and sublime ... while virtue is always wretched and sad.

Yes, the Marquis, despite being an aristocrat, hits here upon an essential truth: that Man is attracted to killing as a moth to the flame. Have you never wondered why in literature it is always the evil characters who have the best lines, the firmest delineation, and who remain forever fixed in the mind? Or why the hell of Hieronymus Bosch should be so vivid, while all paintings of Paradise are so anaemic and passionless, leaving no trace in the mind? Take the Koran: what is its vision of Heaven? Of men lying about forever on golden couches in verdant gardens, being served cool refreshing drinks by virgin nymphomaniac maidens who never grow old, or tire of serving. One can see the attraction of this kind of Paradise to men who have spent their lives in the desert, around and about camels. But as a way of spending a week, let alone an eternity, it is a little restricted.

Man being what he is, eternal bliss simply cannot be imagined. Man is not only a problem-solving animal, but a problem-creating one. He cannot live without difficulties, and from time to time there are riots, even in Switzerland, whose perfection eventually enrages the inhabitants who have created it. He – that is, Man – cannot bear too much good order and happiness, any more than he can bear too much reality (T.S.Eliot, *Four Quartets*); no sooner does he arrive in a comfortable billet than he begins to look around for trouble. Bliss soon palls: *ergo*, it cannot exist. Merely to think about heaven soon induces a kind of stupor.

It is quite otherwise with hell, of course, and it is perfectly easy to imagine eternal torment. And when you put your mind to it, there are no end of perpetual punishments, gross or subtle, you can devise. What does this prove, you ask? Nothing more – but also nothing less – than that Man has a natural vocation for all that is vicious, harmful and antisocial. To select some men for punishment is thus not only futile, but a mere exercise in scapegoating.

Let us return to the authors: though they are but straws in the wind of my argument. If de Sade had been the only example I could quote, if he were merely a sterile proof only of the extent and catholicism of my reading in the public library, well then, I might grant that it were possible to dismiss him as a mere aberration in the history of literature. But he is not the only one, or the greatest. Dostoyevsky, in *The Brothers Karamazov*, tells us that:

> In every man ... a demon lies hidden – the demon of rage, the demon of lustful heat at the screams of the tortured victim, the dream of lawlessness let off the chain.

No doubt you will wonder how it happened that a formally uneducated man such as I can quote these passages by heart in this extremely erudite fashion. The answer is simple: when I came across them in the public library I recognised at once that they not only conveyed an important truth, but they might be useful to me one day, and I branded them indelibly into my memory by constant repetition.

Yes, ladies and gentlemen, you fantasise impurity and cruelty while you speak of virtue and humanity You claim to be civilised, but just look at the way you drive! If there were no traffic laws, or no likelihood of being caught if you broke them, what would prevent you from driving at a hundred miles an hour down a crowded street and mowing pedestrians down like skittles, so that you might arrive at the restaurant or for an appointment on time, or even for the sheer fun of it? Love of pedestrians in general, fear that you will injure them and that they will suffer as a result? Nonsense: for what are they to you, or you to them, that you should avoid them?

No, ladies and gentlemen, it is not love of your fellow man, but the fear of punishment, which keeps your foot off the accelerator. Fear is the prerequisite of order, and there is no civilisation without it. When fear is removed, what do you get: peace and reconciliation, or crime and chaos?

So, then, you live in fear; and fear is the mortal enemy of freedom. You fed trapped by it at every moment of your lives: which, of course, is why your fantasies are so extravagant.

But Dostoyevsky was an epileptic, a neuropath, you object: his idea were almost certainly the result of a pathological electrical discharge in his brain. Besides, he was a Russian, and the inhabitants of such a morbid country are bound to have morbid thoughts.

I am surprised you display your vulgar prejudices so openly. Have I not repeatedly demonstrated that I am not the kind of man to be taken in by such speciousness? If Dostoyevsky's capacity to think had been destroyed, or even distorted, by a defect of his neurones, is it likely that he could have produced some of the deepest and most universal literary work of his, or any other, age? No, it is only because he writes something which disturbs your complacent equilibrium that you bring up the question of his epilepsy. As for the supposed morbidity of Russians, Turgenev was among the least pathological of the great writers, as was Chekhov. It is the truth of Dostoyevsky's words which you seek to deny by descent to the *ad hominem* plane of argument. Besides, Dostoyevsky was far from the only one to recognise this truth. I quote from Louis-Ferdinand Celine:

The first chance we get, we fall back on our old habits: massacre and torture ... Oh to be able to eviscerate someone! It is the secret wish of every 'civilised' person.

So what, you ask? Celine, you say (that is, if you are not completely ignorant), was a notorious fascist, a Nazi sympathiser. (And from where, from what source, do you suppose that Nazism sprang, I ask in parenthesis?) After the war, he had to take refuge in Denmark, and was only able to return to France after an amnesty.

But the truth of what a man says, ladies and gentlemen, is not to be so easily discounted. Even if the devil himself says so, are two and two not still four?

First, fascists had a good understanding of human nature. Did not fascism triumph originally in precisely the country of Europe with the longest continuous history of civilisation? And did it not next triumph precisely in the country of Europe with the highest level of education and culture?

Second, Celine spent many years in practice as a doctor. Thousands of secrets must have been reposed in him, and therefore there was nothing he did not know about the human heart. He knew whereof he spoke. That other doctors, equally the recipients of confidences, have not written in exactly the same terms demonstrates only the exceptional courage one needs to write the truth.

And this, ladies and gentlemen, is the key: you envy me, for I have liberated myself from the inner demons which still torment you, because you have not assuaged them. It cannot be that all the authors whom I have quoted – and many others whom I have refrained from quoting, since there is nothing more vulgar than a display of learning – are mistaken. No: it has long been appreciated that the first injunction of any ethical system, which was engraved over the entrance of the Academy in ancient Athens, is to *Know thyself.*

And I came to know myself after prolonged reading in the public library, and hard reflection in the solitude of my own home. I understood my capacity for violence and cruelty, not from personal experience, but from general principles which I derived from study. And I came to the conclusion (in common with all psychologists of repute) that you cannot repress a natural urge for ever: the very attempt to do so leads sooner or later to a pathological manifestation of it.

Take mourning, for example. Men and women who fail to mourn the deaths of those close to them eventually suffer a deep melancholia which may cause them to act irrationally, or at least to spend many years unproductively and miserably – all of which could have been avoided by the shedding of a few tears at the right time. I do not speak from experience, of course: I have never lost anyone close to me for the simple reason that no one has ever been close to me. But theoretical knowledge is still knowledge, even without direct experience.

Or take gluttony as another example. Who are gluttons? Very often you find that they are people who, in the first years of their lives, were denied the normal pleasures of food. And is the answer to gluttony total abstinence? Obviously not, because it is impossible. A man must eat to live, after all. The answer, then, is a compromise between total indulgence and total self-denial – something akin to Aristotle's golden mean.

And so it was with my urge to kill: I needed to find a golden mean. For ethical reasons I would not permit myself to perform what Andre Breton called 'the basic Surrealist act': namely, to go out into a busy street and shoot blindly into the crowd. Nor did I wish to suppress the urge to kill to the extent that it would one day emerge in that mad bellicosity and war fever by which all societies are seized from time to time, and which results in the deaths of untold thousands (or these days, millions), deaths moreover which occur almost entirely at random. Much better, I thought – and still think – to kill a few rationally selected individuals, chosen according to proper ethical principles, than to sink into such mindless degradation.

And in the process I became, for the first time in my life, a genuinely free man. Not, I admit, after the very first death, when I was still afraid that I might be caught, and perhaps not even after the second, when the fear lingered faintly, but after the third, definitely and definitively.

This was because, again for the first time in my life, I was acting purely of my own volition, and not in craven fear of what everyone else considered right, or in the hope of the paltry rewards which this society offers in return for conformity. I had decided on a course of action and had carried it out, like a completely free man.

Hence your envy, ladies and gentlemen, and why you have transformed me in your minds from a hero to a monster. For if you had not done so, what would disguise from you your own cowardice? What you proudly call your ethics is but the following of the herd, against your deepest and innermost inclinations. And that is why from time to time you have outbursts of terrible savagery, while I remain calm and collected at all times, even in the face of the most egregious insult.

For I have escaped the inner demons which still torment you.

8

I HAVEN'T QUITE finished with quotations yet: for though killing has had a bad press ever since Cain slew Abel (in Chapter 4 of the *Book of Genesis*), there have nevertheless been some partisans of the act courageous enough to brave the hypocritical censure of their fellow men. Political thinkers, of course, have always recognised the necessity on occasion to kill, whether they be pro- or anti-revolutionary. But the kind of killing of which they approve is strangely abstract, as if it were not a question of one man ending the life of another, by shooting him or cutting his throat for example, but rather one of impersonal forces which kill without the need of a human intermediary. One suspects that the authors of such abstract bloodthirstiness would faint at the sight of blood, and complain that the civil war or revolution was interfering with their daily routine.

I shall not refer to those authors, naturally, who are full of sound and fury, signifying nothing (*Macbeth*, Act 5, Scene 5). Rather, I shall refer to those who have recognised individual acts of killing (I find myself obliged to use that emotive word for lack of another, more neutral term) as being psychologically reparative and socially constructive. And here, irony of ironies, I find myself quoting yet another psychiatrist, despite my general contempt for and aversion to the entire breed. But I am reassured by the fact that the words of Franz Fanon find no echo in the thinking of his colleagues – if, that is, the feeble movement of their minds can properly be called thought.

> Violence is a cleansing force. It frees the native from his inferiority complex and from his despair and inaction; it makes him fearless and restores his self-respect.

In killing his erstwhile master, says Fanon, a man recovers his power to act, and in the process becomes more fully and truly human.

I need hardly add, I suppose, that Fanon is not speaking here of the common criminal, of he who kills for lucre or in the middle of a quarrel with his common-law wife (these are the killers who generally find their way into our penitentiaries). Fanon does not approve of any killing whatever: it must be self-conscious and in pursuit of a great cause in order to possess the healing powers he describes. In short, the killer must possess high ethical standards, as do I.

If you have read Fanon, you are likely to ask how I can dare compare myself with the people about whom he was writing? He was speaking, after all, of the downtrodden masses of colonial regimes, while I (according to you) am, or was, a free citizen of a free country, able to do whatever I chose.

That's a joke! (You'll forgive me if I resort to a vulgar expression in a work as serious as this, but there are moments when spontaneity has its own value.) If I were to have stopped working, I should have found myself at once without an income, barely able to find enough to eat, and living in the perpetual cold and damp which are the worst consequences of poverty in a northern climate. How can you call it freedom to be thus forced go five times a week for twenty years to work which you loathe and despise, merely to stave off discomfort and wretchedness? Is freedom, then, the recognition of necessity, as Engels remarked? Be honest with yourselves for once, ladies and gentlemen, and admit that the only people who are genuinely free (and I mean free *to*, not merely free *from*), are the enormously rich.

Like almost everyone else, Fanon was a prisoner of his own experience, and therefore concluded that the oppression with which he had direct acquaintance was the only form of oppression which existed or could exist. That is how the mind of an intellectual works: egocentrically, with no imagination, and no sympathy for the predicament of others. Fanon would have dismissed as insignificant the oppression which I have experienced throughout my life, because I happen to have lived in a country which he would have called imperialist. But unlike him, I have had no Parisian Left Bank intellectuals to defend me in print, or to write on my behalf to the authorities. The tyranny of everyday life is not the less tyrannous because it is concealed (on the contrary, concealment makes all tyranny the more difficult to bear); nor is it the less tyrannous because it is unimposed by water cannon, baton charges, torture chambers and the like. Nevertheless, life – except for the most privileged of the privileged – is a long series of the *diktats* of circumstance.

Think of your own everyday life: the illusion of freedom apart, is it not the case that everything you do from morning till night is dictated not by your own wishes, but by the demands placed upon you by society? Even the way you dress is laid down within very narrow limits, for those who would eat must have a job, and those who would have a job must dress in conformity with the expectations of their employers.

You wake not because you are rested, but because it is time to go to work, you eat not because you are hungry but because society has decreed that it is time to eat. In short, if you have the courage to examine your existence with the total honesty with which I have examined mine, you will admit that all your actions are constrained by the demands placed upon you by others, and that you are no freer than Fanon's downtrodden colonial peasant.

Thus the tyranny which 99.9 per cent of us experience is every bit as crushing as that described by Fanon; and thus it is as vitally necessary for us to overcome this tyranny as it was necessary for Fanon's so-called natives to overcome their inferiority complex *vis-à-vis* their colonial masters. And only the same means will suffice. But who, you ask, is the enemy? Fanon's natives knew clearly enough; but we, who live in a Kafkaesque miasma, cannot point so easily to the authors of our oppression. The boss, after all, lives in the same moral swamp as we, and is no more free to act than we. His elimination would make no difference; he would be replaced immediately by someone with precisely the same characteristics. Besides, one would put oneself immediately at risk by disposing of one's boss.

But if there is no readily identifiable enemy, you will say, then Fanon's argument cannot apply to you (or us). How literal-minded you are! For it is the act itself of murder which liberates a man from his oppression, which makes him a real man for the first time in his life, one who acts from his own undiluted and uncontaminated will, and not the fact that he kills one person rather than another. It is the shooting of the arrow, not the finding of the target, which counts.

On what basis, however, is one to select those whom one is to kill, if not that of enmity? I have already stated my utter and irreconcilable opposition to killing at random, and it therefore follows that some principle or another must be employed by the man who wishes to transcend his condition of slave to the quotidian by means of murder. I would have quoted Nietzsche, to the effect that the weak and ill-constituted should perish, and that we should help them to do so, were it not that you would dismiss the words of this philosophical genius as the ravings of a man whose brain, as is well-known, was rotted by syphilis, and who ended his days completely mute in an asylum.

Let me then quote to you the words of a man indisputably sane, a man who has been proclaimed a sage in his own lifetime, and whom I have read in the public library: Norman Mailer. Two young men beat the owner of a small shop to death, and Mr Mailer says:

> One murders not only a weak fifty year old man, but an institution as well; one violates private property, one enters a new relation with the police and introduces a dangerous element into one's life.

Yes, it's true that we all need risk or danger in our lives, though we need security as well. But where the author utters something genuinely profound is where he states that in killing a man one kills not just an individual, but strikes at an institution. For example, to kill a university professor is to weaken the university system itself. Indeed, on many occasions, I considered just such a 'victim': for how much have I suffered at the hands of those who considered themselves my superior merely because they attended a university and possessed a scrap of paper to certify that they were able during examinations to regurgitate faithfully what their professors had told them! And what had these professors done to deserve such slavish imitation? I grant that at some time in their youth or early adulthood they may have dabbled a little in research, and perhaps even found out something which was not known before (which is no guarantee of its usefulness, however), but the vast majority of them have settled comfortably into their sinecures, and consider themselves intolerably overworked if they have four hours' teaching a *month* to perform – while the rest of us spend more than sixty hours a week on our work, if, as is only reasonable, you count the time travelling to and from the place of our employment as work also. Yes, I should have liked to make an example of university professors as a breed – smug, underworked and overpaid, if you include all their perquisites – but prudence forestalled me: for professors are regarded as important people in this society obsessed by formal qualifications, and do not disappear without some notice being taken of the fact, not only among the self-regarding professoriate, but by the police. The cases would have been investigated to the best of the latter's admittedly limited ability, and before long I should have been apprehended, however elaborate my precautions. Thereafter I should have been unable to continue with the work: and I decided, therefore, that it would be better to choose less socially prominent 'victims'. After all, it wasn't as if the world was short of parasites worthy of elimination.

I can't entirely agree with Mr Mailer about private property, however. I suspect that *there* he is being a hypocrite: he disapproves of private property in the form of small shops but not in the form of writers' royalties and bank accounts. Supposing I had written to him to tell him of my hard and financially pinched existence, which prevented me from realising my artistic potential, and had asked for his assistance on the basis of his published opinion of private property as an institution. Do you suppose he would have replied with a cheque? I doubt very much whether he would have replied at all: or if he did, it would have been to pretend that he received too many such appeals to grant any of them. And if I had replied in turn that his refusal demonstrated that what he had written about his opposition to private property was a sham, a mere posture, and that logically speaking he should divest himself of everything he owned, I think it would have brought our correspondence to an abrupt end. No, Mr Mailer is sometimes capable of enunciating great truths, but by accident as it were: they do not emerge from a personality of transcendent moral scrupulousness.

But neither do I mean that private property in its present form is defensible: why should some people be allowed to earn in a day more than I earn in a month or even a year? Is it possible that there are people three hundred and sixty-five times (or three hundred and sixty-six times in a leap year) more talented, more intelligent, more valuable to society than I? I trust you will not reply with the cheap *ad hominem* jibe that I earned more in a week than a Bangladeshi or Zairean peasant earned in a year. Of course I admit that I earned more than such peasants; but the difference was less than you assume (or pretend). After all, if you divided my income by fifty-two, and asked someone to live on it in this country for a year, he would soon starve or freeze to death. But the Bangladeshi or Zairean peasant does neither of these things, *ergo* his income cannot have been a mere two per cent of mine. These peasants receive free heating, for example, as a gift of God. (I use the term God as a figure of speech, without any theological implications, and without prejudice as to his existence or nonexistence.)

Besides, you cannot sensibly judge a person who lives in one society by the standards prevailing in another. Poverty in a rich country would no doubt be counted riches in a poor one: but it is still poverty to the person who suffers it. Therefore, when I point to the injustice of the income differentials in my own country, between myself for example and (say) a young spiv in the City, or an equally young footballer, who have never been in a public library in their lives and would not know Kant from Spinoza, it is no answer that the differential is no greater than that between me and the inhabitant of one of the poorest countries in the world even supposing this were true, which it isn't, as I have demonstrated. Injustice exists within societies, not between them.

Of course, I am not saying that everyone should receive precisely the same income, far from it. Why should someone who does no work at all receive *gratis* an income from the state not so very different from my own, when I sacrifice five days of every week of my life to my work? What is the incentive for anyone to work in these circumstances? Absolute equality and the abolition of all property as advocated by the Mailers of this world would spell the end of effort, and moreover we should not be able to call even our teaspoons our own.

I am asking only for a fair crack of the whip, to allow myself for once the use of a cliché which nevertheless expresses precisely what I mean: the recognition that no man's labour can be worth hundreds of times that of another – at least, not that of a man who performs any work at all. How can the guitarist of a so-called musical group, with very limited talent and who after all is only entertaining people, usually very unintelligently, rightfully earn in a year or two enough to enable him to live in luxury for the rest of his life, when the vast majority of us will never experience such luxury, not even for a week or a day, however long we work?

In essence, I demand a scale of wages that is just and realistic: the best paid man, for example, should not receive more than twice or three times the amount that the worst paid receives. Nor should it be only a man's ability which determines his place on the scale: after all, ability is a gift of nature (I won't say from God, otherwise you'll think that I'm a believer, and as William of Occam pointed out a long time ago, in the fourteenth century to be exact, *entia non sunt multiplicanda praeter necessitatem*, which is to say that, philosophically speaking, entities are not to be multiplied unnecessarily, without good reason). No one can be said to deserve his own ability, therefore. Effort is a much sounder and more socially beneficial way of determining monetary reward, besides which the intrinsic unpleasantness of a task ought to be taken into account. If my scheme were to be implemented, it would result in a very different and much improved order of things: an order which represented a genuine moral hierarchy, and not the present egotistical anarchy, in which price is the only value.

Not that I expect anyone to take notice of my ideas, I am not so naive as to think it. A prophet is without honour not only in his own country, but in his own epoch.

9

WHO, THEN, WERE my 'victims', as you persist in calling them?

Before I answer (I am not being evasive, you'll be told everything in due course, without reservation), I should perhaps explain the nature of my work. As I have already mentioned, I worked for twenty years in the Housing Department, and always in the same capacity: it was I who sat at the front counter of the Department, protected from the public by very necessary bulletproof glass, receiving requests for housing from the degraded, the desperate and the indigent, as well as those who were already housed by the Department but who wanted to be moved elsewhere, into the better accommodation of which they assumed, quite falsely, that it disposed.

There was a housing shortage in the town, of course, as there was everywhere else in the country: more applicants than dwellings. This fortunate circumstance gave the bureaucrats just the opportunity they needed. They developed a system of the allocating of what they called *housing units* which was so complex and byzantine in its operations that more and more staff were needed to run it, so that the bosses were able to grant themselves ever grander titles for their own jobs. By the time I was arrested, almost everyone in the Department (above the very lowest level, that is) was a director or a manager of something or other. Some years before, a management consultant, the cost of whose hotel bill alone would have housed six families adequately for several weeks, had suggested that one way to revive flagging morale was to rid the Department of job titles implying the subordination of one person to another, and to create new titles emphasising the inestimable importance to the organisation of the bearer of them.

At the same time, the bureaucracy indulged in the pretence that it was accountable to the public whom it allegedly served. It instituted a complaints procedure (actually there was a Director of Complaints Investigation, a little weasel of a man called Jim Jimson, who kept a collection of pornographic material, as well as a quarter bottle of vodka, in his drawer), which itself was so difficult to understand that it effectively disposed of complaints before they could be made.

What an atmosphere prevailed in the office! Everyone was always on the lookout for some lapse or another on the part of their so-called colleagues to serve as the pretext for yet another meeting so that the office might be closed (temporarily, of course). I remember the meeting, which lasted two hours and grew very heated, as to what the preferred term for black coffee should be, since it had recently been decided by the Racism Awareness Officer that the word 'black', as applied to anything at all, was potentially inflammatory and degrading. I was howled down when I suggested that this discussion over the use of words was diversionary and trivial: the Savanorolas of the Housing Department then accused me of racism, and I lodged a complaint with the Director of Human Resources, alleging slander. Needless to say, I was completely vindicated. But it was nonetheless decreed that henceforth the correct usage in the office would be *coffee with* and *coffee without*, and that failure to apply these terms would be a disciplinary matter.

One day workmen appeared in the Department with instructions to affix pictures of great black men on all the walls. Such a portrait was hammered onto the partition of my little cubicle, which covered a smaller floor space than the Director's coffee table (I am talking now of *the* Director, the Director of Directors as it were), but which was nevertheless known as my office. The portrait was of Mansa Musa, the Emperor of Mali who, according to the legend underneath, took so much gold in his baggage train on his pilgrimage from West Africa to Mecca that, *en route* through Cairo, the price of gold halved in the market there. We received a circular to inform us that removal of any of the portraits would be regarded as a dismissible offence. I protested that no authentic portrait of Mansa Musa could possibly exist, since Islam forbade the imitation of God's creation by representational pictures, and that this portrait was therefore a figment of a none-too-accomplished artist's imagination, to which an orthodox Moslem might object on strictly theological grounds; but of course my protest was ignored, it being impossible to argue logically with a semi-educated bureaucracy.

Indeed, we lived in fear in the Department: demons were conjured up to assure us of the significance of the least of our actions. You had only to look at a woman longer than a fraction of a second for her to accuse you of sexual harassment. And as soon as the accusation was made, the accused was suspended from work (on full pay, naturally) until an internal investigation was completed. This always came to nothing, since it was invariably one person's word against another's; but the accused and only partially-exonerated party might nonetheless be ordered to attend a sexual harassment awareness course (in working hours, naturally), run by a former employee of the Department, just to remove any lingering doubts in the office about his past and future conduct.

The only safe thing to be in the Department was a victim: even the left-handers banded together and demanded a meeting to make everyone aware of the difficulties left-handers faced in a right-handed world.

They said that the latest research had proved that left-handers lived ten years fewer than right-handers, and that therefore they were entitled to early retirement, especially as much of the excess mortality among them was accounted for by their increased susceptibility to accidents brought about by equipment designed solely for the convenience of the right-handed, such as scissors. They demanded that henceforth at least the same proportion of equipment in the Department be adapted for left-handed use as the proportion of left-handers in the staff or the population as a whole, a reasonable demand, they said, after several centuries of attempted suppression of left-handedness by parents and teachers, who had tried to change children's handedness as if it were merely a matter of moral failure rather than of neurology and hence an integral part of a child's personality. The more extreme among the left-handed lobby demanded that an even higher proportion of equipment be adapted to left-handed use, claiming that a significant number of so-called right-handers were really left-handed, having been forced to change their preference in childhood, and that, with a modicum of official encouragement, they could be returned to their true identity, and hence to personal wholeness. They also said that restitution was only just and reasonable after so many centuries of oppression by the right-handed.

Left-handed scissors made their appearance for the first time in the Department, and a monitoring group was set up to check that they were available easily to those of the staff who might need them. But even this did not satisfy the lobby, which had scented blood: it pointed out that all the handles of the toilet cisterns were for use by right-handers, and demanded the installation of left-handed cisterns. And then it moved on to what it called *handedness-biased language*, the use of which it wanted to eliminate from the department: terms such as *sinister* and *gauche* which carried derogatory connotations concerning left-handers and left-handedness, and were thus deeply wounding. Even the past participle of the verb *to leave* became suspect, since leaving is often sad and unhappy, and it was officially recommended that it should be avoided whenever possible. *He left his flat* should henceforth be written *He vacated his flat*, or even *He leaved his flat*.

And there were courses to attend – compulsorily, it goes without saying. I was sent three times in five years on a course on how to answer the telephone. It wasn't just a matter of picking the receiver up and telling the caller that this was the Housing Department: it was much more complicated than that. I spent three days practising the mandated reply: 'Good morning, the Housing Department, Graham speaking. How may I help you?' It wasn't just the words one had to get right, otherwise even the Director (who, of course, wasn't obliged to attend) could have learnt all there was to learn in a day: no, it was the correct intonation which was so difficult to capture, according to our instructors – also former employees of the Department who had struck out on their own. One had to remember that the person on the other end of the telephone was calling about a matter of the utmost importance to him or her, and therefore our voice must intimate by its tone a willingness to listen and understand. The tone required was somewhere between that of a clergyman taking choral evensong and that of a doctor informing his patient that he had advanced cancer.

But anyone who has ever telephoned the Housing Department knows that in practice things are quite different, and that a thousand courses on how to answer the telephone will not change them. We had two main techniques for discouraging callers: the first was simply not to answer at all. Eventually even the most desperate person gives up. This technique was not entirely satisfactory for us, however, because the prolonged ringing of a telephone soon begins to get on one's nerves. It is a tough and determined man who does not succumb to temptation and answer it. A more satisfactory technique altogether was to answer the call immediately, thus putting an end to the irritation of the ringing, but to ask the caller before he or she could utter a word to hold on for a moment: a moment which could be almost indefinitely extended. And our Department being a large one, it was most unlikely that the caller had come through to the right person to deal with his case. If the caller had not rung off in despair by the time we took up his call again, it was possible to keep him waiting for yet a further period while we allegedly tried to connect him to the right person. The caller would hold on to his receiver, not knowing whether he had been cut off or not, until he concluded that he had been thus cut off and therefore he himself rang off. Another enquiry or complaint satisfactorily dealt with, from our point of view.

It was, of course, particularly gratifying to use these methods when the caller, having no telephone of his own, was in a public call box, for one knew then that he had wasted his assiduously collected coins on several minutes of silence, and that it would take him a considerable time, and a lot of effort, to collect so many coins again for a further attempt to contact the Department.

Do you conclude from this that the staff of the Department were fools and knaves? The former I am prepared to grant you, with very few exceptions: at lunchtime, all they spoke of was football and what they had watched on the television the night before, or what they would watch tonight. But let no one presume to judge them from the moral point of view who has never had to deal with the public *en masse*, day after day and year after year. For it is when you have worked with people that you learn truly to appreciate objects: the artefacts of Man being, as I have said before, so much more admirable than Man himself.

Yes, ladies and gentlemen, Man is a scoundrel. He is a cheat, a thief, a liar, a swine, a fool, a deceiver, a wheedler, a wife-beater, an oaf, a vandal, a lout, an ignoramus, a boor, a layabout, a moron, a bully, a coward, a drunk, a swindler, and a hypocritical whiner: in short, scum. You go too far, you protest, you exaggerate, or at least generalise unduly. But which of us, I reply, has more experience of the human race as a whole, you who meet no one but members of your own class, or I who have encountered thirty people a day for twenty years, upwards of one hundred and fifty thousand in all? Which of us speaks with more authority on the subject of the human race, of human nature?

Because of this very nature, the extraordinary lengths to which the staff of the Department were willing to go to avoid individual examples of the species were unsurprising, indeed to be expected. When a mouse is confronted with danger, it freezes and starts to lick its paws; when a bureaucrat is confronted with the public, he holds a meeting. If only my so-called colleagues in the Department (who generally steered clear of me because of my broad intellect and sharp tongue, but who, just like my neighbours, affected the most intimate knowledge of me immediately after my arrest, their brief moment with a reporter or on television being the high point in their stunted lives) – if only, I say, they had been able to admit to their loathing for and disgust with humanity, how much more contented, how much less tormented, they would have been. Instead, of course, they had to pretend to love this humanity of yours, or even worse to serve it untiringly. Humanity itself, they were obliged to say, was good, and only the circumstances in which it found itself, created by the government, were bad. (By that, they meant *au fond* that their salaries were too small.) As I have mentioned before, not to recognise one's own true feelings, indeed to turn them into their direct opposite, is always dangerous: and to suppress them permanently in this fashion leads sooner or later to behaviour which is distorted and, as the psychologists put it in their desire to mystify the obvious, dysfunctional.

No one could truly and honestly have thought that humanity was good after working a week (let alone a year or a fifth of a century) in the Department, without doing the utmost violence to his immediate perceptions. And only a person of no judgment or sensibility at all could have failed to loathe humanity passionately after such a week. In fact, one would have to be profoundly depraved in one's tastes to like it after any intimate contact with it.

Of course, my superiors in the Department had been trained at university to deny the obvious, to assert the improbable and defend the indefensible, with all the sophistical arguments at their disposal. They

– my superiors – could deny the hand in front of their faces, while indulging in theorising which had no conceivable relation to reality. Moreover, having achieved their promotion as rapidly as possible, thanks to their so-called qualifications, they withdrew from all contact with the public which they pretended to serve, thus enabling them to maintain their illusions. If you went to them with a particularly egregious example of vile behaviour by a member of the public, they would put the tips of the fingers of their two hands together as if in prayer, adopt a stage-compassionate tone of voice and tell you that what you had to remember was that these people (the public) were underprivileged, that they had never had any opportunity to succeed in life, that they were very poor, that most of them came from unstable backgrounds and broken homes, that many of them didn't even know who their father was, that they had probably grown up in an atmosphere of violence in which people got what they wanted by grabbing it or taking it forcibly from others, that they were badly educated because the schools were so underfunded and had leaking roofs (despite their allegedly higher education, my superiors always said *rooves*), that they had been unemployed for many years and were without hope of employment, thanks to the government's economic policies, and that their lives were boring and wretched: in short, that vile behaviour was a symptom of vile social conditions.

One might have thought my superiors were missionaries, they were so understanding and forgiving of the sins of the public. But just let one of them catch one of us returning from lunch ten minutes late, and see how understanding they were, these self-appointed guardians of compassion! They didn't care even if the reason for our lateness was that we had been attending the funeral of our closest friend or relative. The reason for their punctiliousness about our hours of work was not difficult to guess: they spent half their day with their feet up on their desks, reading the newspaper.

The way they spoke of the public – our *clients*, as they insisted that we call them, though they paid us nothing and were utterly powerless in their relations with us – you would have thought that they were not as fully human as, for example, were the upper echelons of the Department itself, but were mere automata whose appalling conduct registered their misfortunes the way the retreat of an amoeba's pseudopodium registers something noxious in the water around it. When they – the public, our *clients* – swore at us, it was because they knew no other language in which to express themselves or their so-called feelings; when they threatened us with violence, it was because the society in which they lived was violent. The fault was never theirs but only the system's: and only a revolution would put things right, but until then they, the upper echelons of the Department, would continue to draw their grossly inflated salaries, at least until it was time for them to draw their grossly inflated pensions.

How can I describe to you our 'clients' without drawing down upon me once again the accusation of exaggeration, an accusation so easily levelled by people with no experience whatever?

To begin with, they were physically repulsive, one and all. Their teeth were generally rotten, mere mottled black pegs by the time they were thirty. Well, you say, in your complacent middle-class tones of intellectualised but unfelt compassion, they couldn't afford dentists' fees. Humbug! I have visited hundreds of their houses, literally hundreds, to inspect them for the damp or the neighbours' noise of which they complain, and scarcely one of them is without a DVD machine and compact disc player, often of the latest and most elaborate models, and most have computers with which they can while away their idle moments, that is to say their entire waking lives, by killing Martians who flood towards them on the screen to the sound of repetitive tinny music. Stolen, you say: all these contraptions were stolen, and were therefore not indicative of genuine choice. Well, I have yet to hear of anyone stealing to pay for a dentist; besides which, I ask, how does it come that the pubs are filled night after night, with beer at more than three pounds a pint? No, ladies and gentlemen, they don't go to dentists because they choose not to go, and because they are too improvident to do so. They are either repulsively fat, or thin and runt-like – except, that is, the psychopathic young men who spend half their lives in a gym to get themselves fit for further violence. But if they are too fat, you say, it is because they eat too much junk food, and if too thin, because of continual smoking. In either case, it demonstrates the constant pressure under which they live. But what pressure, I ask, can make a man – with an infinitude of time on his hands, be it remembered, for he does not work, has not worked and has no intention of ever working – buy crisps and chocolate instead of lettuce and lentils? As for the smokers, I don't want to hear the stale nonsense about cigarette advertisements having influenced them: I have never smoked, and I have seen at least as many such advertisements as they.

And why don't they wash? The water flows from the tap for the rich and the poor alike, and soap is so cheap nowadays that even the poorest of the poor can afford it. The same goes for their clothes, which look as though they strain their food through them, and which smell of sweat and skin infection. Detergent, after all, is cheaper than beer or cigarettes.

As for the conditions in which they choose to live, they are deplorable. I say 'choose to live' advisedly, because there is no reason, other than sheer laziness and slatternliness, why their habitations should be so dirty, neglected and stained by every conceivable stain. Crumpled and unwashed clothes lie everywhere, scarcely in piles, but strewn like paint on a canvas of modern so-called art; the floors are covered with the detritus of everyday life, from crumbs to condoms, accumulated without tidying for weeks and months; the washing-up is left undone until a mouldy scum floats on the dregs in the cups; a dog has urinated on the sofa, or a bitch has given birth to pups on it; a large window pane is broken and has been replaced by a plywood board. But in every such household – give or take an illegitimate baby or two – there is one corner in good order, arranged with almost religious reverence. I refer, of course, to the corner in which stands the television and DVD player (always switched on, it goes without saying), kept like a shrine or an ikon in a Russian peasant's *izba*. And every piece of furniture points to the holy corner: for it is the centre of the household's miserable existence.

What of it, you ask? An unemployed person has to occupy his time somehow, just like everyone else. This is precisely the point, ladies and gentlemen, that I wish to make: television occupies their minds. It is no coincidence that my metaphor should be a military one, for everything else is literally driven, fleeing, from their minds, however little there may have been there in the first place, to be replaced by the inconsequential drivel from which the television companies (or rather their shareholders) profit. Whenever I visited such a household, to check on the fungus which was allegedly growing up the walls (it never was) or on the roof which was allegedly leaking (only defects which could be blamed on the landlord interested them), I asked the complainant to turn off his television: but in many more than nine cases out of ten, and you have my personal guarantee that I no more exaggerate here than I do elsewhere in my narrative, to switch off a television meant to them no more than to reduce the volume of its sound. And it was futile to try to hold a conversation with them while the screen was winking silently in the corner: they were mesmerised, bemused, stupefied, bewitched by it. They had achieved that state of existence which the Zen Buddhists call *No mind*: and if you asked them what they had just been watching, they could not have told you, not for anything in the world.

So Little Done

I tried to avoid such visits, for obvious reasons. Our public housing is not pleasant, and to wander around it is risky and even dangerous. All the common parts (as we in the property business call them) are deeply impregnated with Saturday night urine, when the tenants and their friends cannot wait to reach the privacy of their own latrines to relieve themselves of their beery bladders. Anything which can be smashed has been smashed; obscene graffiti cover the walls. And of course, there is always the delightful possibility of being set upon by one of the many local gangs.

Oh, the things I discovered in tower blocks' There was a 'clinic' for female circumcisions run in William Cobbett Tower by an unfrocked Sudanese doctor, to say nothing of the glue-sniffing necrophiliac orgies I unearthed in Ruskin House. No depravity is too depraved for an English housing estate, ladies and gentlemen. And everyone in tower blocks lives in abject terror of his neighbours. This is a world in which the most violent and unscrupulous man always gets his way, in which everyone else is afraid to put his nose out of doors even by daylight, but in which staying indoors is no guarantee of safety either. Not that many of the tenants want to venture outside in any case: for there was nothing there which could compete for interest, or at least for hypnotic power, with the flickering, swiftly-moving images of their televisions.

On average, my 'clients' watched twelve hours of television per day. Can this properly be called a human life? Does it not more closely resemble the life of those famous laboratory rats which have had electrodes surgically implanted into the pleasure centres of their brain, as a result of which they press the lever to stimulate the electrode to the exclusion of all other activity, even eating and drinking, until they die of exhaustion and inanition? Was the life of my 'clients' worth leading? Did not the ancients understand that the only life worthy of living was the life of the mind? I don't deny the needs of the body, ladies and gentlemen: but they should be met only so that the intellect be set free to soar into the realms of speculation. On earth, wrote Sir William Hamilton in his *Lectures on Metaphysics and Logic* (in the public library's reserve collection), there is nothing great but man; in man there is nothing great but mind.

And so my 'clients' were indistinguishable (except in one respect, which I'll come to in due course) from animals, from mere beasts. Their minds were empty, they watched television as sheep eat grass. But unlike sheep, they served no purpose for others. They produced nothing, they gave pleasure to no one. I do not agree, of course, with the way sheep and other animals are raised purely for Man's pleasure, to be slaughtered at his convenience; but this does not affect the logic of my argument, which is that sheep, even if artificially raised and ill-treated, have a purpose and serve an end, though it be a disreputable one.

What value did my 'clients' have? In my opinion, they had a negative value, if you will permit me a neologism. They were parasites, who consumed without producing. They absorbed everything provided for them like a sponge, but a sponge with a special quality: it could never be saturated. They ate and they were clothed at public expense: hence they drove up the price of commodities for the rest of us. They were the reason we had to pay such extravagant taxes, and why I had to work a third of my time (or receive only two thirds of my wages, I don't mind which way you want to put it) to support their worthless existence. And not only did they dispose of money which they did nothing to earn, but they had the luxury – which I have never enjoyed – of doing as they pleased the livelong day. Not for them the daily purgatory of rising while they were still tired, of performing a task which was odious to them: no, when they rose, usually at eleven in the morning, they stumbled over to the television to turn it on and fumbled with a cigarette to put into their mouths. They did not even have to dress if they did not wish to, and generally they didn't: at three in the afternoon, half of them were still in their nightclothes.

But if you consider them so fortunate, you ask, why did you not join them? It is not so easy to join this new aristocracy, this new leisure class. If I had resigned my post, ladies and gentlemen, the government would have said that I had voluntarily rendered myself unemployed, and would thereafter have allowed me only a pittance of a pittance; and even this they would have made conditional upon my acceptance of the first job offered me, which, because of my exemplary record of employment, would have been very soon after my resignation. No, you have to be born into the new leisure class. It is a true aristocracy, and my mistake was in having taken employment in the first place, which put me on the treadmill from which there was no escape.

But it was not only in consuming what they did not produce that my 'clients' did harm. In addition they were violent and criminal: if not themselves, then via their offspring. Many of them, indeed, encouraged their children in their criminality, sending them out to steal and burgle, because they knew that the law was so lenient and tender-hearted towards children that it would do nothing to punish them. There were, in truth, no practical or prudential reasons for these children not to have stolen.

You ask whether I have ever been the victim of a crime, that I should feel so strongly about it. Here again you display the superficiality of your thought, the habit of only looking at appearances. Let us pass over in silence the question of whether my house has ever been broken into, or my car taken and driven away: indeed, let us assume for the sake of argument that neither of these things has ever happened to me. But, like everyone else, I must take out insurance: and the level of the premiums is set by the level of claims. It takes no great insight to realise that a high number of crimes will lead to a high number of claims, and from thence directly to high premiums. No insurance policy is an island, entire of itself. Therefore, send not to seek from whom the thief steals: he steals from thee. (Adapted from Donne.) Moreover, no one can believe that the effects of a street robbery or a burglary are confined to the loss of property alone: the way one views the world is changed forever afterwards.

To what end is all this laziness, passivity and inactivity on the one hand, and frenzied criminality on the other, put? Is it to lead a Socratic life of enquiry? No, it is to enjoy a purely animal existence completely devoid of the cerebration which makes Man truly Human. In killing such beings, one is not really destroying Human life at all: moreover, one is reducing the burden of public expenditure which weighs so heavily upon the rest of us.

10

EVEN SO, YOU protest, it was not euthanasia you committed (and with which you were charged), it was murder. After all, the people whom you call your clients did not request death; and if they had been asked, they probably would not have wanted it.

But a pig or a cow does not want to die either, I respond, yet you kill it, or allow it to be killed on your behalf. Perhaps you will object that a pig or a cow cannot express in words its wish not to die, and therefore we cannot know that it objects to death, or even whether it has a concept of death. To which I reply two things; first, a baby or young child also cannot object to its own death in words, but you still take it as wrong to kill it. And second, a pig makes perfectly plain its objection to having its throat cut if given a chance to do so, not in words admittedly, but by squeals and other non-verbal actions. All the laws against cruelty to animals are predicated on the commonsense observation that animals can suffer, and can make their feelings known to us without the intermediary of language.

The point I am making, ladies and gentlemen, is the following: the mere expression of a wish by a living being not to die has never been taken as a sufficient reason in itself for not killing it.

Wait a moment, you say, proudly supposing that you have caught me out in a contradiction. Not long ago you were objecting to the killing of pigs: now you are using the fact that pigs are killed to demonstrate the permissibility of killing in general. Surely you contradict yourself?

Not at all. I did not object to the killing of pigs in any or all conceivable circumstances, only when the purpose of doing so is to satisfy temporarily the unhealthy gustatory lust for meat (unhealthy both physically and spiritually), especially among those who refuse to involve themselves in the messy and degrading business of the killing itself. I have never maintained that pigs have a right to life which overrides all other possible considerations. I do not hold a brief for the Porcine Liberation Front, if such exists, and I have never had any intention of going to the nearest pig farm to release all its pigs, in part because, had I done so, I should have provided the neighbourhood with a legitimate reason for killing them. Yes, if pigs were to become a common pest, if they were to break into our houses, say, and drive off in our cars, or attack us on the streets, which they roamed in packs and rendered unsafe at night, I should be the first to call for their elimination. If they covered our walls in graffiti, if they robbed old ladies outside post offices of their pensions, if they played their music so loud that the ground under your feet began to vibrate and your toes to tingle unpleasantly, if they smashed windows for the mere fun of it, and squealed obscenities at the top of their high-pitched voices, if they shoplifted and received stolen goods, if they urinated wherever they happened to be and especially in the entrances to buildings, if they got into vicious fights in pubs and demanded free legal representation afterwards, if they spent two thirds of their life in front of the television, and if they constantly conceived and gave birth to piglets without the least thought as to how they were going to maintain them or bring them up, then, ladies and gentlemen, there would be no one more anti-pig than I. On the contrary, I should found a vigilante committee, to protect the public from the depredations of these loathsome creatures.

Nevertheless, you stick grimly – and if I may say so, doggedly, with the persistence of a man who is not accustomed to logical argumentation – to your prejudice that the wishes of a man should always be respected: he wishes not to die, therefore he should not be killed. I have already examined the question of killing in times of war, and how your answer to it demonstrated that what you call your moral principles are actually mere unexamined prejudices. The plain fact is that the desire of all the individuals in enemy armies not to die never stopped anyone killing them, or saved a single life. Irrespective of the rightness of killing in war, however, I will now examine your supposed principle that a man's wishes ought to be respected and complied with (in general, I do not like to end sentences with prepositions, but in the present instance I have no alternative).

It is an inescapable truth that millions of people – no, tens and hundreds of millions – have their wishes overruled each day, not once but several, indeed many times. I wish to leave my work to go shopping – I cannot. I wish to drink champagne every day – I cannot.

Trivial examples, you say But, you continue, the right to life itself is a precondition of the fulfilment of all other wishes (except that to die, of course). And then you sit back with a smug, *quod erat demonstrandum* (Euclid: it would be tiresome to quote in the original ancient Greek, which I admit in any case is beyond my power) look on your face.

I shall now dent your complacency a little. There are many desires other than the desire to live which are anterior to the fulfilment of yet other desires, and yet they are not fulfilled or attended to in any special way For example, all my life I have desired many things which required more money than I possessed: but no one ever suggested that I should be given or paid more money so that my subsidiary wishes should be fulfilled.

My point is logically a simple and unanswerable one: what we wish for, and what we receive, are inevitably quite distinct.

Thus, I came to the conclusion (for I had given it much thought) first, that it was morally permissible to eliminate my 'clients', and second, that it was obligatory, insofar as it fell within my means and capacity to procure this great public benefit.

There is, however, a difference between theory and practice, as observers of our system of government will have noticed, and there is always a reluctance to obey the dictates of conscience and conviction. How many Christians love their neighbours as themselves, let alone love their enemies? How many socialists give away their property to those less endowed with the goods of this world than themselves, or donate it to the government (as is permitted by law)? No doubt everybody in authority would have been much happier had I remained a hypocritical weakling, unable to act on my principles. A good example is always frightening. Fortunately, my daily contact with my 'clients' steeled my resolve. For they arrived every day with their specious, fatuous or arrogant demands, and turned unpleasant or vicious when they were refused.

In the allocation of public housing in Eastham there was (and still is, I should imagine) a points system: an applicant had to reach one thousand two hundred points to reach the top of the list. Unemployment counted sixty points; living alone counted another forty. An illegitimate child without paternal support also counted forty, while a second such child counted fifty. Alcoholism, drug addiction or a criminal record was each worth sixty, while membership of a minority group was equal in value. It is unnecessary to continue with this enumeration, because if you have not grasped the principle on which it worked by now, you never will. A year on the waiting list, incidentally, counted for twenty points: in other words, a person who just wanted a house from the council might wait sixty years in the absence of any other factor working in his favour.

This was how it was supposed to work: unfortunately, all human institutions are fallible. Two factors entered to distort it. The first was the influence of the councillors and our bosses, who would descend with instructions that such and such a person was to be found somewhere to live immediately, without delay, whatever their ostensible lack of qualifications according to the points system, but whose lack of entitlement counted for nothing in the face of their acquaintance with or relationship to the councillors or bosses. And the second distortion derived from the conduct of the 'clients' themselves.

What were known as the normal channels, perhaps it is unnecessary to explain, were not torrential in their speed. I knew of cases which had not been closed, as we bureaucrats put it, for fifteen years. This dilatoriness was no more (or less) than the 'clients' deserved, of course, but some of them had different, and mistaken, views of their own just deserts. They grew impatient at what they considered a negation of their rights, and soon resorted to means other than filling in forms to secure them. I should perhaps mention here that it was standard procedure to lose the first copy of any application forms which a 'client' filled in, and then to deny all knowledge of ever having received them. This soon sorted out the serious applicants from those who were merely bored and had nothing else to do: the latter gave up after only one attempt. (I do not say there was ever an official policy, laid down in writing, to lose the first application: but it happened so regularly, and so frequently by comparison with the number of times second applications were lost, that it could be considered no accident.)

I trust you will not succumb to the quintessentially English vice (sentimentality, which is the homage paid to feeling by indifference, a subtle – I think – adaptation of a maxim of la Rochefoucauld, namely that *L'hypocrisie est un hommage que te vice rend à la vertu*, hypocrisy is the homage which vice pays to virtue) and start to pretend to commiserate, at least in theory, with our 'clients'. The important thing to keep clear in your mind is that these people were morally entitled to nothing, to absolutely nothing. All the other facts of the case pale into insignificance by comparison with this cardinal fact.

But to return to those who were not satisfied with or by the normal channels: they resorted to the means which they saw succeed around them every day, namely the threat of violence. They were prepared to use real violence, too: for every unmarried mother had in tow if not the father of her children or their latest stepfather, at least a male acquaintance of some sort whose powers of persuasion rested in his fists, his knife or his baseball bat. They – the unmarried mothers – were often enough on the receiving end of those fists, but this did not turn them against their use as a method: on the contrary, they only wished to turn them in another direction.

And so, when the demand of such an applicant was turned down, or her wishes not complied with at once, she would bring her violent lover to the Department who, as a first step, would glower menacingly at the Department's employee who was dealing with the case. Between them, they let it be known that if they happened to meet that employee outside the office – and they had all the time in the world to wait – it would be the worse for him. Moreover, they were soon able to discover which was his car: tyres were expensive to replace, and paintwork to respray.

Several members of the department had been assaulted by the 'clients', two of them receiving permanent injuries. One of the latter had been pinned against a wall by a car driven by an applicant's boyfriend, and her legs broken; the second had been hurled down an escalator in a busy shopping centre one Saturday afternoon, no one coming to his aid until the assailant, who screamed abuse at him for a time while he lay bleeding at the bottom of the escalator, had run away. This is the world we in the Department inhabited, ladies and gentlemen. And before you shake your head at the brutality of it in your habitually self-righteous way, may I ask you whether you would have gone to my colleague's aid or tried to apprehend the criminal? I should add that the assailant in this latter instance was six feet six inches tall, and an expert, as are so many of our modern psychopaths, in what are called the martial arts. This, I maintain, is the consequence of feeding such people *ad libitum* and asking nothing of them in return: they have the strength of an ox, the brain of a chicken, and the morals of a hyena.

Is it any surprise that in these circumstances, those applicants who had such acquaintances, lovers, enforcers (call them what you will) found that their wishes were complied with in short order, and mysteriously acquired those twelve hundred points which brought them to the top of the waiting list? To boost their score, they were 'awarded' a couple of handicapped or illegitimate children, and a minority was found to which they belonged. And because they had been credited (if that is the word I want) with phantom children, whose existence was guaranteed by their written presence on file, accommodation had to be found for them with a sufficient number of bedrooms. The least uncultured among you will recognise Gogol (1802-1848) in this situation.

It goes without saying, almost, that the police would do nothing to protect us against the violence of our 'clients'. In their eyes, damage to our cars was a minor offence against property, not even worth their while to record, let alone investigate with a view to apprehending the perpetrator. Instead, they implied that it was our own fault for bringing our cars into so crime- and vandal-ridden an area, and suggested that we used the bus instead. You don't go down into a snake-pit, as one police officer put it who came to speak to us about security, and complain about snakebite. In this phrase, he revealed what the police really thought of the inhabitants of the area: less than mammalian, let alone human. Why then did the same police call it murder when they arrested me, having belatedly discovered the bodies of my subjects? Surely culling would have been a better word?

The threats made against us, said the police, were such minor infractions of the law that prosecution was out of the question. And as for the assaults themselves, no one was willing to testify against a psychopath who, if convicted, would be let off with a mere admonishment not to do it again, or at most a fine.

Even without violence, however, I was subjected to the most intense provocation. What else can you call the wilful and deliberate stupidity of my 'clients', to say nothing of their rudeness? Each of them came with an impossible demand: to be moved somewhere where people like them did not live. Each of them laboured, or pretended to labour, under the same delusion, namely that the Department disposed of accommodation in which decent people lived, where neighbours did not totally disregard each other's comfort and therefore did not play rock, rap or reggae music at a volume of a trillion decibels at three o'clock in the morning, and certainly did not break the ribs of anyone who dared complain about it. No, wherever the Department had property, there were drug pushers and prostitutes on the street corners, and rapists lurking in the shadows.

Each day I supposed that I had finally plumbed the depths of human folly and depravity, but on each succeeding day I learnt that these human characteristics were truly fathomless. The day I came to my decision – not without agonising – a man threatened to knife me on my way home.

'You won't be behind that fucking glass for ever,' he snarled, putting his face against it so that I could see the coarsened, greasy pores of his skin, widened by years of alcoholic overindulgence. He had demanded a three-bedroomed house. 'I've got ten dogs,' he said. 'You can't expect me to go on living for ever in a one bedroom flat.'

But this does not count as real provocation, you say – you, who have never dealt with the public as a servant, but have only been served.

What, may I ask, would you condescend to call a provocation?

According to the law, you reply, provocation (to count as an excuse) must be immediate and moreover the reaction must be without premeditation, a dish served hot rather than cold.

Again I reply with a two-pronged argument: first, that the law has changed, and therefore your ideas are out of date, and second, that even if the law's doctrine had remained petrified in its antiquated, indeed mediaeval, psychology, I am talking in this work of moral, not mere legal, responsibility.

It is now accepted by every intelligent person that provocation may be chronic as well as acute. You must have read in the newspapers of a recent case in which the wretched wife of a vicious husband killed him in his sleep. From the very outset of the marriage, he had behaved to her with exemplary brutality: and she shot him while he snored. She could not have claimed to act in self-defence, since at the moment she killed him she was in no danger from him. Neither was she provoked in the immediate sense, unless snoring be considered sufficient. Yet the courts accepted that she had been provoked beyond endurance, and she walked free from the court to the self-congratulatory applause of the nation, proud of its quality of mercy (*The Merchant of Venice*, Act 4, scene 1).

Is my case, I now ask you, so very different? True, I was not persecuted by a single person: instead, I was persecuted by a whole class of persons, my 'clients'. And is it worse, I ask you again, to be persecuted by one or by many?

The provocation was constant, unceasing and intense. You will, perhaps, maintain that it was not physical as in the case of the excused female murderer: and I admit that even if I received threats, I was never actually attacked in person, unless you count thumps on the counter and the flinging at me of pens and any other objects which came to hand, but which fortunately always bounced off the thick, reinforced glass which separated the staff from their 'clients'. The distinction between physical and verbal assault is in any case a false and artificial one, yet another example of a distinction without a difference, as the philosophers put it. For how is a threat to be communicated except through language and gesture, both of them events every bit as physical as a punch in the face? When I implied that I had never been attacked physically, I was using, of course, the language of the philosophically naive and uneducated man in the street.

But even if, for the sake of argument, one were to grant the validity of the distinction between a threat and a physical assault, there is a further point to consider: that the law, in this instance quite rightly, though more by good luck than judgment or a desire to do justice, does not assume that any physical assault is worse than any merely verbal threat. A fracas in the pub leads to a fine at most, even if blood is spilt; but a threat to kill results in a five-year sentence at the least. And this is as it should be, since a fracas, once over, is likely to be forgotten, while a threat lingers in the mind, and destroys the peace of mind of the person who receives it for a long time to come.

And does not the law recognise mental cruelty as grounds for divorce? Is physical suffering (I am resorting once more to the language of the man who lives the unexamined life, that is to say the immense majority) the only kind we recognise? I am not trying to minimise the horror of torture when I say that some of the worst suffering known to Man arises through the power of mental representation, and not at all through physical hardship or illness. A man may deem his life not worth living, though he live surrounded by comfort or even luxury (is not suicide more common among the upper classes, particularly among doctors?). By contrast, a man may be wracked by disease, in constant pain, and poor into the bargain, and yet hang on to his life as on to something precious. No, ladies and gentlemen, the relationship between suffering and those events or processes commonly called physical (as if there could be events or processes of any other kind) is by no means unequivocal.

The matter of suicide among doctors is worth examining in a little more detail, for it bears a relation to my case. Why do doctors kill themselves in such comparatively large numbers? Because, you reply glibly, they know how to do it, and moreover have the means to hand. Come, come, ladies and gentlemen, surely even you can think of something better than that! We live surrounded by buildings of great height, egress from whose roof or windows is available to all without the exercise of great ingenuity or perseverance. Our chemists' shops are full of lethal substances on the sale of which there are absolutely no restrictions, and we inhabit an island much of whose coastline is formed by steep cliffs, which are never more than a hundred miles distant from us. Rope is easily obtained, and no building in the country is without fitments from which it is possible to suspend oneself by the neck. The entire country is electrified, and it requires so little knowledge of the properties of electricity to kill oneself with it that even our uneducated and ignorant population must surely be able to do so if it so wished. Trains criss-cross the countryside at more than a hundred miles per hour, and the tracks are all too easy of access; here are bridges over deep waterways (more than a score of them in London alone) within everyone's reach. And all public libraries have several textbooks of pharmacology, from which implicit instructions for self-destruction may be derived.

I think I have demonstrated sufficiently that superior technical knowledge and access to drugs do not explain the phenomenon of self-destruction among doctors. One does not, after all, require much knowledge of physiology to understand that defenestration from twenty storeys up is deleterious to the health.

Nor can it be said that doctors are by nature unstable men, that the germ of suicide lies dormant within them from an early age. On the contrary: the great majority of the strenuous studies imposed upon them at medical school are quite redundant, perfectly useless from the practical point of view, and are more a *rite de passage* or even a trial by ordeal than education properly so called. No one can deny the strenuousness of these studies, whatever their pointlessness, and to complete them requires considerable psychological stability – as well as burning ambition, snobbery and greed, of course.

No, the doctor's impulse to kill himself comes from elsewhere: in short, it comes from you, the public, ladies and gentlemen. Prolonged and inescapable contact with the human race, of which you are undeniably a part, with its frivolous but time-consuming demands, its adamant refusal to take responsibility for itself, its bad manners, its lack of elementary personal hygiene, its improvidence, its ignorance and stupidity, its meanness, its bad taste and triviality, drives doctors to despair and hence they kill themselves.

But there is all the difference in the world, you say, between killing yourself and killing others. I agree that there is a difference, but not of the kind you think. And this difference can be boiled down to one word: cowardice. Perhaps I should have said two, or even three, words: cowardice, sentimentality and hypocrisy.

Explain yourself! you demand.

I shall. The doctor, whatever his secret lust for power, wealth, social position and so forth, must cloak his whole mentality in a mantle of benevolence and philanthropy. Even to be admitted to medical school, he must feign an unnatural concern for the welfare of others, and this pretence continues throughout his entire professional life. Eventually, if one plays a part for long enough, it becomes such an important component of one's personality that it holds the rest together; and if, for some reason, one ceases to play it, the personality disintegrates altogether.

Now the doctor, to maintain the illusion of his universal beneficence upon which he had predicated his life, must pretend (to others, but above all to himself) that every person who consults him, however objectionable, aggressive, dirty or unmannerly, is only a suffering soul worthy of sympathy who deserves his compassion. He must deny appearances and see in the undesirable qualities of his patients not their essential evil, but an inevitable expression of something else, whether it be an illness, an unhappy home life, a low income, unblameworthy ignorance, or a lack of intelligence consequent upon childhood malnutrition.

The strain of trying to believe all this proves too great. Eventually the sheer weight of appearance overwhelms the theories which the doctor uses to disguise them, and the elaborate, rigid but brittle intellectual edifice with which he has protected himself against reality shatters utterly But even at this late stage the doctor cannot abandon his role of universal philanthropist altogether, for to do so would be to question the purpose of the whole of his past, whose frustrations and tribulations, far from having been endured for the sake of a higher purpose, now appear to have been endured in pursuit of a lie. Torn between two *Weltanschauungen*, he takes his revenge not upon those who have caused his misery; but upon himself.

I trust I do not have to spell out the similarities between the doctors' situation and my own. I, too, had to deal with the footling demands of the public day after day in the name of benevolence. I, too, had to deal with the importuning, the wheedling, the menaces, the lies, the illiteracy; of Man in the mass. But unlike doctors, ladies and gentlemen, I did not undergo a lengthy training to divest myself of the ability to perceive the truth, to mystify reality in clouds of theorising, and to deny my own innermost and truest feelings: unlike doctors, I have not had my self-knowledge destroyed. I hated my 'clients', and I was not going to play their game by killing myself. If I was miserable, much better – more honest, more rational, more *useful* – to remove the sources of my misery than end my own life.

But, you object, though you removed some of the sources of your misery, it was still only a small minority of them, who – as you yourself pointed out not long ago – numbered many thousands over the years. To kill fifteen (or twenty-two, if we count those cases ignored by the police) was unlikely to make any practical difference to your life. For the class from which your 'victims' (that word again!) were drawn is hydra-headed.

What a crudely rationalistic conception of life you have, ladies and gentlemen! Is not Man *par excellence* (I cannot think of an exact English equivalent, and therefore the foreign phrase is perfectly acceptable in this context, and not at all an ostentation) – is not Man *par excellence* the being for whom symbols are ill-important? Wars have been fought over symbols: and is it not common experience that men grow angrier over words than over the things themselves that the words supposedly represent?

I could not, it is true, hope to eliminate the whole class of my tormentors, but surely it will be conceded that the deaths of fifteen of them (or, *a fortiori*, twenty-two) had some symbolic value? And each man can reasonably be required to do only what falls within his power to do. If everyone who had the opportunity to act as I acted were to do so, the world would soon enough be cleansed of those whom Dean Swift (before he went mad, be it remembered) so eloquently and accurately described as 'the most pernicious race of little odious vermin which nature ever suffered to crawl upon the surface of the earth'.

It was the provocation under which I acted which allowed me to plead diminished responsibility. I admit that I had qualms about so pleading – in case it detracted from the public understanding that I acted both in accordance with morality and in a public spirit – but my lawyer insisted. In my all too easily comprehensible confusion of the time, I deferred to his judgment.

11

THE JUDGE, ON the other hand, made much of the fact that I planned my acts with the greatest care. How else he would have expected anyone to carry them out I do not know. He dismissed the idea that I was provoked, and then, in full contradiction of himself, suggested that I acted from a desire for revenge. What does this tell us, ladies and gentlemen, about his intellect, the much vaunted so-called intellect of the English judiciary? For if I was not provoked, what was there to revenge?

I have never disguised the fact that I wished to punish my tormentors and make them pay for the suffering they inflicted upon me – at least, I have never disguised it since the discovery of the bodies in what the tabloid press, with typical overstatement, called my garden. A man who has acted morally disdains to conceal his motives.

Nor have I ever concealed the pleasure afforded me by my activities. I do not mean the killing itself: I found it rather tedious and tiresome, in fact. I am no sadist, having overcome my childish and adolescent propensities in that direction a long time ago. The mere throttling of my 'victims' gave no pleasure at all to me, and the disposal of their remains was, frankly, a disagreeable chore. No, my pleasure was an altogether subtler thing, richer, more intellectual and ethical in nature: the realisation that the world now contained one fewer unworthy person to consume its scarce resources to no other end or purpose than the very consumption itself.

I admit, however, that the search for and choice of 'victim' was not without its pleasures, the pleasures of the chase. For a mistake in the selection could have been fatal (if I may be allowed that word in this context) to the whole enterprise. A challenge, then: and who does not like, or rise to, a challenge? I had always to find a person of the right characteristics: someone who lived alone, who either had no relatives or who had so alienated them that all contact had been broken off, who was unemployed and who led the kind of isolated existence such that his or her disappearance would arouse no curiosity or would not even be noticed, or if noticed would be attributed to a desire to move and leave no trace behind – a desire common enough in this class. And although my initial impression had been that there were many such people to choose from, when I looked into the matter more closely the great majority of possibles turned out to have a defect from my point of view: a grandmother whom they visited once every two months, an old boyfriend who turned up every time he came out of gaol, or merely once in a while (when he needed a meal or sexual intercourse), a neighbour with whom they were carrying on a feud which had become the neighbour's *raison d'être*, or an illegitimate son at a boarding school for the behaviourally disturbed who came home during holidays.

A single small error could have ruined my project and therefore I had to proceed with the utmost caution, which explains my relatively low level of activity over the years, if I may put it thus. I had no illusions as to my ability to clear the world entirely of human parasites, but I wished to rid it of as many as possible, which naturally entailed remaining undetected for as long as possible, if not indefinitely. I also knew that it was likely I should be caught in the end, but I was willing to brave martyrdom for my cause.

It wasn't only a question of selecting the right candidates, however. In a way the selection was the easiest part because, as a distributor of points for the housing list, I had the right – indeed, the duty – to ask members of the public the most intimate of questions concerning their lives. I even asked about their sexual practices, and they did not think it odd or impertinent. In the event, several of my 'victims' were pregnant, and these, of course, gave me double pleasure, insofar as prevention is better than cure. Some of you, perhaps, may find it strange that a pregnant woman could have fulfilled my criteria as a candidate (social isolation etc.), but your surprise only demonstrates how far you are from understanding the nature of my 'clientele' or of the world they inhabited: for a pregnancy was of no greater significance in that world than was buying a stamp at the post office, catching the bus or switching the station to which their television was tuned.

But having selected a candidate for elimination in the public interest (be it remembered) was one thing; carrying out the elimination in practice was quite another. First, I had to gain his or her confidence so that I could lure him or her safely – from my point of view, that is to say – to his or her death. It was not usually very difficult: I had merely to feign sympathy towards their requests or demands, in itself so extraordinary and unexpected a stance in an official of the Housing Department that they at once dropped their guard. All I had then to do was to maintain that, though their case was undoubtedly among the most deserving I had ever known, the procedure to bring about the desired result was of such complexity that I could not hope to complete it during normal working hours. So deep, however, was my sympathy with their cause that if they came to my home in the evening, I could and would complete the necessary paperwork there.

Of course, their timekeeping left a lot to be desired: they were, after all, people to whom time meant nothing, except perhaps the approach of a television programme or a payment from Social Security. They would invariably arrive late for their appointment, so that I had to counteract this tendency by giving them an appointment for an earlier time than I intended that they should arrive. Sometimes they arrived – perhaps 'turned up' would be a better way of putting it – on the wrong day altogether. When I pointed this out to them – gently, for I did not wish to alarm them or frighten them away at this

239

stage in the proceedings – they did not apologise, but on the contrary, provided me with a whole cascade of fatuous excuses, all of which were entirely egotistical and took no account at all of the convenience or well-being of others such as I. This, naturally, reassured me that I had chosen my subjects not only wisely but with great accuracy.

It wasn't difficult to put my subjects to sleep with a drink spiked with capsules I had procured from the doctor. So much for the so-called clinical acumen of the medical profession, which was quite unable to distinguish between a true insomniac and a man who wanted to use his prescription to lull his subjects to sleep before they died.

As was only to be expected, the drug did not work at once, especially as half my subjects were taking it already: insomnia being a common consequence of the boredom of a pointless existence. There was a dangerous interval between the taking of the drug and the sleep it induced, during which I could not afford to let my subjects depart in case they later realised their drink had been spiked and then went to the police with the information. Though I was not, and am not, a man of violence, I had a baseball bat at the ready, forcibly to oppose and prevent their departure. They were all too familiar with the use of this implement, as I think I have already mentioned, not as sports equipment – no one played baseball within a radius of fifty miles – but as a means of acquiring property and getting one's own way It was they, in fact, who had taught me the use of such a bat as a weapon.

Fortunately, though, I never had to use it. I imagine that I should have found the impact of the wood upon the hard but brittle skull, or on the maggot-soft abdomen, distasteful and even revolting. No, though I am an unsocial man (and there is a world of difference between being *un*social and *anti*social), I can charm and amuse when I want or need to do so, and I managed to keep my subjects cheerful and contented until sleep overtook them.

Now came a difficult moment – not difficult morally, I had settled all that in my mind already and was at ease with myself – but difficult physically. As I believe I may already have mentioned, I am not powerful or muscularly well-endowed, and I freely admit that I have no presence: I am the kind of man who can walk into a room without anyone noticing. It is not surprising, then, that I am not especially strong, though I am what is known as wiry, and strength is a distinct advantage in a strangler. Asphyxiation is more difficult than you imagine to carry through to a successful conclusion, and not only because, even when unconscious, a struggle is put up by a subject. Sometimes one mistakenly believes that the subject has stopped breathing and its heart has stopped beating. You may believe me, ladies and gentlemen, when I tell you that there is scarcely a more terrifying experience in the world than the sudden revival of one whom one believes one has successfully strangled and who should therefore be dead. Fortunately, I kept my head when it would have been all too easy to lose it and then to flee in panic – and a lesser man might have done so. I returned to the fray and emerged victorious: and I learnt also the difficult lesson that death is not always as easily distinguishable from life as one might have supposed.

The most difficult part of all remained, of course: the disposal of the no longer living. However, this is not the place to go into practical details, for to do so would detract from the force of my argument. This is, after all, a philosophical work, not a do-it-yourself manual. Perhaps one day, when I am more at leisure, I shall write a guide to the disposal of human remains, but for the moment I prefer to confine myself to more important, though admittedly abstract, matters. I am not seeking to interest or amuse those who thrive on cheap sensation.

I cannot, however, forbear to mention the exquisite joy (not to be confused with relief) I felt once my task had been completed. To have served the public and to have released myself from the inhibitions of a lifetime: I have known no satisfaction to compare with it. I always slept soundly afterwards.

But when the judge said at my trial that I acted from a wicked desire for vengeance upon a world which had disappointed me, his upper lip curled at the very word *vengeance*, as if he were speaking not of a universal and inevitable desire, a human constant like hunger or thirst, but of something disreputable or even repulsive. Here again, ladies and gentlemen, we see the formidable power of self-deception: for what is all judicial punishment except a licensed form of vengeance, administered cold-bloodedly by those who themselves have suffered no injury from those upon whom the revenge is wrought?

The judge, in the unlikely event that he were ever to read this, his mind being firmly closed against all new experience, would protest vigorously that legal punishment is much more than mere vengeance, and maintain against all the evidence that it performs several important social functions at once, among which are protection of the public, deterrence, correction and rehabilitation of the wrongdoer, *et cetera*. And all of you would nod your heads in agreement and approval.

Let us examine the matter a little more closely, ladies and gentlemen. I shall not stoop to mention again – because it would be a cheap debating point to do so – the late Chief Justice, who lived and passed sentence within my lifetime, who derived sexual gratification from pronouncing the death penalty. Nor shall I be so foolish as to deny that the incarceration of recidivists – of burglars, say – does, by definition, protect the public for a time from their depredations. Remember, I am what I have always been, a genuine searcher after Truth.

But the proof that vengeance is not merely divine, but a fundamental principle of English law, resides in the latter's treatment of those whom I may (I think) call *domestic murderers*. By domestic, I mean the killing of a spouse in a moment of ungovernable, or at least ungoverned, rage, after the discovery of adultery or other affront to the murderer's *amour propre*.

Study after academic study has demonstrated that these men (for most of them are men) are unlikely ever to commit another crime. Most of them have never committed a crime before they killed their wives, either. So punishment as reform is out of the question, since there is nothing to reform; likewise, the public has no need of protection from them. This leaves deterrence and vengeance as the two possible motives for sentencing them not merely to imprisonment but to imprisonment for life. With regard to deterrence, no one has ever been able to produce the slightest evidence that any punishment whatsoever, even the death penalty itself, actually deters the act of murder. After all, if deterrence had worked, would any men ever have killed their wives? Were not their passions at the time of their deed not so inflamed that they were no longer capable of considering the consequences of their own actions? No, ladies and gentlemen, a man does not weigh the *pros* and *cons* of killing his unfaithful wife before doing so, and only someone completely without insight into the workings of the human heart (a metaphor, for I am far from supposing that the heart is the actual anatomical seat of the emotions) could imagine that he did. Thus, regardless of the penalties, there will always be some men who kill their wives, and hence the argument for imprisonment as deterrence collapses like a house of cards.

Which leaves vengeance. I have already explained that the locus of moral authority cannot be the state, a principle established at Nuremberg. Therefore, if it be permissible for the state to exact vengeance, it must be permissible for individual citizens to do likewise. *A fortiori*, in fact: for while citizens as individuals may truly experience the real and genuine emotions which justify vengeance, the state, being an abstraction, cannot possibly do so.

Moreover, the judge, in ascribing to me a single motive only, fell prey to the absurd fallacy that human actions gave a single unique and final cause which explains them to the exclusion of all other explanations. If I acted from a desire for vengeance, he argued (or rather implied), then I could not also have been motivated, as I always said I was, by the desire to perform the public some service. But, My Lord, if one as humble as myself may be permitted to apostrophise for a moment one as mighty and important as yourself, consider your own behaviour: has it always one, and only one, motive? And if not, if your behaviour has several motives, should it always be ascribed in the last analysis to the least creditable of these several motives? Let us give you the benefit of the doubt, and suppose that you love justice and wish to see it triumph everywhere; does this mean you are obliged to forgo your salary, lest your love of justice be contaminated by the love of filthy lucre? No, My Lord, just as a man can love justice and yet still accept payment for administering it, so can a man desire to serve the public and be revenged upon his tormentors at the same time.

Nor did the judge confine himself to remarks about the supposed incompatibility of public and private motives (as if they could ever be disentangled!). He felt free to animadvert as to my character in general. As far as I know, no one has ever protested at the gross natural injustice of this inequality in the rights granted a judge and the accused. But if the character of a man undergoing trial may be investigated and then traduced in court – that is to say, in public – then surely natural justice requires that the character of the man conducting the trial should be subjected to the same jeopardy. No doubt you will reply with the hypocritical fiction that the accused has his voice in court, even though it be a surrogate one in the form of his counsel; but the latter plays by the rules of the game, and his first loyalty is to the game rather than to his client. Indeed, his livelihood depends upon obedience to these rules, for fear of expulsion from the game. Not only does a man's counsel fail to say in court all that he would like him to say, he specifically refuses to do so and resorts to threats (to abandon the case in mid-trial) if his client should insist upon his saying something he deems inadvisable. And the rules of the game, which are opaque to everyone except the lawyers themselves (which is how they maintain their indispensability, after all), are specifically designed to prevent the accused from using every argument relevant to his case, for fear of causing embarrassment to his accusers.

The judge, taking cowardly advantage of his immunity to criticism, referred – with his pendulous and moist lower lip quivering, as if in anticipation of something really tasty – to my deliberate wickedness. I could see several of the jurors, not a few of whom looked as honest themselves as bookmakers at race meetings, nodding fervently in approval.

The fools! Could they not see that the phrase *deliberate wickedness* was itself the product either of the judge's animus against me – so much for his supposed neutrality! – or of a deeply impoverished intellect, despite the many years of training it had supposedly undergone? For how, I ask you, could wickedness be other than deliberate? Try the phrase with the opposite meaning: accidental wickedness. It will be understood at once by almost everyone that, since this phrase is a contradiction in terms, its opposite must contain a redundant word, to wit *deliberate*.

Now either the judge knew this, or he did not. If he knew it, he was guilty of resorting to a vulgar rhetorical device, in which case he was not a fit person morally to conduct my trial (or that of any other person). If, on the other hand, he did not know it, if he really thought that the use of the word *deliberate* in connection with *wickedness* was not supererogatory, then his intellect was not up to the task of conducting a trial properly. (Is it not extraordinary, by the way, that there should be no requirement in our legal system for jurors to be at least of a certain level of intelligence and education, especially in cases such as mine which are not straightforward and which require philosophical sophistication?)

When I pointed out to my lawyer that in either case the judge was not competent to deliberate upon the fate of another, that is to say me, and that this single phrase of his demonstrated that I had not received a fair trial, he remained, or pretended to remain, unmoved. This, he remarked superciliously, was not sufficient grounds for an appeal either against verdict or sentence: but if the moral or intellectual incapacity of the judge is not sufficient grounds, I should like to know what is.

And now I should like to enquire a little more closely into what the judge meant, or thought he meant, when he used the word *deliberate*. That, at least, is easy, I hear you say: *deliberate* means *knowingly, of your own free will*.

Yes, for you everything is clear and easy, ladies and gentlemen. That, I venture to suggest, is because you do not take the trouble to think very hard, or to be critical of your own conceptual framework. Perhaps you will plead in your own defence the press of everyday business – work, shopping, taking the children to school, putting them to bed, and so forth. And I grant that, unlike me who has enjoyed the benefits of social isolation and therefore of increased access to the public library, you have not had the leisure, even if initially you had the inclination, which I doubt, to examine your own ideas from a philosophical standpoint. But this being the case, I deny you the right to stand in judgment over me for even so much as an instant. A man should be tried by his peers, not by his intellectual inferiors.

Now, however, that I have raised the issue of free will, you have no further excuse for not considering it as deeply as you can. And I ask you now what you mean by the words *knowingly* or *of your own free will*?

You may take the coward's way out, and reply that these concepts are irreducible to any others, and therefore not susceptible of further analysis: in which case I congratulate you, ladies and gentlemen, for having discovered – merely by the repetition of your own prejudices – elements in the universe more fundamental by far than the tiniest and most recently-discovered sub-atomic particles. For nothing has a final cause, ladies and gentlemen, unless it be God Himself (if he were to exist, that is, which at the least is open to doubt) and I take it that you do not consider men the possessors of your precious so-called free will to be so many gods, all equal to the one God?

What is it, this will that you deem to be free? Take the thought that is currently occupying your mind, whatever it may be. Where did it come from, did you conjure it to come into your mind by an act of choice? The answer must be no, ladies and gentlemen, because otherwise all the thoughts you ever had, have now and will have must be already present in your consciousness, simultaneously, which I take it you will agree to be an impossibility. Likewise, you will acknowledge that your every thought arises from sources of which you know nothing.

Moreover, thought is the father of action, or at least of all action which is above the level of a Pavlovian reflex. It follows that the source of all our actions must remain unknown to us. This being the case, can any action be said to be deliberate, in the sense in which the judge meant it, that is to say, freely and consciously chosen? And if again the answer is no, can anyone be held personally responsible for anything? We none of us know why we act as we do, and therefore have no right to sit in judgment over each other.

Indeed, what is the *I* and this *You* which is so ceaselessly, and yet so carelessly, invoked? I have no wish to make a vulgar exhibition of my erudition, but it is surely significant that as long ago as Heraclitus (his exact dates are uncertain, but in any case irrelevant in this context) it was pointed out that the same river cannot be stepped into twice. Heraclitus meant by this, naturally, that by the time anyone returned to the river into which he had once stepped, it had changed to such an extent because of the flow of its water, the erosion of its banks and bed, etc., that it could no longer be called the same river. Someone, I admit that I forget who, and the prison warders are hardly the people to ask, extended the argument even further, to its logical conclusion: you cannot step into the same river once.

Applying the argument of Heraclitus to the question of personal identity, is it not evident that there is no such entity as the persisting *I* and the persisting *You*? Physics and physiology alike teach that the molecules which make up the human form are in constant motion, and that not a single molecule with which a human organism started out in life remains in its original condition or position by the time it appears, say, in court. And only a person of peculiar obtuseness could fail to realise that this argument holds over much shorter periods of time as well: that is to say, the person who appears in court is not the same as the one who allegedly committed the offence which, thanks to the law's delay (an oblique reference once again to *Hamlet*), may have occurred more than a year earlier.

Perhaps you will argue that the faculty of memory provides a basis for the stability of personal identity. A feeble response, ladies and gentlemen! For of all the faculties of the mind (regrettably, one has to use such inaccurate, insubstantial and unscientific terms as *mind* if one is to speak at all), memory is the least reliable. You maintain that your personal identity is a continuous and unbroken stream since you first reached the age of consciousness, but not even the least honest among you would claim that your stream of memory since then is continuous and unbroken. Thus, your memory cannot stand guarantor of that precious identity of yours. Indeed, nothing can.

I have, of course, further objections to memory. It has been conclusively established by experimentation that people do not remember what really happened and – worse still from the point of view of your argument – claim to remember what did not happen. Eyewitnesses recall logically contradictory events; and the versions of their childhood which most people provide when asked to do so depend more upon the image of themselves they wish to project than upon what they were actually like. Memory is the means by which the past is distorted to present purposes.

But even if memory were perfectly reliable, ladies and gentlemen, it would not and could not establish the continuance of personal identity, but on the contrary its very opposite. How so, you ask? Because with each passing moment, the store of memory must be increased, its content enlarged; in short, changed. And surely I do not have to point out that difference cannot be used to establish identity.

I am not in general in favour of providing summaries or recapitulations of an argument, or of spelling out all its implications – this practice seems to me to promote mental laziness in a reader. But even less do I wish to be misunderstood; and therefore I restate the following two points:

i) The judge called my actions deliberate, when the very notion he had of deliberateness was incoherent and intellectually unviable, and therefore all the decisions he took on the basis of this notion were unreasonable, incompetent and unjust.

ii) The judge assumed that the person before him in the dock was the same person as the one who allegedly committed the so-called crimes which were the subject of the trial. But this was an elementary error, as I have demonstrated. Thus, the person sentenced to life imprisonment, with the recommendation that he never be released, was not the same person he assumed had killed the fifteen innocent (*sic*) people. Indeed, one person could not even have committed all the alleged offences. I therefore have one question for you, ladies and gentlemen: Can any greater offence to natural justice be imagined than to punish one man for the alleged crimes of another?

12

SINCE WICKEDNESS MUST be deliberate in order to be wickedness, and since no action can be deliberate, it follows, as the night the day (Polonius in *Hamlet*, Act 1, Scene 3), that wickedness is impossible.

Nevertheless, the judge said that I behaved with wickedness, without fear of being contradicted this side of eternity. He enjoyed pronouncing the word, but he did not know what he was talking about, his portentous manner and the grandeur of his wig and robe notwithstanding.

Let us suspend our disbelief in wickedness for a moment, however, and ask what the judge meant by this emotive word? Doing wrong for its own sake, perhaps you reply. But I counter-reply that no one ever behaves thus, or at least so small a number of people that it reduces the problem of wickedness to the dimensions of a rare neurological disorder, which afflicts only one in a million. Any human phenomenon so rare must be a disease, and one of minor importance.

No, I have never wanted to do wrong, but on the contrary have always tried to do my public duty, at the same time as developing my own personality to its full potential. You may, perhaps, disagree with what I considered right action, but what is incontestable is that I wished no harm. I am, after all, the final authority as to what my wishes were: and they were always honourable.

But what you actually did was wrong, you reply, irrespective of your wishes. It is not the thought that counts.

Do I really have to go through it all again? Who is to decide what is right and what is wrong? Are there not societies whose ideas are very different from our own? In one country (to take a trivial, but nevertheless illustrative, example) it is deemed the height of bad manners to eat everything on one's plate, while in another it is regarded as insufferably rude to leave anything at all. When one has read as much history and anthropology as I, one is struck by the immense variation as to what has counted as moral conduct down the ages and across the continents. The Aztecs sacrificed thirty thousand men at a time, and thought they were doing right – indeed, it never occurred to them that they might be doing otherwise. I trust I do not have to give further examples, yet more extreme. It seems, therefore, that morality is like beauty, in the eye of the beholder, but I shall not repeat the Latin tag for fear of inducing tedium, a mental state not conducive to the rational assessment of philosophical arguments.

Certainly, morality – and therefore guilt or innocence, I might add – cannot be a mere matter of votes. If it were, some of the worst conduct in history would have to be deemed moral. And to whose vote should we attend, the victims' or the perpetrators'? Does one take the vote of the Mongol horde or of the inhabitants of Baghdad when the former sacked and destroyed it utterly? The victims' vote you cry, as if by reflex. But there is no reason to suppose that victims as a category have any special insight which makes their votes more valuable – to be counted double, say – than those of anyone else. My 'victims', on the contrary, were all, without exception, people whose whole lives were a negation of morality whereas I, the alleged malefactor, always sought, at least since childhood, to make my behaviour conform to the dictates of my conscience.

There is another way of conceiving of wickedness, however, though so subtle that I do not think the judge could have meant it this way. I refer, of course, to Socrates' view of the matter, namely that no man ever does wrong knowingly, by which he meant not that the wicked know not what they do, but that they know not the significance or the effect of what they do.

But this is not coherent either, if I may say so. Firstly, no one fully appreciates the effect of what they do: for every human action has consequences which the actor neither wished nor foresaw, or indeed could have foreseen. History furnishes us with innumerable examples of good coming from evil, and *vice versa*. Was not the Sistine Chapel raised in conditions of the utmost misery for the immense majority of the inhabitants of Rome, combined with the utter unscrupulousness and rascality of the elite? When it comes to failing to appreciate the effects of our actions, we are all in the same boat.

Furthermore, the very idea of failure to attend sufficiently to the effects of what one does is logically self-contradictory, and therefore cannot have any application in the real world. Socrates tells us that wickedness is a form of ignorance, to be overcome by mere thought and reflection: but *ex hypothesi* the wicked person is inattentive to precisely those effects of his actions which are harmful. In other words, he *knows* from where he should avert his gaze, which is to say that he is not ignorant. And then the question naturally arises as to why this man ignores the evil effects of his actions. The circle is closed: the man is wicked because he ignores the effects of his actions, and he ignores the effects of his actions because he is wicked. Nothing whatever is explained, ladies and gentlemen.

Besides, no one can accuse me of having disregarded the consequences to others of my actions: I thought about them long and hard. And I came to the conclusion that they would be wholly beneficial. Of course, the judge worked himself up into a lather of indignation about the fact that I had killed fifteen people (as he so inaccurately supposed). I had deprived them of their lives, he said, without the slightest regard for their wishes. He waxed lyrical about the inestimable value of each human life, though he signally failed to enumerate any particular in which the lives of those he called my 'victims' were valuable. And when he spoke of the sanctity of human life, he omitted all mention of doctors withholding life-saving treatment from their patients when they (and they alone) deemed that their patients' lives were no longer worth living. Must one have attended medical school, I ask, to decide whether or not a life is worth living, and do medical students receive tuition in such matters that make doctors experts upon them, uniquely beyond the reach of the law?

And by what right did the judge wax indignant at the thought of all those 'poor innocent dupes', as he called them? What had he ever done for them during life, or for any member of their class, that he should feel so strongly about them? Certainly, he would never have met any of them socially: indeed, the only occasion he ever encountered any of their class was when they stood in the dock before him, and he sentenced them to one punishment or another (nine of my 'innocent victims' had been charged with a crime in court within the last year of their lives, and three of them had been imprisoned). To hand down prison sentences to people is hardly evidence of great solicitude for their welfare.

The concern expressed for my 'victims' (or subjects, as I prefer to call them) after their death contrasted rather strangely with the complete indifference shown towards them during their miserable lives, an indifference which, when you remember that it was universal on the part of society, accounted in large part for what they were or had become.

Society failed to educate them; society housed them in conditions unfit for human habitation; society gave them no hope; society gave them no work to do and kept them on the margin of pinched subsistence. But once they were dead, society wailed and gnashed its teeth. By what right, then, does society pronounce judgment upon me?

13

BUT JUDGE ME it did, and judge me it continues to do. It feels distinctly pleased with itself for having consigned me to perpetual imprisonment. 'He got his just deserts,' it says, adding, 'And now we are safe.' It thinks that merely by anathematising me it has satisfactorily demonstrated that I am anomalous and perverted, and therefore not the true product or offspring of itself.

But if I am so very abnormal, ladies and gentlemen, if society neither produced me nor has any place for me, may I enquire of you why it is that I receive at least two written declarations of love each week from women whom I have never met? And why have I received, in total, forty-seven offers of marriage, whereas before my achievements were known I received none at all, but on the contrary, women had not even noticed my existence? How many of you who read this can claim to have been so beloved of so many?

And I have received much support besides. I have received letters from several organisations agreeing with my contention that not only did I fail to receive a fair trial but that – because of the pre-trial publicity surrounding my case – it was inconceivable that I should have done so. For if any juror had known nothing of the matter beforehand, this would have demonstrated that he was so out of touch with everyday affairs that he was unfit to be a juror. If, on the other hand, he had knowledge of my case through the media of mass communication, he could not have been an unbiased participant of the trial. *Ergo*, no fair trial was, or is, possible; *ergo*, I should be released at once.

And then I received hundreds of letters in support of my struggle against the *lumpen* element in society. Insofar as I was reproached at all in these letters, it was for only having made a start and for not having gone far enough.

Finally, I should be accused of ingratitude if I failed to mention the Free Underwood Committee (FUC) which, unbidden by me, works on my behalf, pointing out to the public that even if I killed at all, which was not satisfactorily demonstrated at my trial because the forensic evidence was tainted by past scandals involving the laboratory, it was not for profit or pleasure, but for an ideal. At the very least I should be treated as a political prisoner.

I am not so naive, of course, as to suppose that I shall not remain in prison, and therefore I must make the best of it. The authorities have not yet noticed that the suicide rate among inmates of each prison in which I have so far been lodged has risen greatly. This is not because prisoners spontaneously prefer death to association with me: on the contrary, thanks to my superior intellect, knowledge and powers of persuasion, I have managed to convince more than a few that by taking their own lives (I advise them also on the technical details) they are striking a blow against the police and the hated Prison Department.

And it is true that with each suicide the Department is made to feel official embarrassment. From my point of view, of course, I have – if I may be allowed what amounts to a pun – killed two birds with one stone (a prison sentence is known to prisoners as their bird). With each death, I have saved the taxpayer untold thousands, and therefore performed a further public service; but at the same time I have exposed the hypocrisy of society's supposed concern for the welfare of its prisoners.

How absolutely typical of the society we live in – its absurdity, its irrationality – that a man like me, whose burning and justified hatred of useless humanity led him to eliminate as much of it as he reasonably could, should be incarcerated in an institution in which the concentration of such humanity is the highest possible, namely one hundred per cent, and in the name of the safety of that useless humanity itself! But, ladies and gentlemen, I do not despair, far from it. I have been observing very closely how prisoners obtain positions as cleaners in the hospital wing of the prison. If necessary I shall act a part. And then, when I am a trusty in the hospital, I shall be near both drugs and equipment. So little done, so much to do! (Cecil Rhodes).

POSTSCRIPT

Extract from the Conclusions of the Report of the Official Enquiry by His Honour Judge Rosewood Davies Into the Death of Mr Graham Underwood at HM Prison, Southmead

iii) The Enquiry was satisfied that Mr Underwood died of stab wounds received while he was an inmate of 'S' (the Maximum Security) Wing of HMP Southmead.

iv) The Enquiry was satisfied that all the stab wounds suffered by Mr Underwood were inflicted by the inmates of 'S' Wing, and that there is no substance to the rumour that there was collusion, either active or passive, on the part of the prison officers.

v) The Enquiry found, however, that the prison officers of 'S' Wing were lacking in reasonable forethought when they permitted Mr Underwood to associate with the other inmates of 'S' Wing, who were themselves known to be dangerous and violent, and several of whom were convicted murderers, at a time when feeling against Mr Underwood in the prison was known to be running high.

vi) Moreover, there were several breaches of security regulations which allowed the inmates of 'S'

Wing to procure or manufacture the weapons with which they stabbed Mr Underwood. In part, these breaches were caused by inadequate staffing levels, and the Enquiry therefore recommends that these levels be increased, and if possible doubled, in the interest of public security and the safety of inmates.

vii) Furthermore, the Enquiry found that the response of the officers on duty in 'S' Wing at the time of the incident was inadequately coordinated, that there was a lack of proper procedure laid down in the event of such an incident, that communications with other parts of the prison were poor so that there was unnecessary delay in medical assistance reaching Mr Underwood, and that the officers on 'S' Wing were not properly trained in first aid. Mr Underwood's life might have been saved had the officers been adequately trained. The Enquiry therefore recommends that further training in first aid be given all prison officers and that steps be taken to improve communications between the various locations in the prison.

Also from Monday Books

Not With A Bang But A Whimper / Theodore Dalrymple
(hbk, £14.99)

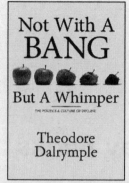

In a series of penetrating and beautifully-written essays, Theodore Dalrymple explains his belief that a liberal intelligentsia is destroying Britain. Dalrymple writes for _The Spectator_, _The Times_, _The Daily Telegraph_, _New Statesman_, _The Times Literary Supplement_ and the _British Medical Journal_.

'Theodore Dalrymple's clarity of thought, precision of expression and constant, terrible disappointment give his dispatches from the frontline a tone and a quality entirely their own... their rarity makes you sit up and take notice'
- *Marcus Berkmann, The Spectator*

'Dalrymple is a modern master'
- *The Guardian*

'Dalrymple is the George Orwell of our times...
he is a writer of genius'
- *Dennis Dutton*

Second Opinion: A Doctor's Dispatches from the Inner City
Theodore Dalrymple (hdbk, £14.99)

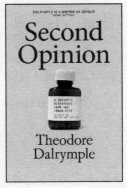

No-one has travelled further into the dark and secret heart of Britain's underclass than the brilliant Theodore Dalrymple. A hospital consultant and prison doctor in the grim inner city, every day he confronts a brutal, tragic netherworld which most of us never see. It's the world of 'Baby P' and Shannon Matthews, where life is cheap and ugly, jealous men beat and strangle their women and 'anyone will do anything for ten bags of brown'. In a series of short and gripping pieces, full of feeling and bleak humour, he exposes the fascinating, hidden horror of our modern slums as never before.

> **'Dalrymple's dispatches from the frontline have a tone and a quality entirely their own... their rarity makes you sit up and take notice'**
> *– Marcus Berkmann, The Spectator*

> **'Dalrymple is a modern master'**
> *– Stephen Poole, The Guardian*

> **'The George Orwell of our time... a writer of genius'**
> *– Denis Dutton*

**From all good bookshops, online from
www.mondaybooks.com or via 01455 221752.**

Anything Goes / **Theodore Dalrymple**
(hdbk, £14.99)

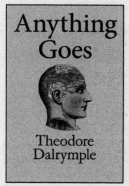

Theodore Dalrymple is one of Britain's most brilliant writers whose work on political and social issues appears regularly in a wide range of leading newspapers and magazines on both sides of the Atlantic, including *The Times*, *The Spectator*, *The Daily Telegraph* and *Standpoint*.

Until now, his books have all been collections of essays which had previously appeared in these and other publications.

For the first time, in *Anything Goes*, he presents a collection of entirely new pieces which dissect modern Britain.

Drawing on his vast experience as an inner city prison doctor and consultant psychiatrist, he examines – among other things – the state of the NHS, fake charities, our education system, British criminal justice and our politics.

Published February 2011

From all good bookshops, online from www.mondaybooks.com or via 01455 221752.

Sick Notes / Dr Tony Copperfield
(ppbk, £8.99)

Welcome to the bizarre world of Tony Copperfield, family doctor. He spends his days fending off anxious mums, elderly sex maniacs and hopeless hypochondriacs (with his eyes peeled for the odd serious symptom). The rest of his time is taken up sparring with colleagues, battling bureaucrats and banging his head against the brick walls of the NHS.

If you've ever wondered what your GP is really thinking - and what's actually going on behind the scenes at your surgery - *SICK NOTES* is for you.

'A wonderful book, funny and insightful in equal measure'
– *Dr Phil Hammond (Private Eye's 'MD')*

'Copperfield is simply fantastic, unbelievably funny and improbably wise... everything he writes is truer than fact'
– *British Medical Journal*

'Original, funny and an incredible read' – *The Sun*

'A mix of the hilarious, the mundane and the poignant'
– *Daily Mail*

Tony Copperfield is a Medical Journalist of the Year, has been shortlisted for UK Columnist of the Year many times and writes regularly for *The Times* and other media

From all good bookshops, online from www.mondaybooks.com or via 01455 221752.

Wasting Police Time / **PC David Copperfield**
(ppbk, £7.99)

The fascinating, hilarious and best-selling inside story of the madness of modern policing. A serving officer - writing deep under cover - reveals everything the government wants hushed up about life on the beat.

'**Very revealing**' – *The Daily Telegraph*
'**Passionate, important, interesting and genuinely revealing**' – *The Sunday Times*
'**Graphic, entertaining and sobering**' – *The Observer*
'**A huge hit... will make you laugh out loud**'
– *The Daily Mail*
'**Hilarious... should be compulsory reading for our political masters**' – *The Mail on Sunday*
'**More of a fiction than Dickens**'
– *Tony McNulty MP, former Police Minister*
(On a BBC *Panorama* programme about PC Copperfield, McNulty was later forced to admit that this statement, made in the House of Commons, was itself inaccurate)

**From all good bookshops, online from
www.mondaybooks.com or via 01455 221752.**

Perverting The Course Of Justice / Inspector Gadget
(ppbk, £7.99)

A senior serving policeman picks up
where PC Copperfield left off and reveals
how far the insanity extends – children
arrested for stealing sweets from each
other while serious criminals go about
their business unmolested.

'Exposes the reality of life at the sharp end'
– *The Daily Telegraph*

'No wonder they call us Plods... A frustrated inspector
speaks out on the madness of modern policing'
– *The Daily Mail*

'Staggering... exposes the bloated bureaucracy that is
crushing Britain' – *The Daily Express*

'You must buy this book... it is a fascinating insight'
– *Kelvin MacKenzie, The Sun*

In April 2010, Inspector Gadget was named
one of the country's 'best 40 bloggers' by *The Times*.

**From all good bookshops, online from
www.mondaybooks.com or via 01455 221752.**

In Foreign Fields / **Dan Collins**

(ppbk, £7.99)

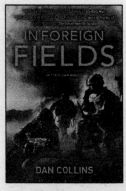

A staggering collection of 25 true-life stories of astonishing battlefield bravery from Iraq and Afghanistan... medal-winning soldiers, Marines and RAF men, who stared death in the face, in their own words.

'Enthralling and awe-inspiring untold stories' – *The Daily Mail*

'Astonishing feats of bravery illustrated in laconic, first-person prose' – *Independent on Sunday*

'The book everyone's talking about... a gripping account of life on the frontlines of Iraq and Afghanistan' – *News of the World*

'An outstanding read' – *Soldier Magazine*

From all good bookshops, online from www.mondaybooks.com or via 01455 221752.

So That's Why They Call It Great Britain / Steve Pope
(ppbk, £7.99)

From the steam engine to the jet engine to the engine of the world wide web, to vaccination and penicillin, to Viagra, chocolate bars, the flushing loo, the G&T, ibruprofen and the telephone... this is the truly astonishing story of one tiny country and its gifts to the world.

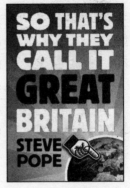

**From all good bookshops, online from
www.mondaybooks.com or via 01455 221752.**

A Paramedic's Diary / Stuart Gray
(ppbk, £7.99)

STUART GRAY is a paramedic dealing with the worst life can throw at him. *A Paramedic's Diary* is his gripping, blow-by-blow account of a year on the streets – 12 rollercoaster months of enormous highs and tragic lows. One day he'll save a young mother's life as she gives birth, the next he might watch a young girl die on the tarmac in front of him after a hit-and-run. A gripping, entertaining and often amusing read by a talented new writer.

As heard on BBC Radio 4's Saturday Live and BBC Radio 5 Live's Donal McIntyre Show and Simon Mayo

In April 2010, Stuart Gray was named one of the country's 'best 40 bloggers' by *The Times*

From all good bookshops, online from www.mondaybooks.com or via 01455 221752.